"Take Off Your Clothes . . ."

Hayden rasped in that menacingly soft voice. "Or I'll do it for you."

"Hayden, please. Don't be angry with me."

"I'm not . . . angry."

And dust never blows in Texas, Brianne thought frantically as she edged along the side of the bed. "I know what you're thinking about me and your friend, b-but it isn't true. You see—"

"I passed *angry* five minutes ago," he continued as if she hadn't spoken. He stepped closer, the muscles in his arms quivering as he fought for control. "I think *murderously insane* more describes how I feel right now."

Brianne's knees went weak. She'd really done it this time. "Hayden, please. You've got to listen to me. What you overheard wasn't real. It was planned. It was a scheme to make you jealous . . . make you want me."

His hot gaze raked her body. "Well, *chica,* it worked." Lashing out a hand, he pulled her against him. "I do want you." His warm breath teased her lips. "I want you naked and trembling beneath me, your long legs wrapped around mine, your body burning with need."

He shoved her from him. "But I wouldn't want you to get the wrong idea about our relationship."

Books by Sue Rich

The Scarlet Temptress
Shadowed Vows
Rawhide and Roses

Published by POCKET BOOKS

Rawhide and Roses

Sue Rich

POCKET BOOKS

New York   London   Toronto   Sydney   Tokyo   Singapore

This book is a work of fiction. Names, characters, places, and
incidents are either products of the author's imagination or are used
fictitiously. Any resemblance to actual events or locales or persons,
living or dead, is entirely coincidental.

An *Original* Publication of POCKET BOOKS

POCKET BOOKS, a division of Simon & Schuster Inc.
1230 Avenue of the Americas, New York, NY 10020

ISBN: 0-671-75914-0

First Pocket Books printing September 1993

10 9 8 7 6 5 4 3 2 1

POCKET and colophon are registered trademarks of
Simon & Schuster Inc.

Cover art by Lina Levy

Printed in the U.S.A.

This book is dedicated to:

The real Uncle Lecil—my uncle,
Lecil Thomas Woodruff.

The real Billy Wayne—my cousin,
Billy Wayne Franklin.

My granddaughter, Chelsey Breann,
who inspired my heroine's name.

Rich Marusak, of the Kemp Public
Library in Wichita Falls, for all
his help with research.

My critics, Dianna Crawford, Sally
Laity, Kat Martin, and Mary Lou
Rich for their friendship and
honesty.

My editor, Caroline Tolley, and my
agent, Rob Cohen, who always prop
me up when I start to sag.

And, as always, to my wonderful
husband, Jim Rich.

___1___

*D*ark shadows closed in around Brianne Logan, thickening the air she fought for in strained gulps. For just a heartbeat, she lost her courage and nearly bolted into the night, back to the desolate streets of Wichita Falls, but the gnawing ache in her belly sprouted claws, and she knew she would do it. She had to.

Brianne anxiously searched the windows of the farmhouse for any sign of light, any movement from within.

Nothing.

She tightened her shaking hands into fists. Curse them for going to bed so early—for making it easy for her.

Rising from her crouched position near the barn, she tucked a limp, blond curl beneath her hat and cautiously stepped toward the open yard. Her legs wobbled precariously. Heavens. She had to get hold of herself. She'd never be able to continue if she kept shaking like a bank clerk during a robbery.

She hiked up the baggy men's britches she wore, then ignoring the stench of manure and hay surrounding her, she squared her shoulders. It would be all right. It would only

1

take a minute. There wouldn't be much blood, and when it was over, the ache would go away.

Holding onto that resolve, she dashed silently across the dirt yard, wincing as sticks and pebbles cut into her bare feet. When she reached the chicken coop, she flattened up against it to catch her breath and still the wild hammering in her chest. Only a few more steps.

She crossed herself, just in case God wasn't in a forgiving mood, then charged into the chicken house.

Blackness engulfed her. A frenzy of wild squawks and flying feathers assaulted her from every direction. Terrified that the noise would wake the farmer, she lunged forward.

Her toes touched something wet and gooey an instant before her legs careened out from under her. She landed with a flop on her belly. Something squashed through the thin shirt covering her unbound breasts. The odor of chicken droppings nearly gagged her. "Oh, *ick.*" Trying not to think about what she was lying in, she pushed herself up. And slime oozed between her fingers.

She cringed, then, from her knees, dove toward the screeching fowl. One scrambled over her head, knocking her hat off. Hair tumbled into her eyes. Shoving it out of her face, she fought to catch one of the chickens flapping crazily in front of her. At last she latched onto a fat, wiggling bird.

Light flooded the shed.

Brianne sprang to her feet and whirled around. The hen she held fluttered to the ground, then scurried away. But Brianne didn't take her eyes off the half-dressed man glaring at her from the doorway . . . or the shotgun pointed straight at her heart.

If the farmer was surprised to see a girl dressed as a boy standing guiltily among his egg layers, he hid it well—but not the wide-eyed woman who stood behind him holding a lantern.

"Land sakes, Clarence. It's a gal."

"I got eyes, Maude," the skeletal man snapped. "But it don't change nothin'. She's still a thief. Now send Junior fer the sheriff."

The older woman, in a nightdress buttoned clear to her

pointed chin, edged forward. She set the lantern onto a crate by the door. Gathering the folds of her gown, she sent Brianne a sympathetic look before hurrying out.

It was too much. After months of sleeping in sheds, barns, or under porch steps, scrounging to exist, and having gone the last two days without food, everything caved in on Brianne at once. The farmer's form wavered. An eerie floating sensation dissolved the ground beneath her feet, and she grabbed for the support of a nearby post.

"Don't be makin' no sudden moves, gal, or ya'll be pickin' lead outta yer innards."

Holding onto consciousness by a thread, Brianne nodded numbly. But just the thought of being arrested sent another wave of dizziness crashing over her. They'd send her back.

The horror of that vision snapped her to awareness. "Please, mister. Let me go. I didn't mean any harm. I was just so hungry . . ."

The farmer's features hardened. "What makes ya any different from the rest a us?" He swept a hand skyward. "Case ya ain't noticed lately, the whole dang country's starvin'. Them raidin' Injuns 'bout ruined ever'one in these parts." He returned his bony fingers to the shotgun. "Yer sorry tale don't wash with me, gal. An' it won't hold water with the sheriff, neither. Ta ol' Harley Smith, a thief's a thief. Ya'll be lucky if'n he don't hang ya by that scrawny neck a yers."

"They don't hang people for stealing *chickens.*"

"I suppose most sheriffs don't. But ya never know 'bout Harley." The farmer's narrow lips spread over protruding teeth. "He sorta makes up his own rules. Does a right fine job a keepin' riffraff outta our town, too. Folks 'round here don't give no sass ta his ways."

Fear mingled with disbelief. He was lying. He had to be. But she couldn't hold onto the thought. Images of her life if she were sent back kept intruding. Her nervousness grew, and for just an instant, she wondered if hanging might not be preferable.

Long minutes ticked by, Brianne not daring to move, the farmer doggedly alert. Chickens cackled and flapped. The smell of droppings thickened the air, and it seemed like hours before she heard the rumble of an approaching horse.

Clarence straightened, a satisfied sneer curling his lips. Keeping the gun pointed at her, he leaned his head toward the door. "In here, Harley!"

The plodding hooves grew closer, then stopped. In a frightened daze, Brianne listened to the sound of creaking leather, the jangle of spurs, then the heavy thud of footsteps. Her palms grew damp.

The farmer moved aside to allow a massive form, well over six feet, to enter the room.

Brianne had never seen anyone so big—or so ugly. The blubberous man had to weigh at least three hundred pounds. A huge, flabby belly drooped over his belt, stretching the buttons on his faded shirt until pasty white flesh bulged between the gaps. Bloated lips sucked on a cigar stub, while watery dirt brown eyes surveyed her from head to foot.

"Will you lookee here." He elbowed the skinny farmer. "You ever seen tits like that on a chicken thief 'afore?"

"Can't say as I have," Clarence snickered.

Self-consciously, Brianne gathered the front of the too-large shirt, attempting to pull the gaping neckline together. For the first time since she'd stolen the garments, she regretted the action.

The sheriff waddled forward, his stomach jiggling. A meaty hand lashed out, gripping her by the upper arm, nearly lifting her off her feet. "You're gonna be right sorry you messed with these good folks here, gal. We don't cotton to no thievin' whores 'round these parts." He wrinkled his nose. "Gawd, you stink."

"So do you," Brianne snapped without thinking. The smell of his foul breath gagged her almost as much as the odor wafting from his armpits.

His nails dug into her skin. "Shut up, *thief.* I don't take sass from no outlaw. You got that?"

Fearing she might be sick, Brianne swung her face away and nodded.

"I figured you might." Turning abruptly, he hauled her through the door to the yard. He spat out the cigar stub, then spoke to the farmer. "Hold her till I get on, then toss her up."

Brianne nearly smiled at that. The farmer didn't seem strong enough to lift her, much less *toss* her. But that notion died the instant she felt his bony hand replace the sheriff's on her arm. He was stronger than he appeared if the grip pinching her flesh was anything to go by.

The leather groaned as the lawman hoisted his heavy frame up and slopped onto a saddle that looked ridiculously small beneath his sizable rear.

"Okay, Clarence, hand her up."

"Git over there, gal." The farmer shoved her into the side of the lawman's huge horse.

The sheriff caught her by the hair and pulled upward.

"Ow!" Brianne winced against the pain and kicked out.

Skinny fingers grabbed her by the hips and thrust her upward over the pommel like a sack of grain.

The saddle horn gouged her ribs, and she gasped in pain.

Smith's big belly rumbled with laughter, then his knee slammed into her temple as he shoved his foot into the opposite stirrup.

"Curse you!" Brianne blinked away tears and tried to rise to ease the pressure on her ribs. A heavy hand immediately halted the effort when it snagged the back of her britches and dragged her over the large man's knees.

"Stay put, gal, less you're lookin' to ride somethin' a little harder than that horn." He yanked on the reins and the horse turned, then his voice boomed out. "See you in church tomorra, Clarence."

"I hope the roof falls in on you," Brianne mumbled.

Obviously ignoring her, Smith kicked the horse into a gallop.

The short ride into Wichita Falls was the most excruciating Brianne had ever endured. With each plod of the horse, the pommel stabbed her side. Breathing became nearly impossible. Her empty stomach rolled at the odor of her own putrid smell and the consuming pain that threatened to steal her coherency.

And if that wasn't enough to contend with, the fat bastard

kept patting her rear and chuckling. "You got a nice tight ass, sweetcakes. Could be you and me might work somethin' out for your bail."

"I'd rather hang."

His knee came up again, slamming into her forehead. "That can be arranged, whore." Hauling back on the reins, he stopped at a rail before the jail house. "Yes, ma'am. Since you don't think I'm good enough for the likes of your skinny ass, that can sure be arranged."

Pouring himself from the saddle, he jerked her down and marched her into a small room at the front of the building then roughly propelled her onto one of two stools facing a pine desk.

He lifted a ring of keys off a peg, then settled his immense form into a spindle chair and tilted back on its two hind legs. Studying her. "What's your name, thief?"

In her unstable condition, she'd forgotten she wasn't in her own hometown, and it had never dawned on her until this moment that the sheriff wouldn't know her identity. A tiny surge of relief eased her tension some. If the sheriff didn't know who she was, then he also didn't know where she came from. Thank goodness. At least she could come through this ordeal without having to go back. More confident now, she defiantly clamped her lips together and lifted her chin.

The front legs of the sheriff's chair hit the floor with a crash, and he lurched forward threateningly. "Answer me, damn you!"

"No."

Harley Smith's face reddened with anger. His mouth worked but no words came out. Then, pulling his hands toward him, as if afraid he might wrap them around her neck, he planted them on the arms of the chair. He sat there for a long time, breathing heavily, until he appeared to have regained control. Then suddenly his eyes took on a rabid gleam.

He hefted himself to his feet and picked up the keys from the desk. "You'll be sorry you crossed me, gal. Real sorry."

He shoved her through a door at the rear of the building and held her pinned to a wall of bars while he opened a cell.

After locking her inside, he just stood there watching her, until his gaze drifted to something behind her. He twisted his mouth into a smirk. "Hey, Malo. You got a roommate."

Startled, Brianne swung around. Light from a wall lantern poured over a dark figure sitting near the back of the cell. Fear pricked her skin. Never in her entire eighteen years had she seen a more deadly-looking man.

He sat in a shadowed corner at the end of a cot, his back against the wall, one long leg propped up, stretching blue denim tight around a sinewy thigh. A muscular arm rested on the raised knee allowing his long-fingered hand to dangle lazily.

The light reflected on his gray shirt, illuminating hard features and a sinister scar that ran along his left jaw. Her anxiety grew, and she hesitantly met his gaze.

Cold, gunmetal blue eyes stared into hers.

Brianne pressed herself against the bars.

The sheriff cackled. "Well, little-miss-chicken-thief, I'd like you to meet Malo Navaja, one of the meanest bastards ole Lucifer ever put on this earth." He smirked at the dark man. "Go ahead, Malo, tell our lady friend here why I sent to Fort Jacksboro for a Texas Ranger."

The prisoner remained menacingly silent.

Harley Smith grinned. "A little shy, are you? That's okay, I'll tell her." He sent Brianne a gloating sneer. "Seems our friend here's gonna hang soon as the Rangers get their hands on him. They don't cotton to the way he likes to carve people up with his straight razor."

Brianne's midsection jumped. She'd heard of Malo Navaja. Her maid, Maria, had told her how he'd once slit a woman's throat, then cut off her breast. She'd also gone on about the numerous men he'd killed, and how he'd used his deadly razor to remove various parts of their bodies. That's how he, a white man, had earned the Mexican name Malo Navaja, *evil razor*. Her gaze flew to the man in the corner. Through the shadows, she saw his mouth curve into a slow smile.

The sheriff snickered, then patted his belly. "Well, I'm gonna go grab me a bite. You two have fun." He headed for the door.

"Wait!" Brianne cried. "My name's Brianne Logan." She spun around and clutched the bars. "My father's Assemblyman Art Logan from Santa Fe."

She could have bitten off her tongue. *What have I done?* A movement sounded from the rear of the cell, and she nervously glanced at the man behind her. But his position hadn't changed. Only his smile had disappeared.

"Sure you are," the lawman mocked, reclaiming her attention.

"I am. I swear to you." Frantically her mind searched for something to convince him. "Send him a telegram. He'll prove it." Anything to get her out of this cell with that butcher.

A frown puckered the sheriff's brow.

"Please?" she pleaded. "I'm telling you the truth. Art Logan will prove it."

The sheriff looked uncertain, then a lecherous gleam entered his eyes, and they slid down to the gaping front of her shirt. "Well now. Suppose we go in that little room"—he gestured toward a side door—"and talk 'bout this."

Brianne's grip on the bars tightened. She flicked another peek at the killer. "My father won't like it if you—"

"Just send the telegram, Smith," Malo Navaja ordered softly from behind her.

The sheriff froze.

Brianne whirled around.

The dark man had risen to his feet, his tall muscular body crowding the cell, his spread-legged stance threatening. "The telegram, Sheriff. Nothing more."

At first, disbelief crossed Smith's fat features. But the prisoner's quiet warning must have frightened him, because he eased back a step. "Yeah, well, I'll think about it—after supper." Not glancing at either of them again, he left the room.

Brianne felt the confines of the cell choking off her breath.

She was alone with a man who *mutilated* people. Her knuckles grew white as she gripped the bars. Every nerve in her body tingled with fear. She closed her eyes and pressed her forehead against the cold metal in an effort to stop shaking.

"Sit down, *chica*," the murderer commanded in a smooth voice. "I won't come near you." He paused, then a spark of amusement laced his tone. "I can't get past the smell."

For a breathless moment, Brianne wondered if it were possible to die from relief, then lowering her hands, she clasped them tightly while silently vowing to attend church every Sunday for the rest of her life.

But what if he was just trying to catch her off guard? Lull her into relaxing so he could pounce on her? Unable to trust his insulting statement, yet fearing what he might do if she didn't obey, she edged toward the rope bed and perched stiffly on one corner, keeping her attention fixed straight ahead and listening for any threatening movement.

Rope creaked across the cell.

Her body clenched. She sent a panicked glance toward the killer, then breathed again when she saw that he'd only returned to his seat. Too, she couldn't help but notice the way his gaze boldly roamed the damp, muck-covered front of her shirt.

"The chicken that shit on you must have been a big one."

Brianne tried to smile, but couldn't. She swallowed and turned her head.

When silence stretched into nerve-twisting minutes, she peeked over at him. He had crossed his arms, leaned against the wall, and lowered his lashes. The flickering glow from the lantern danced over the tough planes and angles of his face, glinting off the thick dark hair that toppled onto his brow.

Suddenly his eyes opened to meet hers. "Why're you wearing men's clothes?"

Brianne flinched at the sound of his voice, then forced herself to calm down. She considered his question. But what could she say? Because she'd run away from home? Because she'd feared being molested? Because a woman traveling alone would have sparked unwanted attention that might have somehow reached her father? "They're comfortable."

"They look like hell."

"Your opinion doesn't matter." She clamped her mouth shut. One of these days her swift tongue was going to get her killed. *If not this day.*

Fortunately, the man seemed to ignore her brazen outburst. But her relief was short-lived when he sat up suddenly and glared at her.

"Do you even know Art Logan?"

"Of course I do—"

"Describe him."

Brianne stared in disbelief. "Why?"

He rose to his feet.

"Medium height, white hair, bull-like shoulders and arms," she babbled hurriedly. "Why are you asking all these questions? You heard what I told the sheriff—"

"Lady, don't play me for a fool. I know you're not Logan's daughter." He advanced a step. "Now who are you? And what's your link with him?"

"What do you mean, I'm not his daughter? That's absurd. I most certainly—"

"Shit. Do you think I'm stupid?" The corded muscles in his arms drew tight.

Brianne pressed back and clutched her shirt as if to protect herself. No. He didn't look stupid. He looked ready to do her tremendous harm!

"Get this straight, lady. I *know* you're not Brianne Logan." The breath hissed through his teeth. "I watched them bury her."

2

"What?" Brianne jerked forward on the bunk. "You couldn't have! *I'm not dead.*"

He closed the distance between them and grabbed a handful of her hair. Blue eyes blazed into hers. "Who are you?"

God help her. What could she tell him? He wouldn't believe the truth. "Please—"

He released her so suddenly, she nearly toppled off the cot. Clutching the mattress for support, she fought to gather her scattered senses. Did he speak the truth? Had there been a funeral for Brianne Logan? Dear God. Had her mother been told this? "W-when did this funeral take place?"

The outlaw strode to the window and stared out. "A couple months back."

"In March?" Right after she'd run away. When he didn't answer, she pressed on. "Let me guess. You never saw the body, just the coffin?"

He spun around. "I saw Logan's daughter. Saw her mangled body and mutilated face."

"Oh, my God." Brianne felt faint. They'd buried another woman and said it was *her*? Why? Did her running away have anything to do with it? Oh, God. Her father couldn't have done something so brutal just to protect his precious reputation from scandal. Yes, he could, a little voice argued. "Listen, mister—" A sound halted her words, and she saw Malo glance toward the bars.

He tensed.

Almost afraid to look, she warily followed his gaze.

A heavily bearded blond man stood on the outside of the bars, his hairy arms crossed over his chest. Glazed, pea green eyes revealed disbelief. "I don't know how ya do it, Navaja. Only *you* could end up in jail with a switch-tail ta keep ya company."

Her cell mate's stance eased into an icy calmness. "Yeah. Some of us have all the luck. Get me out of here, Sawyer."

The younger man hesitated for an instant. His eyes lit with a hint of smug satisfaction, then casually unfolding his arms, he exposed the keys to the cell and unlocked the door. "Ya better thank yer razor that Pedro sent us for ya. He got his dander up right good after ya busted up the tradin' post this mornin'."

He swung the door open. "Gawd, Navaja. Yer dadgum Wanted Poster's plastered all over them walls. Ya shoulda hightailed it right outta there. Didn't ya see 'em? Didn't ya know even a lazy sheriff like Smith'd sell his balls for a reward like that? Hellfire, Malo, a body'd a thought ya wanted ta get caught." He tossed the keys onto the opposite bunk. "The others are gettin' right tired a breakin' ya outta jail. If it'd been up ta them, they'd a left ya ta hang."

Malo retrieved his gray Stetson and perched it on his head, tugging it low. "It'd take a helluva lot more than one fat sheriff to pull that off." He smiled evilly. "And your gang woulda lost a few members when I escaped." He started toward the open door, then stopped suddenly. His gaze swung to Brianne, and he frowned. Moving to her side, he gripped her by the arm and hauled her to her feet. "Let's go, *chica.* You're coming with me."

She pulled against his grip. "No!"

He tightened his fingers. "You don't have a choice. Now

move your ass." He pushed her forward but didn't release her.

"What are ya doin'?" Sawyer blurted. "Ya cain't take *her.*"

Malo went still. "You gonna stop me?"

His deceptively soft tone sent chills up Brianne's back. God. What had she gotten herself into over one lousy chicken?

Sawyer bristled for the barest instant, then retreated a step. "Ya know what Half Bear thinks 'bout women on a raid. He ain't gonna like this."

I don't like it either, Brianne wanted to scream.

Malo curled his lips into a mean smile. "That's the Comanche's problem."

Comanche? *What Comanche?* Brianne thought wildly.

Still maintaining his hold on her arm, the outlaw shoved past his barrel-chested partner. "Let's go, Clyde. The sheriff's not gonna stay gone forever."

Brianne swallowed a surge of hysteria. Why was he taking her? What did he want? What would he do to her?

The one called Navaja shoved her into the main office, then stopped abruptly.

A gaunt man dressed in dirty, baggy clothes turned from the front window, his gun drawn.

Nothing could have prepared Brianne for the shock of seeing such a horribly distorted face. She instinctively recoiled and glanced away, but the image of the puffy, jagged purple scar that slashed across his features from his left eye to his right jaw remained imprinted on her brain.

"What the hell's this?" the disfigured man rasped.

Clyde Sawyer shrugged. "Ya wanna tell Navaja he cain't take the girl, Frank? Go ahead."

"Christ, Navaja. What'a you want her for?" He holstered his gun and walked toward them. "Jest look at her." He caught her by the chin and twisted her face toward him. "She's covered in crap and ugly as a rotten stump."

Tears stung her eyes from embarrassment and pain as his fingers dug into her flesh.

Malo grabbed the man's arm.

A frightening silence filled the room as the two men stared at each other. A muscle throbbed in her captor's temple. "Never touch what's mine."

Brianne's nerves went crazy. She didn't know which scared her more, the disfigured man or the one who'd just staked his claim.

"Let her go," the killer rasped in a dangerously soft voice.

The scarred man glared his hatred, but released her.

Tossing Frank's hand aside, Malo pushed Brianne to the desk, then down into the sheriff's chair. He retrieved an ivory-handled straight razor from the top drawer and stared down at it as his thumb traced the etching of a coiled snake on the smooth, polished bone surface.

She clung desperately to the seat of the chair, recalling Maria's tales of how Malo Navaja never, *ever* left witnesses.

The others backed up a few steps, their features marked with apprehension as they watched him finger the weapon then slip it beneath his belt.

Reaching behind her, he pulled a gun and holster from a peg and strapped it on, tying it low on his thigh. Without a pause, he dragged her up by the wrist.

Brianne cringed as he forced her toward the entrance.

One of the others said something low that she didn't quite catch, but it sounded like a threat. She felt Malo's hand tense and knew that he'd heard it, too. But that was the least of her concerns. Her thoughts were too full of what she'd heard about outlaw gangs—and what they did to women captives.

She tried to dispel visions of them ripping off her clothes and ruthlessly, savagely assaulting her again and again as each in turn violated her body. Panic surged, and she grabbed onto the door frame as Malo attempted to shove her through. "No! Please, let me go! I didn't do anything to you. Please, please, don't do this."

On a disgusted breath, he pried her hand from the wood and jostled her out the opening.

She fought tears as he hauled her along beside him.

As they moved silently down the sparsely populated

street, she eyed every door from the adobe trading post to the smattering of houses to the livery stables, praying for rescue. But they were closed and locked up for the night or, like the sheriff's place, off the main street and out of sight. Besides, in a town as small as Wichita Falls, even if someone did witness the jailbreak, they wouldn't do anything about it. There just weren't enough people. Smith had been a fool to think he could hold a dangerous criminal like Malo Navaja.

Near a grove of trees at the edge of town, she saw the silhouettes of two more men and several horses. Her terror soared, and for the first time since leaving Santa Fe, she regretted running away. She was at the mercy of the outlaws, and her only protector—if he could be called that—was a vicious killer who would probably murder her when the others were done with her.

She swung her gaze frantically, looking for any means of escape.

Malo's fingers dug into her flesh. "Don't even think about it, *chica.*"

Brianne prayed as she'd never prayed in her life. Stumbling along next to him, she begged for the sheriff to come with a posse of a hundred men—a band of Texas Rangers to appear out of nowhere—a regiment of soldiers. Anything. Even an Indian attack sounded promising.

A horse nickered, snapping her out of her desperate appeal. In the bright moonlight, she met the shocked gaze of another gang member.

"Amigo?" the short Mexican directed at her captor, but continued to stare at her. He seemed to fumble for words, then spoke around something in his mouth. "Er, the *gringa,* she has shit all over her."

The man holding her didn't even acknowledge the wiry desperado. His attention remained fixed on the fourth one in the group.

Nervously, she slid her gaze to the tall, heavily muscled Indian.

He turned his black eyes on her, his harsh, angular features stiff. "Get rid woman."

Malo smiled slowly. "In time."

Brianne's knees buckled. Only the tight grip on her arm kept her upright. *Oh, God.*

The Indian's chin raised, his chest swelled beneath a rawhide vest, his bare arms bunched, straining the beaded bands around bulging muscles. He obviously didn't like defiance.

Malo didn't seem to be intimidated by the fierce snarl on the Comanche's face. His free hand rose to his belt, and he slowly fingered the handle of the razor. "If that's a problem for you, Half Bear, we could always discuss it down by the river."

An undefined expression flickered across the Indian's features. Wariness? Grudging respect? Hatred? Without comment, he turned and vaulted onto his horse. But, by the rigid way he held himself as he rode off, she knew the matter wasn't settled.

When the others had mounted, her captor led her to a palomino, then released her wrist long enough to snag her by the hair. He shoved a boot into the stirrup and swung up. From his towering position, he considered her, then examined her smelly, stained shirt. His gaze drifted to the Mexican. "Hey, Pedro? Where'd you make camp this time?"

"El campo, senor?" the man answered coolly, pushing the object in his mouth to one side. "Is downstream, maybe three miles."

Malo nodded and nudged his horse forward. "I'll meet you there."

Brianne winced when he tugged her hair, forcing her to stumble along beside the horse. Sharp rocks and dead weeds stabbed the soles of her bruised feet. Curse the man!

When they reached the water's edge, the others started across, but Navaja reined in. Still gripping her hair, he dismounted and moved behind her.

Brianne trembled. What was he going to do? Had he brought her to the river so he could kill her and dispose of her body easier? Her heart pounded frantically. Paralyzed with fear, she awaited the slice of the razor across her throat.

Abruptly, he released her hair, then seized her by an arm and the seat of her britches. He pitched her headfirst into the Wichita.

She screamed, arms flailing, as the shallow, frigid water engulfed her. She came up sputtering. "You beast! You rotten bastard!" She clamped a hand over her mouth, knowing she'd just ensured her own death.

The other riders reeled their horses around, and a burst of laughter erupted.

Malo stood on the bank, hands on hips. "Your smell's enough to gag a cockroach." He snatched something out of his saddlebags and tossed it to her. The grayish bar of soap splashed close to her chest. "Clean yourself. Or do you want me to do it?"

Brianne pulled in a relieved breath and lowered her hand. He wasn't going to kill her. Yet.

"Hey, little gal. I'll help ya!" Clyde shouted, a line of teeth flashing through his beard.

Pedro glared at the bearded man. "Do not listen to this *hombre, senorita.* He is not so kind. Pedro, he will be gentle, *si?*"

She shuddered. The thought of a man's hands on her turned her stomach to jelly. Especially these men.

"She doesn't need your kinda help," Malo grated harshly. "Now get the hell outta here." He whirled on her. "Wash."

A rush of anger heated her cheeks. She'd be damned if she'd let him boss her around. If he was going to kill her, let him do it now and save her further miseries. Defiantly, she glared at him. But her courage wilted when he mounted his horse and rode directly at her. She grabbed the soap and began scrubbing vigorously.

Another round of chuckles burst from the men. The Mexican spit out whatever he'd had in his mouth and raised a hand in farewell, the silver conchos twinkling on his black jacket. *"Ole', amigo.* We see you at camp, no?"

Nearly blinded by fear and anger *and* embarrassment, Brianne didn't hear Malo's response and was barely aware of the gang's departure. Her only thoughts were of escape.

Of course, she realized that was all bravado when her

captor stopped his horse dangerously close. She couldn't possibly overpower him—or outrun him. But she *could* pray for a bolt of lightning to strike his arrogant head.

"Get the shit outta your hair, too."

Brianne glowered up at him, but for once, and wisely—or was it cowardly—said nothing. With a disdainful toss of her long hair, she dunked her head then lathered the lye soap into her curls. After all the weeks without a decent bath, it felt wonderful to be really clean, but she'd cut out her tongue before she'd let him know it.

Ignoring the big man on the horse as best she could, she rinsed her hair. When she'd finished, she controlled the urge to throw the bar in his face and handed it to him instead. Their fingers brushed, and a jolt skittered up her arm. Her gaze snapped to his.

Confusion flickered in his eyes briefly before he quickly glanced away and went about replacing the soap in the saddlebags. That done, he reached down and caught her arm.

"I'd rather walk."

"Too bad." He dragged her up in front of him.

His horse sidestepped as water cascaded from her clothes, and she felt them mold to her body. She moaned inwardly, wishing desperately for the filthy, torn chemise she'd finally been forced to discard over a month ago.

Fortunately the outlaw didn't seem to notice her shameful appearance. He merely banded her waist with his arm and snapped the reins.

Slightly eased by his lack of interest, Brianne relaxed. Maybe she'd been wrong about him. Maybe he didn't plan to ravage and kill her, after all. *Or was he just biding his time?*

An early May breeze seeped through her wet shirt, turning the air cool. She shivered and instinctively pressed into the warmth of his broad chest. When she realized what she'd done, she stiffened. But, at her next thought, she almost smiled. Soon, he would be every bit as wet, cold, and miserable as she. She squirmed against him.

He shifted in the saddle, and a firm warmth nudged her bottom.

Her eyes flew wide, and intuitively, she straightened her spine.

The fingers at her waist curled into her side. "Be still, *chica.*" His voice sounded husky, strained. "For both our sakes, be very still."

3

*B*rianne clutched the saddle horn. Be still? She'd never move again! No one in her right mind would play childish games with a killer like Malo Navaja. What was the matter with her?

She leaned forward on the horse, away from his tight body, and willed her pounding heart to slow. He hadn't done anything really threatening so far, and she'd like to keep it that way.

As they silently rode north along the river, Brianne tried to distract herself from her uncertain fate by studying the area. She became aware of the heavy smell of sagebrush, damp leather, and the distant odor of woodsmoke. The roar of gushing water drew her attention, and she turned to see the rapids and cascades that had given the town of Wichita Falls its name.

"Why were you stealing chickens?"

Brianne jumped at the sound of Malo's voice. Quickly gathering her wits, she cleared her throat. "Chicken. One. And I was trying to steal it because I didn't have the money to buy it." She recalled how she had planned to kill the bird and roast it—a task she'd never been forced to do with so many servants around the house. "I guess when you're hungry, you'll do just about anything."

He reined the horse around an eastward bend in the river. "When'd you eat last?"

"Day before yesterday. I pulled weeds for Widow Foster, and she gave me a hunk of bread."

"Don't you have a home?"

"Not anymore."

A light flashed through the trees up ahead, and Brianne caught a glimpse of a low-burning fire. A heavy pounding hammered in her chest. The camp.

As they drew nearer, she could see outlines of the men sitting around the flames. Piles of boulders and fallen trees loomed in the background, casting eerie silhouettes against the sparkling river just beyond. She gripped the pommel, trying to hold her panic in check.

The palomino stepped in a hole and stumbled. Malo braced her with his arm. "Where's your mother?"

For an instant, Brianne forgot her terror as old pain rushed to the surface. "She disappeared two months ago." She lowered her gaze to the saddle horn. "Her name's Suzanne Logan. *Art Logan's* wife, and I've been searching for her. That's one of the reasons I ran—left home."

She glanced up to see the outlaw's mouth draw into an angry, disbelieving line. For pity sakes, what did it take to make this man believe her?

He started to speak.

"'Bout damn time you showed up, Navaja."

Brianne swung her head around to see that they'd entered the camp. Good heavens. Was this another member of the gang? The one who just spoke from his sprawled position by the fire was an older fellow with gray-brown hair sticking out from beneath a dusty hat.

Her palms grew moist when his tiny sunken eyes hooded by heavy brows explored her clothes, stopping to linger on the swell of her breasts pressing against the wet cotton shirt. Not for the first time did she wish her Creator hadn't been quite so generous.

"Goll dang. Look at them teats!" The deep wrinkles

around his mouth stretched into a lewd grin beneath a long drooping mustache, and he jumped to his feet. "Ya gonna share that, Navaja?" The older man raised his arm, revealing a stub that should have been his left hand.

"Gawd, Lou," the hairy Clyde Sawyer chuckled from across the fire. "You'd have ta figure a way ta get it up, first."

"Ya think so, ya young skunk? Well, take lessons, boy." In one swift movement, he was beside her, yanking her from the saddle.

Brianne shrieked and lashed out.

He wrestled her to the ground, his stubby arm pressed against her throat. "Come on, Frank. We got us some screwin' ta do."

Two other men came toward her, their faces leering.

Nearly insane with fear, Brianne twisted. Screamed. Kicked and bucked. "Get away! Don't touch me!"

One of the men caught her hands up over her head and pinned them down while Frank pushed the older man aside and straddled her. His evil face lowered threateningly, his breath foul. "I wanna be first, Pa." He brutally squeezed her breast, then cackled lewdly.

Out of nowhere a spark of silver flashed in the light, and the man on top of her froze, his eyes bulging in horror as someone jerked his head back.

Brianne swallowed a gasp.

Malo Navaja stood behind the disfigured outlaw, clutching his hair with one hand and holding a razor to his throat with the other. "You don't listen, kid," he grated in an icy tone. "The girl's mine . . . till I tell you different."

Frank's Adam's apple bobbed beneath the blade. "Sure, Navaja. Anything you say."

Malo's gaze met Brianne's with concern, then glittered dangerously as it moved over the other men, stopping on the oldest one. "You got any arguments?"

The bearded one, Clyde, released her hands and retreated. "Not me."

The one-handed outlaw stared at the blade pressed against Frank's throat. "Let my boy go, Navaja. We got the message."

Frosty blue eyes stabbed the older man. "Make sure you remember it." As quickly as the blade had appeared, it vanished. Her captor shoved Frank off her and every muscle in her body quaked as he pulled her to her feet. For just an instant, she felt secure in his protection, but quickly came to her senses. He was responsible for this!

"Sit on that log," he ordered, pushing her toward a fallen tree on the other side of the campfire.

Not in any position to argue, she moved forward. She met the hate-filled gaze of the Comanche who was propped lazily against a tree. Near him, Pedro stood, his expression oddly satisfied.

Brianne's belly trembled. For some unexplainable reason, the Mexican frightened her. Reaching the log she sat down, trying to avoid their vulgar stares. Her father's tyranny suddenly seemed minor compared to this. She could feel their eyes on her, feel the glow from the fire heating her face.

After tying his horse, Malo walked in her direction, then stopped as if startled. He searched her face in surprised wonder, then swore softly. "Damn."

Self-consciousness pinched her. She knew she must look awful with her curly, near-dry hair all tangled around her face and the soggy clothes sticking to her body like a coat of paint. She lifted her chin. What did she care. She certainly wasn't out to impress these lechers.

"Ah, *amigo.* The *senorita,* she is an angel, no?" Pedro said as he popped something into his mouth.

Angel? Brianne thought bewilderedly. The man must be blind.

Malo straightened and shot the Mexican a nasty sneer. "What's for grub?"

Pedro traced the line of a mustache above his full upper lip, his eyes on her chest. "Same as always—hardtack and beans."

A shiver ran through her at Pedro's heated perusal. She felt violated.

Ignoring the Mexican, her captor grabbed up two metal plates from a pack on the ground and moved to the black pot sitting half out of the fire.

She was torn between fear of Pedro, of her fate, and the smell of bubbling beans. Her gaze drifted to the simmering cast-iron kettle, and the gnawing ache in her stomach grew to a low growl. Her mouth watered as she watched Malo slop the brown beauties onto the plates, then tear off two chunks of bread from a loaf.

"Why you bring *la senorita, amigo?*" Pedro asked.

Navaja sat down beside Brianne, handing her a plate. "Claims to be a politician's daughter. Figured he'd pay to get her back." He scooped in a mouthful of food.

"What politician?"

"Assemblyman Art Logan."

The little Mexican's gaze moved to Brianne, but he didn't appear surprised. In fact, by the glint in his black eyes, it was almost as if he'd known all along who she was. But his next words belied that fact. "Navaja, he is sure?"

The killer kept eating. "Tell him your name, *chica.*"

Wanting desperately to defy him, yet terrified of the consequences, she cleared her throat. "Brianne Logan."

"Ah." Pedro nodded. *"Si, la senorita,* she bring *mucho dinero,* no?"

"Not as much as that army wagon we're goin' after tomorra," Frank spat. He turned to Half Bear. "What time we leavin'?"

"First light. Sun is two hands high when we reach bluecoat's wagon."

Brianne breathed a sigh of relief now that the talk had turned away from her. And she couldn't help feeling a tiny spark of hope. *Not* that they were returning her to her father, but that they, hopefully, wouldn't harm her if they wanted to collect a ransom. Of course, he wouldn't pay. She was sure of that. He didn't want her, never had, and her showing up again would ruin him, especially after he'd already buried her in front of the whole town of Santa Fe.

Besides, even if he dared to own up to the mistake, *if it was a mistake,* which she doubted, he still couldn't let her come back, not after spending days—and nights—alone on the trail in the company of outlaws. The scandal would, in his eyes, destroy his chances for governor. But her captors didn't need to know—and it gave her more time to plan her escape. Somewhat relaxed, she began to eat.

Clyde Sawyer, stretched his hands out before the fire. "I sure as hell hope this job goes better'n the last 'un. El Hefty's gonna have our butts if we foul this 'un up."

"*El jefe,*" Pedro corrected.

"The boss can't blame us for screwin' up that payroll robbery." Lou jabbed his stubby arm at midair. "How was we supposed to know them goll dang soldiers had more men hidin' less'n a mile away?"

"Half Bear make sure no more follow this time," the Comanche interjected.

A breeze caught a strand of Clyde's hair and slapped it across his mouth. He spit it out and glanced at the Indian. "Gawd, I'll be glad when this is over. I cain't wait ta get outta this hellhole and find a place we can make camp more'n one night in a row."

Brown's stained teeth flashed beneath Frank's disfigured nose. "Kept the sheriff from spottin' us, didn't it?"

"Yeah, but what 'bout now? Smith's gonna be out scoutin' for Navaja." He flicked a scowl at Malo.

"The lawman, he is no worry." Pedro thumbed his hat off his forehead. "The town, she is too small. Not so many men for the posse. No deputy. This sheriff, he will not come alone."

"We're still gonna be takin' a helluva chance goin' up against them soldiers."

"That's why we took on another man," Frank answered, darting a look at Malo. "To even the odds and—"

Malo plopped his empty plate down on top of Brianne's. "Wash 'em."

She bristled, then glanced toward the river that meandered beside the camp, wondering if she could escape. But she knew it wouldn't work. The others, or Malo, would come after her. And catch her. So far, her captor hadn't been cruel—had even protected her—but an attempt to run might change that. She rose, nervously eyeing the men. No. She'd wait for a better opportunity—and surely there would be one.

After she cleaned the utensils with sand and rinsed them in the river, she returned to the fallen log and sat down, trying to make herself as inconspicuous as possible. Though she didn't lift her gaze from the ground, in her peripheral vision she saw Malo pick up his bedroll and saddle, then walk behind a sheltering row of mesquite.

"Amigo? Our company, it bores you?"

Malo reappeared from behind the edge of the trees, then strode toward Brianne and pulled her to her feet. He turned back to the smaller man, the corner of his mouth tilted upward. "Tonight, I need a little privacy."

Her chest nearly exploded with fear. "But what about my father? He won't pay a ransom if you—"

"He's not gonna know, *chica.*"

Pedro grinned. "Ah, *amigo.* What Pedro, he would give to be *you* for one hour."

Malo quirked a brow. "An hour isn't long enough." Ignoring the others, he guided her toward the trees.

Brianne pulled frantically against his hold. "P-please don't do this."

"Don't fight me, *chica.* You'll only get hurt." His gaze seared hers. "And the end result will be the same."

She bit her lip and tried to steel herself for what was to come. It didn't do any good. Images of what he might do flashed through her mind, again and again.

He led her to his spread blankets. Vaguely, she noticed that he'd put his saddle at one end of the covers to use for a pillow.

When he stopped, she just stood there staring at the place he'd prepared. Horrifying visions of another place, another man, rose, but she swiftly shoved them aside. If she thought of that now, she'd fall apart.

Retaining his hold on her with one hand, Malo began unbuttoning his still-damp shirt. Too paralyzed to move, she watched the material part to expose smooth bronze skin and dark, silky hairs.

Distantly, she became aware of the men's muted voices, the low chirp of crickets, the occasional crackle of the fire. Of the savage beat of her own heart.

He was going to rape her. Dear God in heaven, he was going to accomplish what the other man hadn't!

All her fears stormed to the surface. Nearly crazed with panic, she lashed out blindly with her fist. "No, curse you! No!"

The blows could have come from a child for all the attention he paid them. He didn't even wince, but merely tightened his hold. "Yes, *chica*, yes," he mocked in a hard voice. "Now take off your clothes."

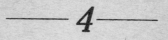

*T*exas Ranger, Hayden Caldwell, studied the woman standing before him. Though she held her chin at a defiant angle, she couldn't conceal the underlying fear in her wide gray eyes. With all that liquid gold hair curling around her smooth face and those soft lips drawn into a willful pout, he was hard-pressed not to act on his baser instincts and kiss her senseless. But she looked so damned young, so vulnerable.

Guilt stung him. Hell, when he'd assumed the real Malo Navaja's identity, Hayden had never dreamed he'd end up kidnapping a girl from a jail cell, nearly frightening her to death—or lusting after her.

For just an instant, he considered letting her go. He didn't really believe she was Art Logan's daughter. She was probably just a runaway who heard the name somewhere. Then he recalled her description of the assemblyman, and Hayden's resolve rooted. She might not be the bastard's daughter, but she damned sure knew him. Possibly intimately. That alone made her valuable.

But what if she told the truth? Hayden's conscience

28

nagged. What if she *was* Logan's daughter? Taking her back could very possibly place her life in danger. The assemblyman may have killed another woman in Brianne's place to cover the scandal of her running away. From what, Hayden couldn't say, but whatever the reason, it might be damaging to the politician's future plans. The man couldn't allow her to show up again.

For a brief moment, Hayden faltered, but he quickly regained control. The risk didn't matter. He couldn't let it.

An ache settled around Hayden's heart. He'd taken over investigating the Hawkins Gang after his brother, Billy Wayne, had been murdered by Logan or one of his men.

Hayden's pain—and rage—grew when he thought of Billy's wife, Kathy, and their two small children. Kids that would grow up without a father. All because of scum like Art Logan. Hayden owed it to Billy.

"Let me go," the woman demanded, yanking him back to the moment. Those smokey gray eyes stared up at him from beneath sooty lashes as she obviously struggled to hold her fear in check.

Compassion tugged at his heart. She was so frightened. Hayden clenched his jaw. *It didn't matter.* He needed her. Releasing a tired breath, he met the girl's gaze. "Get undressed."

Tremors racked her slim shoulders, and Hayden felt another jab of guilt. He brought a hand to the nape of his neck. "Listen, if you don't get those wet things off, you'll catch a fever by morning." Realizing how soft he sounded—a way the real Navaja never would—Hayden hardened his voice. "And I'll be damned if I'll drag a sickly woman all over the countryside."

"Then don't," Brianne countered automatically.

A low sound rumbled from his throat.

She wrapped her arms about her, willing herself to stop shaking, but it didn't do any good. Her muscles ignored the command. She was going to be sick. She just knew it.

"Either take them off, *chica,* or I will."

Swallowing a lump of terror, she forcibly directed her

numb fingers to the buttons on her shirt, but she couldn't make them work. Her thoughts tumbled wildly. She had to get away. She couldn't let him—

"Here, take this." He held out one of the blankets from his bedroll.

At first she didn't understand. Then it hit her. He was offering her privacy. Relieved, she opened her mouth to thank him, but quickly snapped it shut. Why should she? It was his fault she was in this position. Greedily snatching the cover, she spun around.

"I won't tell you again, woman."

Afraid he'd make good his threat, she timidly lifted the blanket over her head, forming a dark cocoon, then clumsily peeled the wet clothes from her body. But she held onto them, refusing to relinquish even the smallest amount of protection. Holding her damp things with one hand, she awkwardly wrapped the blanket around her with the other.

She turned to him. "Why are you doing this to me? I haven't done anything to you. Surely you're man enough to get your own woman without using force." She hated the way it sounded like a compliment, but it was true. Few women could resist a man as attractive as he.

"Force?" His gaze traveled down to her bare shoulders. "I've never had to. Yet."

She stared at him blankly. "You're not going to make me . . . You won't—"

"No." He snatched the wet clothes from her hand. "Get into bed." He moved to a nearby shrub and spread her shirt and britches over it.

Relieved, though not completely reassured, she pulled the blanket tighter around her shoulders, then quickly scrambled onto the pallet and burrowed under another cover. Was she being too gullible? Her mother had always claimed that was her worst fault. Well, that and her excessive curiosity, and her sharp tongue, and her impulsiveness, and her . . . But he *had* said he wouldn't take her by force. She slid him a wary glance.

He stood with his back to her, peeling off his wet jeans.

Oh, God! She clamped a palm over her mouth and quickly averted her gaze.

His hand tugged at the edge of the blanket. "You're gonna have to share this."

Brianne gave a startled squeak, but she couldn't bring herself to look at him. She'd never seen a naked man—not even *that night*—much less lain next to one. "Please . . ."

"Move over."

Biting her lower lip to keep from crying out, she gripped her own blanket, then scooted to the side until she was nearly off the pallet. She held herself completely still, trying desperately to ignore the body sliding down beside her. But when his bare leg brushed hers, Brianne couldn't hold back another outcry. "No!"

Navaja dragged in an exasperated breath, then rolled away from her. "Go to sleep, *chica.*"

For a breathless moment, she didn't move. Every inch of her body waited for him to pounce. After several long minutes, when he didn't stir, she finally began to ease her rigid position.

Unfortunately, with relief came the growing awareness of the man next to her. In the small space that separated them, she could smell his leathery scent that reminded her of warm earth, see the blanket's slight movement with each breath he took. She knew if she just reached out, she could touch his bare back, feel the heat.

Good heavens! What's the matter with me? She forced aside the indecent thoughts and diligently concentrated on plans of escape. Listening to his slow, steady breathing, she wondered if she could possibly get away from him after he fell asleep.

She watched the slight shift of his wavy black hair. He looked so comfortable with those overlong locks nestled against the curve of his saddle, but she couldn't tell if his eyes were open or closed—and she wouldn't be able to tell unless she peeked over his shoulder. No, her better judgment warned. For all she knew, he could be lying there wide-awake . . . waiting.

A branch snapped nearby.

Her eyes flew to the line of trees separating them from camp.

Malo sprang up—and rolled on top of her.

"No!" Brianne threw up her hands, causing her blanket to separate. "Oh God, help mmmm—"

His mouth covered hers in a hard kiss. The naked warmth of his body thrust down on hers.

Brianne twisted savagely, whimpering under the brutal pressure of his lips. She kicked out. Bucked. Clawed at his shoulders.

He caught her by the hair, holding her head still, then kissed her again, forcing the tender flesh of her lips against her teeth.

Another twig cracked.

Malo jerked his head up and swung it to the side, his body tense. "What the hell do you want?"

"Ah, *amigo*. Pedro, he disturbs?" The little Mexican stepped out of the shadows, his mocking tone matching the nasty grin on his face. His eyes raked Brianne. "But, Half Bear, he say, go tell Navaja, his watch, it begins at two."

Though she shook with terror, Brianne felt the muscles in Malo's stomach relax.

"I'll be there. Get the hell outta here." Malo returned his attention to Brianne. His gaze bore into hers. But even through her fear, in the dim moonlight she could see a silent appeal in his eyes, one that promised he wouldn't hurt her if she didn't fight him in front of Pedro.

Terrified—though baffled, she steeled herself not to resist when he again lowered his mouth to hers.

Soft, slow, almost chaste, the gentleness of his kiss took her by surprise.

Distantly, she heard Pedro's footsteps recede.

Malo lifted his head and stared down at her. "Sorry, *chica*. But if Pedro thought I wasn't . . . er . . . enjoying myself, he'd see to it that he or one of the others did."

An apology was the last thing she'd expected, and it left her more confused than ever. Why did he want the others to think he was ravaging her when he obviously wasn't going

32

to? Not that she was complaining, but why would he protect her when he was the one who took her in the first place?

Puzzled, she met his eyes. Instantly, she realized her mistake. He was too close, too appealing . . . too naked.

The heat of his bare flesh covering hers stirred unfamiliar sensations. She could feel the movement of his taut stomach on her own as he breathed, his silky chest hairs brushing the peaks of her breasts, the strength in his thighs pressed intimately over hers.

An unexpected shiver raced through her belly, and a force seemed to hold her in place, hold her gaze locked to his. The air became thick, hot.

His fingers tightened in her hair. "Damn."

The sound of his muttered curse was like a slap to her senses, bringing her to full awareness. Frightened, she turned her head to the side, her voice a shaky rasp. "Please, get off me."

He rolled away and sprang to his feet.

Brianne closed her eyes, clutching the blanket. She didn't dare look at him. She couldn't. Her body still tingled crazily. What was happening? She should be scared to death instead of intrigued, *aroused*.

But something, maybe instinct, told her this man wouldn't really hurt her. Lifting her lashes just the tiniest bit, she peeked up at him, feeling a wave of relief when she saw that he'd pulled on his jeans.

He stared down at her. "Get some sleep, *chica*." He started to walk away, then hesitated before leaning over to pick up her clothes. "And don't try anything foolish. I'd hate to have to hurt you."

Hoping she'd heed his threat, Hayden headed for the bottom of a mountain of boulders, away from camp—and the girl.

Hot blood still pumped through his loins. Shit. He hadn't been this fired up since he was a kid. And all because of a meaningless kiss. Feeling like a fool he released a disgusted breath. He had more important things to think about. Like how he was going to stop that robbery tomorrow without getting the girl killed—or himself.

He gave a moment's thought to leaving her alone in his bedroll, wondering if the others might bother her, or if she'd be reckless enough to attempt escape. Probably, but he'd be close if anyone came snooping around. Nor would she get very far if she tried to run, not in full moonlight—without her clothes.

After again spreading her garments out, he climbed up into the cradle of a rock formation and settled in until time for his watch, confident that he could handle most any situation that came up. He always had. After all, he wasn't a fourth generation lawman for nothing.

But then, Billy Wayne had been, too. What good had it done him? Except earn him an early grave. Hayden could still remember the day when Captain McNelly called him into his tent and told him about Billy. The anger—the pain—had nearly sent him to his knees. Billy was his little brother . . . his only brother. And Kathy, Billy's wife. God, what would she do without him? Her whole world was wrapped up in that smiling jackass.

Hayden felt moisture sting his eyes, and he blinked rapidly. Damn Art Logan. And damn the bastard that pulled the trigger—whose identity Hayden had yet to discover. But he would. Oh, yes, he would.

He recalled what McNelly had told him about Billy's investigation into the Hawkins Gang, and how Billy believed that Art Logan was behind them.

The very next morning Hayden had set out for Santa Fe, determined to prove Billy's theory and see Logan and his cutthroats swing.

A day's ride out of New Mexico's capital, in a little town called Las Vegas, Hayden had laid over for the night. While there, he saw Pedro Torres, one of the five gang members that Billy had sketched and sent to McNelly.

For two days, Hayden watched and listened to Pedro and the other men he'd joined up with in one of the cantinas. Finally, on the third day, the gang's conversation had turned to *el jefe*, their silent leader.

"What's El Hefty got fer us next?" the scarred Frank Hawkins had asked.

Pedro lowered his voice. *"El jefe,* he say we need another *bandito* for de big jobs."

"What fer?" Lou Hawkins had protested angrily. "We gotta split the take betwixt the five of us—and the boss—as it is. Sometimes, I wish me an' Franky hadn't never hooked up with you an' the Injun. We was doin' fine before."

The Mexican rolled his eyes, then scooted his chair closer to the table. "Pedro, he no question *el jefe.* Just obey. And *el jefe* say *mucho* bad *hombre* in *la carcel*—de jail, Santa Fe. He say Pedro, get Navaja out. Three days. When town at funeral."

Hayden smiled, recalling how shocked he'd been at the time to learn that Navaja had finally been caught. Automatically, Hayden's hand rose to the scar along his left jaw. A memento from his last encounter with the vicious bastard. But on that day in Las Vegas, he hadn't been thinking about his scar. He'd been planning.

Hayden hadn't known at the time whose funeral would conceal the gang's jailbreak. Not that it had mattered. What *did* matter was that Hayden had to get to Santa Fe and have Navaja secretly moved, then assume the killer's place in the cell. Since Billy's report revealed that the Hawkinses had never crossed paths with Malo Navaja, Hayden was certain his plan to infiltrate the gang would work.

When he reached Santa Fe the next afternoon, he met with Sheriff Tate, then, after arranging to have Navaja transferred to Fort Marcy, just out of town, and for Hayden to take the killer's place on the following day, Hayden had gotten a room at the Exchange Hotel for the night.

The next morning, he learned that Art Logan's daughter had been killed. *Mutilated.* Someone had viciously raped her, then carved her up and left her in her own bed.

Wondering if Logan, himself, might have somehow been involved, Hayden had gone to see the girl's body, then wondered how Logan could even tell it was his daughter. Nothing remained of her face.

Hayden shifted against the rocks, unwilling to dwell on the gruesome memory. Besides, he didn't have time to linger in the past. He still had that robbery tomorrow to worry about—and hope his message had reached the Rangers.

Shit, he'd purposely gotten himself arrested by Sheriff Smith so the fat man would wire Ranger Headquarters for someone to come after Malo Navaja. It was a prearranged signal between Hayden and the Rangers. Ever since he'd joined up with the Hawkins Gang, that was how he'd gotten word to headquarters. The wires sent by various sheriffs who'd captured Malo Navaja gave the Rangers the approximate location of the next robbery. He just hoped the outlaws didn't start associating his captures with the foiled holdup attempts.

Stretching his legs, he looped his thumbs in the waistband of his jeans. If all went according to plan, the scheme to steal the payroll going to Fort Sill tomorrow would be just another bungled job. Hayden smiled. And sooner or later, the boss man would tire of defeat and hopefully summon Pedro . . . or the entire gang.

Either way, Hayden would have him. *If* he lived through tomorrow.

5

*H*ayden watched the Texas sky lighten to a pale pink, then rose from his seat on the boulder—a spot he'd chosen so he could also keep an eye on the men in camp. Tiredly, he placed a hand to his spine and arched, trying to relieve some of the stiffness. He wished he could have gotten some sleep earlier, before he began the night's vigil. But he hadn't.

He wouldn't have minded sharing his bedroll with the girl, but she obviously did. Uncertainty about her identity bothered him. Was she Logan's daughter or just a whore with a gift for acting? He recalled how frightened she'd been—or seemed to have been—and whether she was pure or tainted, she'd had every right to have been scared. If he'd been the real Malo Navaja, she'd have been raped last night—and this morning, she'd probably be dead. Hayden had seen that mutilating bastard's work too many times.

He slid a look in the direction where the girl now slept on his blankets just beyond the concealing shadow of trees. As much as he hated to frighten her more, he'd have to. He needed to tie her up until after the robbery. He didn't want to chance her getting in the way of a stray bullet.

Expelling a long breath, he strode toward the small grove.

But as he broke through the undergrowth, he froze mid-stride.

She was gone.

A cold, murderous feeling curled in his gut. He'd kill the sonofabitch who'd taken her. He headed for the main camp, an angry cloud blurring his vision. When he cleared the trees, he sent a rapid glance over the area. Half Bear and Pedro stood near the river, talking low. Frank and the others still slept. But there was no sign of the girl.

"Buenas dias, amigo." Pedro sucked loudly on a piece of candy. "Your night, she was good, no?"

"Where's the girl?" Hayden demanded.

Half Bear swung around, his black eyes hard. "Woman gone?"

"Ah, *amigo,* no. You do not let the little bird fly?"

"No," Hayden ground out. "But she damned sure isn't where I left her." He pinned the *bandito* with a glare. "You wouldn't happen to know anything about that, would you, Mex?" Sudden visions of Pedro dragging the girl off flashed in Hayden's mind.

The little outlaw slapped a hand on his chest in an obvious effort to appear wounded, but a gleam of satisfaction flared in his eyes. "Pedro, he does not see *senorita* since Navaja, he take his pleasure." His gaze mocked. "Pedro think Navaja, he maybe not so much man. Maybe the *senorita,* she is disappointed?" He grinned at Half Bear. "Maybe she search for another man, no?"

Like hell, Hayden thought. The girl wanted another bed partner about as much as she wanted a snakebite—at least that's the impression she'd given him, whether real or fake. Feeling a surge of relief that they obviously hadn't seen her, Hayden raked the outlaw with a cold sneer. "She wouldn't have the strength to take anyone else on . . ." He paused meaningfully, ". . . after last night."

Pedro choked on his candy.

Hayden smiled to himself and glanced knowingly at the mountain of boulders. She had to be up there somewhere. She couldn't have made it across the valley without him or one of the others seeing her. The boulders, yes. But not the plains. The moon had been full last night as he well remembered. The whole countryside had been lit up in a bluish light. Hell, a jackrabbit couldn't have moved out in the open flatland without being spotted.

Still, it didn't do his ego any good to know she'd escaped him . . . however temporary. The witch.

Frank rose from his bedroll, clutching a timepiece connected to a chain on his belt. "That payroll wagon's gonna be here in less'n an hour," he mumbled through sleep-thickened lips. "We'd better get a move on." He kicked Lou. "Get up, Pa. Time's awastin'."

Half Bear strode to his horse, then lifted a hand. "I go now. Make sure more soldiers no follow."

"Better make it quick, Injun," Lou slurred, rubbing his stubby arm. "Accordin' ta El Hefty, that wagon's s'posed ta come through not long after daybreak."

"El jefe," Pedro corrected in an exasperated voice. Then turning to Hayden, he grinned cockily. "Pedro, he find *senorita,* no?"

"You got that right, Mex. No."

The *bandito's* eyes narrowed.

Half Bear mounted his horse as Clyde sat up, scratching his heavily bearded face. "Where the hell's the coffee?"

Shutting out the others, Hayden headed for the mountain. He had to find the girl. Fast.

As he passed his bedroll, he paused, noting that one of the blankets, too, was missing. Realizing she must have taken it, he picked up the other one. Instantly it brought to mind how her hair had shone against it last night in the moonlight.

Shit. He didn't have time for this. Dropping the wool, he grabbed up his now-dry shirt and stalked toward the boulders.

Crouched down behind a sharp rock, Brianne watched Malo Navaja making his way in her direction. Her heart pounded wildly. *He knows I'm here, and he's going to find me.*

She shot a frantic glance around. No place to run. To hide. If she even moved, he'd spot her. *God help her.*

A sudden rumble shook the ground.

She scanned the area hurriedly.

The Indian called Half Bear, who had ridden off just moments ago, was returning. He raced over a rise, headed straight for the outlaw's camp.

Her gaze swung to Malo Navaja, and she saw that he, too, must have seen the Indian return. He was retreating, obviously to join the others. Thank heavens.

Momentarily relieved, she watched him until he reached the bottom and gathered his bedroll and saddle. He tossed both on his palomino and tightened the cinch, then swung up. Pulling his hat low, he shifted in annoyance, then sent a disgusted glance in the direction of her hiding place.

When he rode out, the others also mounted up and headed for the flatland below to meet the Indian.

Off in the distance, she could see a cluster of mesquite trees, and realized that must be where they'd hide until time to attack the army wagon.

She squinted against the rising sun, trying to see if anyone—anything—was coming. But all she saw was the Indian, still riding furiously. He met up with the others out in the open and made several abrupt movements with his hands.

Pedro drew his guns. The rest followed his lead.

Except Malo.

He just sat there staring at the mountain. Finally, with a subdued shake of his head, he drew his weapon.

From her concealed position, she could view the entire valley. As she'd expected, the outlaws took cover behind the mesquite just before the wagon plodded up over a hill into view.

Her pulse quickened. She had to warn the soldiers of the ambush somehow. Seeing nothing near her that would be of any help, she jumped to her feet, wishing she'd made time in her hurried escape to find her clothes. Clutching the blanket to her chest, she frantically waved her arm over her head. "Look out!" she screamed.

The outlaws whirled toward her.

"Get down!" Malo shouted.

The wagon driver jerked his head up in shock.

Gunshots exploded.

Brianne gasped and clutched the cover as the outlaws charged out from behind the trees and opened fire on the defenseless wagon. Horrified, she watched the driver fall.

Suddenly, the canvas covering the wagon bed dropped away—and soldiers poured over the sides, guns blazing.

Clyde toppled from his horse.

Pedro whirled his mare around and raced toward the mountain where she stood, then disappeared.

Frank and Lou shot wildly, their horses rearing up and circling fearfully. An instant later, they bolted in the direction Pedro had taken.

Just as they reached the foot of the mountain, Lou slumped forward, and Brianne could see blood staining the back of his shirt.

Half Bear and Malo kept firing, both bent low over their mounts.

Brianne held her breath as she watched Navaja. He was aiming too high—and none of the soldiers fired back at him. It was almost as if they'd expected the holdup. They seemed to be more concerned with the Indian and the men riding for cover. Didn't they know Malo was the most dangerous of the group?

When the last of the outlaws had disappeared from sight around the boulders, Brianne stood up. Now was her chance to get away.

Scurrying down as fast as she could, she rammed her foot into a jagged rock and tripped. Her hands flew out to break the fall. Pain cut into her knee. Stones scraped across her palms. Scrambling to her feet, she ignored the raw burning and the blood that trickled down her leg. Gathering the blanket close, she broke into a dead run and charged after the soldiers, waving one hand wildly. "Help! Help me!"

A horse bolted from behind the rocks, directly in front of her. Startled, she jumped back—but not quickly enough.

Through the dust, an arm snaked out and caught her by the waist.

"No!" She twisted frantically.

41

It didn't help. The man hauled her up the animal's side and held her fast.

Clawing and cursing, Brianne kicked savagely. "No! Damn you, no! Let me go!"

The arm tightened, nearly cutting off her breath.

The horse burst into a gallop.

Brianne swung her fists viciously. She screamed again and again.

The man's arm drew her closer. "Settle down, *chica,* or you're gonna get us both killed."

6

*M*alo?" Brianne whispered with a measure of relief she knew she shouldn't be feeling. It could so easily have been one of the others. Then anger set in. Curse the man. If it hadn't been for him, she might have gotten away. Furious, she struggled in his hold, knowing it was futile. She'd never be able to overpower him.

"Settle down," he commanded in a hard voice, his hand tightening unmercifully on her side.

Aching and defeated, she eased her nails out of the flesh on his arm and grabbed for anything stable. Her fingers closed around leather ties attached to the saddle. She didn't know how angry she'd made him, but she certainly didn't want to make matters any worse by falling off a racing horse.

Hanging on for dear life, she tried to ignore the painful grip on her waist and the stirrup digging into her hip, the jolting that jarred her teeth and the choking dust that billowed up from the dry Texas ground. She ducked her head, but it didn't help. The other outlaws kept closing in around Malo's horse, churning the soil as they dashed for freedom.

43

As if sensing her discomfort, her captor hauled her up over the saddle then onto his lap.

Instinctively, she buried her face into his chest to avoid the dust.

The hand at her waist pressed her closer.

Brianne tried not to think about how secure that made her feel.

Fortunately, the ride was fairly short in duration. Since the soldiers didn't have mounts, they weren't able to follow, and the robbers got away with little effort. Oddly, she wondered at that. If the soldiers had known about the robbery, then why hadn't they had extra men and horses somewhere close by? If she didn't know better, she'd have thought they just wanted to stop the holdup, not catch the outlaws.

Realizing her escape had been successfully thwarted, a surge of loss overwhelmed her. She wanted to cry out her frustration and gnash her teeth at the same time. She'd been so close to freedom.

Navaja drew his horse to a halt, then immediately dropped Brianne to the ground.

She grabbed at the blanket to keep from exposing herself as she hit the hard-packed dirt. But in doing so, she landed on her injured knee. Her eyes stung as pain shot up her leg. "Curse you!" she cried, but the words came out like a raspy whimper.

Fighting back the urge to burst into tears, she drew the cover around her knees, hugging them close to her chest. She'd be damned if she'd give him the satisfaction of knowing he'd hurt her.

Not that he'd have noticed, anyway. He completely ignored her while he unsaddled his horse. Unsaddled his horse? For the first time, she realized they were in a deserted Mexican village. A line of empty adobe huts rose up from the earth to blend with the barren landscape.

She knew this place. It was about ten miles out of Wichita Falls. She'd passed through here once with her uncle Lecil. Though he stopped by Santa Fe often during his trail drives, it was the first and only time Brianne ever remembered going to visit him, and Uncle Lecil hadn't wanted to be separated from them. He'd asked Brianne and her mother to accompany him on his sad journey to visit a dying friend. The trip took them through this very place.

The thought of Uncle Lecil and her mother brought on another wave of agony. When her mother disappeared, Father had told everyone in Santa Fe that Suzanne had gone to visit her brother but never arrived. He said he feared she'd been kidnapped and possibly killed.

But Brianne knew that wasn't true. Her mother never once mentioned going to Uncle Lecil's. She just up and vanished in the middle of the night—clothes and all.

That's why Brianne had been so desperate to find her. But she hadn't known where to begin looking. Uncle Lecil was her only hope. Unfortunately, the journey to his ranch in Fort Worth had been long and difficult for a woman on foot, catching a ride whenever she could. Because of the Indian troubles in northern Texas, there weren't many travelers, and by the time she'd reached Wichita Falls, she'd been exhausted . . . and starved. After earning only one meal in three days, stealing the chicken had been her last resort.

And look what that had cost her. Still, she held onto the hope that her uncle knew something about her mother's whereabouts. Anything.

"Get up."

Her thoughts cleared, and she lifted her gaze to see Malo towering over her, hands on hips. But she didn't move. She couldn't. He was standing on the edge of the blanket.

His eyes narrowed. "If you value your life, *chica,* you'll stop these senseless games. Now get up."

It was the first time he'd really threatened her, and she didn't mind admitting, it scared the stuffing out of her. This man wasn't one to cross. Tugging lightly on the coarse wool beneath his boot, she sent him a pleading look. "Could you move your foot?"

His attention shot downward, and he immediately stepped back.

Holding tightly to the blanket, she rose to her feet, trying not to flinch at the pain that stabbed through her knee.

He grasped her by the arm and, none too gently, marched her toward one of the shabby buildings. Once inside, he thrust her up against a lone supporting beam in the center of the room. "Maybe this time you'll stay put."

Then she noticed the rope he carried.

Sickening panic hit her with the force of a gale. She couldn't bear to be tied up. "Please don't."

Malo seemed mildly surprised, then frowned down at the braided cord draped across his palm. "It's necessary, *chica.*" He looped it behind the post then drew it around her arms and beneath her breasts, again and again, pulling it snug.

Brianne stared straight ahead, trying not to think, not to tremble, as horrifying memories of the last time she'd been bound threatened to steal her control.

"When we're settled, I'll bring your clothes."

The sound of the deep tone startled her. It was so different from the *other* one. She forced her eyes to focus, then glanced at the hated bindings. Though he'd banded her arms with the rope, he'd left them down at her sides. Unlike the last time, at least she could move her hands—and keep the lower half of the blanket pulled together, she thought belatedly. Although it certainly didn't help the gaping upper part that revealed an embarrassing amount of cleavage.

Her captor stepped away, as if to inspect his handiwork. His gaze stopped at her chest. For a long time he just stood there, staring. Slowly, those metal blue eyes rose to meet hers. They flashed appreciatively before sliding again to her exposed flesh.

She pressed against the beam and watched helplessly as he lifted a hand to her breast.

But he didn't touch her. Instead, he gently pulled the edges of the material together.

"Hey, Navaja. Git out here. Ya can poke the bitch later, Pa's bleedin' bad," Frank shouted.

Malo slowly lowered his hand. Without looking at her, he turned and left.

The fear spiraling through her belly slowed to a churn. God, what had she done to deserve this?

Stop it! You're only making it worse. She glanced around at her prison—and that's exactly what it was, a lifeless prison. Dirt floors, crumbling walls, and beams covered by spiderwebs surrounded her. A stale, musky odor thickened the air, and she closed her eyes, taking short, shallow breaths.

Pain shot through her knee, and she bent forward, trying to see her wound. But the blanket covered her legs almost to the floor. Shifting slightly, she released her hold on half the wool, then raised her knee.

Most of the blood down her leg had been wiped away, but what remained left her feeling light-headed. An ugly gash, clotted with moist blood, revealed tiny pieces of rock and sand imbedded in puffy red flesh.

She'd had enough experience with injuries—*God, had she ever*—to know that if it wasn't taken care of soon, infection would set in. She couldn't afford that if she planned to escape. Which she most certainly did!

The room darkened suddenly.

Brianne snatched the blanket together and glanced at the open doorway.

A shadowy figure stood silhouetted in the sunlight. "Ya know anything 'bout doctorin' gunshot wounds?"

Though she couldn't see his scarred face, Brianne had no trouble recognizing Frank's voice. "No."

He stepped inside, his gait slow as he approached her. Light filled the room when he moved from the doorway, and Brianne fought the urge to cringe. The sun's bright glow illuminated the purple, diagonal slash across his face. "My pa's gonna die if'n he don't get help." He glared at her. "Ta my way a figurin', all womenfolk knows somethin' 'bout doctorin'." He bent close. "Sure would rile me if my pa died when *someone* coulda helped him."

Brianne didn't miss the intended threat. Her heartbeat quickened. "I-I've never seen a gunshot wound. I never even saw a man shot until today."

"Ya seen who gunned my pa?"

"No. I saw your friend Clyde fall."

Frank snorted. "That 'no-count? Shoulda been kilt long 'afore now. Was more a hindrance than a help." He stepped closer, and she could see the lines of genuine worry crinkling the corners of his mud brown eyes. "Ya better not be lyin' ta me 'bout doctorin', gal." His foul breath blew across her face. "Ya jist better not."

Brianne didn't even inhale until the man turned and left the room. He made her skin shrivel, but she knew if she really did know anything about doctoring, she would have helped his pa. Not because of any threat, but because it was the decent thing to do. Brianne may have had a bastard for a father, but her mother had been a kind, God-fearing woman. And, thank heavens, most of Suzanne's compassionate traits had been passed on to Brianne.

For the next few minutes, she listened to the sounds coming from outside, sometimes loud bellows, sometimes quiet mumbles, or the creak of saddle leather. But no one came in—and that suited her just fine.

She passed the time studying the bare room, planning ways to escape, digging her toes in the dirt, and blowing the hair out of her eyes.

A sudden vision of Malo Navaja's hands tangled in the heavy locks rose. With it came heated memories of the way he'd kissed her . . . lain on top of her. Naked.

An unexpected shiver skittered through her belly that had nothing to do with fear. She clamped her lips tightly together. Of course it was fear! She couldn't possibly have enjoyed *that*. Not after the other—

The room again went dark as another figure passed through the doorway.

Brianne whipped her head around to see her captor's tall frame walking toward her. In his hand, he held her clothes. Thank goodness. At least now she could preserve some of her modesty.

Without speaking, he tossed the garments on the ground in front of her, then moved to untie her bindings. His warm fingers brushed her wrists, causing queer little tingles to skitter up her arms. She did her best to ignore them.

When the ropes fell away, she gripped hard on the edges of the blanket for composure as well as modesty before turning to face him. "Thank you." She'd meant to sound sarcastic, but her tone came out entirely too sincere.

Angry with herself, she scooped up her clothes, then waited for him to leave.

He didn't move.

She glared at him.

"We gonna stand here all day, *chica?* Or are you wanting my help?"

"I most certainly am not. I'm waiting for you to leave so I can dress."

"You're gonna have a long wait."

"But—"

"Get dressed."

"But—"

"Woman, are you hard of hearing? Or just hardheaded?"

Brianne gritted her teeth. "Neither. I just don't happen to enjoy dressing in front of strangers."

"I'm not a stranger anymore," he said softly.

Blood rushed to her face as intimate memories of the night before wavered in her mind's eye. She could almost feel the warmth of his bare body. Appalled, she whirled around, presenting him with her backside. The barbaric beast didn't have a lick of decency!

Pulling the blanket up over her head, she determinedly held the shirt under one arm long enough to drag on the britches, then wrapped and tucked the cover beneath her arms so she could shove them into the sleeves of the red plaid shirt.

"My God!"

Brianne froze, instantly realizing what she'd done. Oh no. How could she have forgotten? Humiliation surged over her in waves. *Please, God. Don't let him ask.* She whipped the blanket up higher and clutched it so hard her knuckles felt numb. With much more bravado than she felt, she carefully controlled her features, then faced Navaja. "Is something wrong?"

His expression was murderous, his eyes nearly black. "Who did it?" He took a step closer, his anger almost tangible. "Who put those marks on you?"

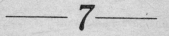

7

*S*corched by an anger he couldn't begin to fathom, Hayden stared down at Brianne. Though she now faced him, he could still see the slim white curve of her bare spine, the satiny smoothness of her skin, and the vicious red marks that couldn't be more than a couple months old, welts that revealed how much she'd suffered at the cruel hands of a maniac. "Who did it?" he asked again, gentler this time, yet unwilling to examine this fierce need to put a name to the person who hurt her.

"I fell out of a tree," she blurted, gripping the shirt closer to her chest.

Hayden stared into those incredible silver eyes. "You're lying, *chica.*" He closed his hands over her shoulders. She felt so small, so easy to damage, it made him want to squash the snake who'd marked her. "Tell me who used the strap."

Brianne shivered beneath his oddly tender touch and soothing voice, but she knew if she answered truthfully, he'd demand she tell him more. She couldn't even think about that last beating, much less tell someone. Inhaling deeply, she met his gaze without wavering. "A disappointed lover."

His hands fell away as if she'd burned him. Revulsion twisted his features, and he abruptly turned away. "Finish dressing," he said in a tight voice. "You're gonna make yourself useful."

His rejection hurt, and she didn't even know why. She barely knew the man. Controlling her wayward emotions, she clamped her teeth together. She didn't care what this killer thought. Not one whit.

Watching to make sure he didn't turn around, Brianne slipped into the shirt and quickly buttoned it. When she'd finished, she dropped the blanket. "I already told Frank that I don't know anything about tending gunshot wounds."

"You can cook, can't you?" he asked, casting a glance over his shoulder.

Brianne fought the urge to roll her eyes. There were a lot of things she did very well, but cooking wasn't one of them. Until shortly before she'd run away, there'd always been a pack of servants filling the house. Instantly, a vision of sweet, smiling Maria bustling around the kitchen in the hacienda rose. Loneliness cut into Brianne. Maria had disappeared the same night as Mother.

Brianne gave herself a mental shake, and recalled Malo's question. She opened her mouth to tell him she didn't know the first thing about cooking, but quickly snapped it shut when an idea flashed. If she gave it a try, she might manage to poison the bastards.

Deciding not to answer directly—one lie a day was enough—she tucked the oversize shirt into her britches and stepped forward. "Where's the stove?"

He stared down at her from his great height, looking for all the world as if he were trying not to smile. "You'll have to make do with a campfire."

"Oh." Hiding a groan, she followed him out the door.

Unseasonably hot wind blew across the dusty soil, raising the acrid scent of dry sage and fresh manure. Brianne brought a hand to her nose and turned her head to dispel the offensive odor.

Several earthen huts clustered on one side of the road. At

the end of the street, she saw the outlaws' horses. They'd been led inside an open adobe building that might have once been a livery.

Half Bear had obviously posted himself as guard over the animals. He sat near the opening with his back to the wall, knees raised. Though his arms rested on his bent limbs, appearing completely relaxed, she wasn't fooled. The Indian struck her as too shrewd not to remain fully alert.

Pedro, dressed in a flashy black outfit, stood nearby, cinching his horse as if preparing to leave, his eyes on her, warmly exploring her body. She suppressed an eerie shiver.

Sneaking another peek at her captor, she decided she preferred his insolence to Pedro's shiftiness. At least Navaja was up-front about his unsavory intentions.

As they neared the end building, Frank stepped out of a doorway to the side, and she could tell by the strained expression on his face that things weren't going well with his father. The flesh surrounding the younger man's scar had paled, his posture slumped. A bleak, hopelessness shadowed his dark eyes.

"Pa's bad, Navaja," he said in a heavy voice. "Real bad."

Malo halted, his features controlled, but he couldn't disguise the flicker of sympathy in his eyes. "Did you get the bullet out?"

Frank shook his straggly brown head. "Cain't reach it. It's hung up next to his ribs. Looks like the bullet went into his back and bounced off a bone."

Though she tried not to, Brianne couldn't stop the flash of compassion she felt for the man. For all his faults, Frank loved his pa. Memories of her own mother rose—and hurt.

A low, pitiful moan sounded from behind Frank, and his skin lightened another shade. "Christ," he half cried. He lowered his head, his throat working spasmodically.

"Have you tried searing the flesh closed?" Brianne offered, not wanting to feel sorry for him but unable to control it.

Frank stared at her blankly.

"I think she wants to know if you've tried cauterizing the wound," Malo clarified, his own voice a little rough.

"No. I gotta figure a way ta get the bullet out first." He jammed skinny fingers into his mat of grimy hair and glanced back at the dark doorway behind him. "Pa'll die for sure if'n I don't."

"Ah, God. Somebody help me," Lou whimpered in a hoarse voice, the pain in his tone unmistakable.

Empathy spurred Brianne into action. Even after what he'd tried to do to her, she just couldn't stand by and watch a man die without trying to save him. Mama would never forgive her.

She placed a hand on Malo's arm and felt the muscle flex beneath her palm as he turned toward her. "With your skill with a razor," she encouraged, "you could get at the bullet."

His arm tightened, and she could almost see the war waging within him. It seemed as if one part of him wanted to soften, wanted to help the wounded man, while the other resisted. Apparently the latter won, for he straightened his stance and hardened his features. "I only use *el navaja* for one reason." With that, he grabbed her by the wrist and started walking.

She pulled back, strangely disappointed at his lack of compassion. "Then let me do it."

He stopped so suddenly, she nearly fell. "What?"

"I-I don't know how to use a razor, but someone's got to help the man."

Malo looked as if he were torn between hugging her and choking her right then and there. With obvious effort, he tore his gaze from her face and directed it at Frank. "You willing to let her cut on your pa?"

Clearly undecided, Frank just stood there. Then, after a lengthy frozen moment, he nodded. "Long as we watch her." His eyes turned hard. "An' if she makes a slip, Navaja, you can use the razor on her."

Her captor swore beneath his breath.

"Good grief," Brianne moaned low. Now she'd done it. "Maybe I'd better not—"

Malo gave her a little shove. "You started this. You'll finish it."

Why did she get the feeling that he was glad to have the

initial decision taken out of his hands? Stumbling along behind him, Brianne summoned up every ounce of courage she possessed for the coming task—which amounted to about a teaspoonful.

Inside the adobe hut, eerie shadows from a small fire slithered over Lou's squirming body. He was stretched out on a blanket near the wall where he lay on his side, curled forward, his knees drawn up.

"Ya got ta help me, Franky." Lou's voice rattled on a half-winded wheeze. "Got ta make the pain go away." His chest labored. "Cain't breathe."

Frank dropped to his knees beside his father and brushed a shaky hand over the older man's brow. "We will, Pa. We're gonna fix ya right up. Ya jist hold on now, hear?"

Lou turned his head and coughed weakly into the dusty blanket.

Malo withdrew the razor from his belt and handed it to her. "I don't think you've got much time, *chica.*"

Swallowing nervously, Brianne took the blade. Malo was right. If something wasn't done soon, Lou would die. Trying to hold her hand steady, she approached the injured man, stopping beside his son. She touched the younger man's shoulder. "We're going to need hot water and clean rags."

Frank jumped as if startled, then, after a last worried peek at his father, nodded and rose. As he reached the door, he shot a meaningful glance at Malo. "Watch her, Navaja. Watch her close. If she even looks like she's gonna cut him wrong—kill her."

Brianne tried to hide a shudder. What had she gotten herself into this time?

Lou moaned in pain.

Forgetting her fears, she gingerly knelt beside him, careful of her own injury, and touched his sweaty forehead. "Take it easy. We'll have that bullet out of there in no time." *At least, I hope we will.*

She tried to control her trembling fingers as she peeled the blood-matted shirt away from his flesh. Her stomach gave a giant heave when she saw the gaping wound just below his left shoulder blade, wondering if the man's son had used a

54

meat cleaver in his bungled attempt to dig out the bullet. The room dipped.

"Steady, *chica,*" Malo said quietly as he placed a hand on her shoulder. "You're not gonna be much help to him if you pass out."

Oddly, the warmth from his hand gave her added strength. Her vision cleared, and some of the dryness left her throat. "I'm all right." Lifting the razor, she unfolded it, then, thrust its deadly end onto the coals of the low burning fire. She kept her attention on the bloody wound, planning the quickest, most efficient path to where she thought the bullet would be. Fairly confident in her summation, she lifted the razor and made a small cut at the edge of the wound. The odor of burning flesh nearly gagged her.

Lou screamed.

"Shit," Malo snapped. "Hold on a minute."

Brianne snatched the razor back and watched in stunned surprise as Malo turned Lou over, drew back his fist, and slammed it against the older man's jaw.

Lou went limp.

"My God! What are you doing?" Brianne cried.

Malo eased to his feet. "Just trying to save you both a little agony." He gestured toward the unconscious man. "Better get to it, woman. He isn't gonna stay out long."

The full force of what Malo had done hit her. He had wanted to save Lou from the pain and make things easier for her. Although she was grateful, she couldn't stop a smart remark from escaping. "I sure hope you're not around if *I* ever need a painkiller."

"I don't use my fists on women."

Brianne fought the urge to laugh. He rapes and kills them, but he doesn't use his fists. How gallant.

It took her what seemed like an eternity to locate and dig out the bullet. But she did. Afterward, she cauterized the wound with the hot tip of Frank's knife—no easy feat with Malo and the younger Hawkins staring holes in her. When she'd finished, the bleeding had stopped. Lou's breathing, though shallow, had nearly returned to normal, and she felt good.

Brushing the hair out of her eyes, she eased down on her heels, satisfied that she'd done the right thing. Her mother would have been proud.

When she and Malo emerged from Frank's hut, she saw that Half Bear had fixed a meal from a jackrabbit.

And Pedro was gone.

Following Malo to the main campfire, Brianne wondered where the little Mexican had gotten off to, but was afraid to ask.

The aroma of roasting meat wafted, and her stomach grumbled in appreciation. One meal in three days definitely had its disadvantages.

As Malo pulled her down next to him, she focused on the plates he was filling with food. Another growl rumbled through her midsection.

"Why'd you run away from home?" he asked conversationally as he handed her a steaming dish.

"I told you, to find my mother," she answered, biting into the juicy meat.

Half Bear snorted.

Her captor's lips tightened. "You'll have to do better than that, *chica*. Everyone's heard the stories of how she took off alone to her brothers and got killed."

"Brianne. My name is Bree-ann. And the stories aren't true. Curse it! My mother would have told me if she was going away. She would have taken me."

He obviously ignored her. "Who's the lover? The one who used the strap on you?"

Brianne flinched at the lie she'd told, then wanted to kick him for being so obtuse. She gripped the plate tighter. "Just one of many." *So much for one lie a day.*

Malo stared into the fire, his expression unreadable. "That's what I figured."

She rolled her eyes and took another bite. Lord save her from ignorant men.

"Must have been hard leaving Logan's fancy hacienda and having to fend for yourself, though." He chewed on a piece of meat then swallowed it. "Did you leave because he found out about the others you'd been sleeping with?" His eyes narrowed. "Is that why you were beat? Why you ran?"

A blush burned her cheeks, and she turned away, avoiding his gaze and Half Bear's leer. It was too close to the truth. She formed another lie, one that had been a part of her vocabulary since she learned to talk. The one her father had beaten into her. "He has never laid a hand on me. I told you who did it."

Half Bear gave a vicious snarl and lunged to his feet, dumping his plate on the ground. "No man pay gold for evil woman." He loomed over her, his eyes dangerously bright. "Half Bear say kill her."

Terror skittered up Brianne's spine. Fearfully, she swung her gaze to Malo.

A wicked gleam brightened his eyes, and his mouth slowly curved into a sinister smile. "Maybe you're right, Comanche."

8

They were going to kill her! Brianne's hands shook uncontrollably, causing the metal spoon to rattle against her plate.

Malo's smile died instantly. "But I don't think we oughta get rid of her just yet. Not till we've made sure her pa—or someone—won't pay."

Half Bear curled his lip. "Woman make Navaja weak." Turning abruptly, he strode off toward the other end of the deserted village.

Brianne's stomach sank with relief. Malo had managed to give her a little more time. But she could have told him right up front that her father wouldn't pay. And if he did it would only be because he wanted to . . . A shudder passed through her, and she forced herself to concentrate on her food.

After regaining her composure and taking a few more bites, and wanting to switch the subject to someone else, she set her plate aside. "Where's Pedro?"

"Away."

"Where?"

"Business," Malo tossed his plate down and rose to his feet, hauling her up with him. "Come on. We're gonna turn in for a spell." He gave her a quirky smile. "Didn't get much

58

sleep last night." He raised his hand and flicked a finger across the tip of her breast. "Not much at all."

The breath whooshed from Brianne, and she wrenched back. "How dare you!" She glared at him, trying desperately to ignore the tingle racing through her belly. "You vile beast! I wished I'd used that razor on your throat!"

A strangely satisfied smile curved his mouth, and he slapped an arm around her waist, hauling her to his side. "Sure you do."

Brianne fought him wildly, but she was no match for his strength. Like a wayward child, he dragged her toward the building where she'd been tied earlier.

The closer they got, the quicker her bravado faded. What would he do to her now? Had he changed his mind and decided to take the Indian's advice? Was this it? The end? Visions of some weary traveler finding her decayed remains inside that smelly little hut flashed through her mind. Her stomach knotted.

When they reached the building, Malo led her inside, then closed the half-rotted door.

The tightness inside her grew unbearable. "What do you want from me? Please don't do this. Just let me go."

His brow flicked upward. "You want your freedom?"

"Of course I do!"

"Then tell me what I wanna know."

"What, for God's sake?"

"Who beat you?"

Brianne closed her eyes to stop a rush of tears. She couldn't tell him. She couldn't tell anyone. Her father would kill her. Nothing was more important to him than his reputation. If he ever got word . . . "I told you. A disappointed lover."

The killer's mouth drew into a menacing line. "Don't play games with me, *chica.*"

"I'm not. I'm telling the truth."

"You wouldn't know the truth if it bit you on the ass."

Clutching her upper arms, she faced him. "Believe what you wish."

He studied her for a long time, then looked as if he came

to some decision. "Maybe I will." His lips arched into a dangerous smile, and his hand snaked out, catching her around the middle. "And if I choose to believe you're a whore, you won't resist, will you?" he grated softly.

Oh, God. Now I've done it. Heat from the length of his body seared her like a branding iron. Her heart thudded painfully. Fear and an emotion she couldn't name pumped through her at a reckless speed. "Why are you doing this to me?"

His lower body tightened, and he caught her by the hair, tugging her head back. "Oh, I think you know why." He stared at her lips. "Yeah. With all your experience, you know."

She opened her mouth to argue, but solid, warm, male lips captured her words. Brianne was so shocked that for a moment she remained motionless, mesmerized by the moist heat moving over her mouth, by the excited tingles fluttering through her belly, by the hot hand sliding down to cup her bottom, by the hard bulge nuzzling . . .

Snapping to her senses, she frantically lashed out, striking his shoulder. She twisted her head to the side. "No!"

He released her so quickly that she fell backward, landing on the blanket. Trying to control the quivers racing through her body, she just sat there, catching her breath and fighting to repress the pain stabbing through her knee.

"What really happened, Brianne?"

She jumped at the cold sound in his voice. "I've already told you."

"No. You've only told me part of what I wanna know. Either you've never had a lover, or you're a very talented actress."

She could tell by the way his mouth tightened that he was angry. "I—"

"Get up."

Afraid not to comply, she stumbled to her feet.

He snatched her wrist.

Before she realized what he intended, he'd tied one end of a rope to her and the other to his belt. "What are you doing?"

"Making sure there's not a repeat of this morning's foolishness, and you'll stay this way until you've told me about your *real* association with Logan."

"Then you'd better marry me, mister. Cause we're going to be together a long time."

He glanced down at her, his expression both surprised and amused. "Yeah." He grinned. "Then we could have a litter of little *Navajas.*"

At the thought of having his children, something inside her rippled. Probably the rabbit she'd eaten didn't agree with her. Lifting her chin, she gave him her coldest stare. "I'd die before I'd have your baby and bring another murderer like you into this world." Brianne sucked in her breath when she realized what she'd said. Heavens. She was going to have to learn control.

"Navaja!" Frank's voice shrilled from outside. "Bring the gal. Pa's come down with fever."

"Yeah, sure, Frank." Malo tugged on the rope. "Come on."

Brianne breathed a sigh of relief that he was obviously going to let her little remark slide. For now.

As she followed him to Frank's hut, Brianne felt a rush of dizziness claim her. A chill seemed to slide over her flesh. She frowned and glanced up at the blazing sun. Why was she suddenly cold? And why did her limbs suddenly feel weak with fever? She shook her head, trying to dispel the strange sensations and the fiery ache in her knee.

"He's gonna die, ain't he?" Frank asked in a quiet, shaky voice when they entered the hut, his tortured gaze on his father.

Empathy tightened her chest, and Brianne glanced down at the man lying on the floor. He moved restlessly under the thin blanket, his face flushed, his lips swollen. Discounting her own listless feeling, she moved closer. "I'll see what I can do. But I'll need lots of cool water and more rags." She tugged at the rope on her wrist, drawing Malo's attention. "Do you think this can wait until after I've tended your friend?"

"He's not my friend," Malo grated. "And no, it can't wait.

You're tied to me for better or worse, *chica*. Unless you're gonna tell me what I wanna know."

Brianne didn't doubt his words. Malo didn't seem like a man who made idle threats. "I've already told you."

"Sure you have."

Frank left the building but returned a few moments later carrying a canteen filled with water and an old shirt. He held them out to her. "These okay?"

She nodded and took the offerings. Then, kneeling down beside Lou, fighting the pain in her knee and the growing unsteadiness in her movements, she tore off a strip of material from the shirt and dampened it, the rope still dangling from her wrist. Ignoring the other men in the room, she concentrated on blotting Lou's face and neck with the cool rag, hoping to draw some of the heat from his flesh.

Hayden watched the girl's gentle ministrations with mixed emotions. One part of him, the Texas Ranger part, wanted to see the murdering bastard meet his Maker, while the other praised the woman for her compassion. Even after all he and the outlaws had done to her, she still tried to help. Why? He damn sure wouldn't have if he'd been in her position. And what made him keep badgering her about her association with Logan? Shit. It didn't matter whether she was the bastard's whore or daughter. Either would serve Hayden's purpose, catching Billy Wayne's murderer.

But somehow, it did matter.

Too, his guilt over the way he treated the girl was mounting. Damn it. Why was he so obsessed with wanting to know who hurt her? And why wouldn't she tell him? Surely she didn't want to protect the bastard. Then another thought struck Hayden. She could be too frightened.

Yes. The more he considered it, the more he knew that was a real possibility. He stared at the girl's silky head, his anger rising. Was Logan the sonofabitch who terrorized her? If so, he'd gut the bastard himself.

Not understanding his outrage or the peculiar protective-ness he felt, he glared down at the rope that bound him to her. This was definitely *not* one of his better ideas.

Wishing he could storm out of the room, he glowered at the doorway. He should have found some way to follow Pedro, to check on the wire the Mexican planned to send. Not that it'd do any good. Hayden had done that before on several occasions. True enough each telegraph office had sent Art Logan a telegram, but the wire was always paid for by someone other than Pedro—someone who apparently sought to earn a little cash by doing the Mex's bidding. And the wires were obviously in code. They had to be over such a public line, and they never revealed anything Hayden could use as evidence.

He clenched his hands. Logan was smart. But he'd make a slip—hopefully soon—and when he did, Hayden would be waiting.

The thought of capturing the gang's elusive boss cooled his temper. The big man wasn't going to like having another robbery foiled. No sir, he wasn't. Nor would he be thrilled over the knowledge that his daughter was alive and well—as Pedro would surely tell him. If she *was* his daughter, which Hayden was starting to believe more and more.

He glanced out the window—toward the hills leading in the direction of Henrietta. It shouldn't take more than a couple of days for the Mex to ride in, wire his boss, receive a return answer, and make it back.

If Brianne really was the bastard's whelp, the assembly-man would want the girl brought to him. He wouldn't have a choice. Logan had to get rid of her and couldn't afford for her "second" body to be found along some trail, not after claiming the first one was Brianne.

He sneaked another peek at her and felt a moment's hesitation when he realized the danger he would put her in if she was telling the truth. Hell, even if she wasn't.

Hayden yanked his hat low, his resolve firm. It didn't matter. He *had* to draw Logan out.

He owed it to Billy Wayne.

"I've done all I can," Brianne's voice penetrated his thoughts.

He turned to see her looking up at him. A streak of dirt

smudged her left cheek, nearly touching the corner of her lush pink mouth. For the barest instant, Hayden had the most ungodly urge to kiss it away.

He shifted his attention to Lou in an effort to regain control of the wayward impulse—something he'd been doing a lot lately. The outlaw was resting quietly, most of the flush gone from his face. "For someone who doesn't know anything about doctoring, you do a mighty fine job, *chica.*" He pulled on the rope. "Come on. It's time to turn in."

The frightened look that suddenly clouded those silvery eyes told Hayden the girl fully believed he was going to assault her the minute he got her alone. But there wasn't a damned thing he could do about it. She'd just have to find out for herself when they reached the hut—*if he could keep a rein on his lust.*

"I'm not sleepy yet," she blurted as he urged her toward their hut.

Hayden was forced to continue his facade. "It's a good thing, *chica.* Because sleeping wasn't what I had in mind."

He felt a tremor pass through her arm, and wanted to shout out his frustration.

"Please . . ."

"Don't say another word," he snapped, wishing for just a second that he was the real Malo Navaja so he could take her and get it over with. Ease his own discomfort and put an end to hers.

But he wasn't.

Stretching out on the pallet he'd spread out earlier, he pulled her down. "Get into bed."

Trembling visibly, she sank onto the far edge of the blanket, then winced as if in pain.

He stared at her hard. Was she hurt?

"Y-you really don't want to do this," she whispered in a shaky little voice, her lower lip quivering. "You're not like the others."

Hayden sighed, knowing he had to end this conversation quickly before he gave up the battle he'd been fighting since yesterday and allowed himself to become lost in those dove eyes and that beautiful mouth. *"Chica,* I'm only gonna say this once. Lay down and go to sleep."

Her lashes flew up in surprise, then she quickly scrambled under the covers.

Hayden rolled over and smiled into the darkness. Good girl. Now, if she just didn't move for the rest of the night, they both might make it through this ordeal.

9

"How can I sleep?" Brianne mouthed into the darkness. Trying to ignore the scratch of the blanket beneath her, she glanced down at the rope binding her wrist to the killer's belt, wondering if she could untie it without disturbing him. Was he even asleep? Lord, she hoped so. She'd been lying still as a dead leaf for hours, staring out the small window at the moon, just waiting for the opportunity to try. Quietly, slowly, she lifted her hand to inspect the knot.

"Put your arm down, *chica.*"

Brianne jumped. He was awake! Curse him. Didn't the man ever sleep? Expelling a breath, she lowered her hand. Tears threatened as her exasperation grew. She had to get away from him. Not only for her own safety, but before they took her farther away from Fort Worth. From Uncle Lecil. He was her only hope of finding Mama.

A vision of Suzanne Logan's lovely face wavered, and Brianne started to cry. *Oh, Mama. I've got to find out why you left me.*

How she missed her mother, her kindness, her healing arms, soothing voice, and soft laughter. Brianne closed her eyes and felt a warm drop slide across her temple. Why had her mother gone? Was Maria with her? Why hadn't she come back for Brianne? So many *whys*.

"You're getting me wet," Malo grated, but she didn't miss the underlying gentleness in his tone. "Get some sleep so I can." He turned onto his side, away from her.

It was stupid, she knew, but that little act of rejection broke her restraint. A sob escaped, then another . . . and another.

"Shit."

Brianne tried to stop crying, she really did. But she hurt so bad. No one wanted her. Had *ever* wanted her. Not her father, not even the dredges of the earth who'd kidnapped her. Even her own mother had left her without a single word.

She moaned and buried her face in a warm, secure haven. Her weeping escalated to gut-shaking wails. She couldn't stop. Couldn't think. Raw emotions poured from her like water over a fall.

Finally, exhausted, her cries wilted into dry hiccupping sobs. Spent, she slumped into the warmth, only then realizing it was Navaja's chest.

The irony of the situation struck her as hilarious, and she began to laugh into the soft material of his shirt. She had been crying her heart out to a man who planned to carve it up.

"Stop it," he demanded harshly. He shook her. "Stop it."

She couldn't. His words, his voice, everything seemed funny. Even the moonlight seemed to bounce as it danced over his intense features.

Pain exploded in her jaw, and her head snapped back. She gasped and blinked in surprise. Her gaze cleared, then settled on Malo, on the taut lines of his face, on the anguished look in his eyes. Dawning struck like another blow. He'd *slapped* her.

Hayden saw the sanity—and anger—return. She was finally coherent.

"You ruthless bastard! If you're going to kill me, then do it and get it over with. I'll be damned if I'll be your whipping post."

"Jesus! You're acting like I wanted to hit you. What the

hell happened, anyway? Up until now, you've shown more defiance and courage than I'd ever expected from any woman in your position." His voice softened. "Don't quit on me now, *chica*."

She just stared at him, trying to grasp his compliment.

The confusion in her eyes made Hayden want to grind his teeth. And he sure couldn't understand why it bothered him to see her brought down to this level. Uneasy with his thoughts, he forced harshness into his tone. "Just turn over and go to sleep. I'm not up to any more female displays tonight."

"Female displays! Why you—"

He clamped a hand over her mouth, halting the words, yet pleased that she'd regained some spirit. But he had to put some distance between them. His body still ached with need from holding her while she cried.

"Listen, woman, and listen good. I don't plan to kill you *right now.* But if you don't back off, I'll do things to that lovely body of yours that you never even had nightmares about. Painful things that would have you begging for death."

He released her abruptly, hating to frighten her, but, at the moment, he was too unsettled to care. One minute he wanted to shake the daylights out of her, and the next he wanted to make love to her.

Brianne tried to still the quaking in her limbs. This man was Satan's own. She scooted as far away from him as possible. How could anyone be so gentle one minute, then so deadly the next? And why had he comforted her, anyway?

A pounding ache began in her temples, and she closed her eyes. She couldn't think about it tonight. Weariness pressed down on her, and she curled on her side, feeling drained, empty. Thoughts of Malo intruded, then drifted into the distance. She'd untangle the reasons behind his erratic behavior later, when her mind wasn't so cluttered. . . .

Light burned her closed eyelids, and she pried them open. She blinked as a shadowy figure floated into focus through the now open doorway.

Brianne lurched upright. Half Bear!

Unable to speak, she frantically scanned the adobe hut. No one else was in the room. Not even her kidnapper. *And her hand wasn't tied to him—but a post.* Her gaze flew back to the Comanche glaring at her from the doorway. "W-what do you want?"

The Indian's full lips twisted into an ugly sneer. "To see woman who cloud Navaja's thoughts." Half Bear's gaze slithered insultingly over her body. "He thinks only of mating."

His moccasined feet moved silently across the earthen floor as he came to stand beside her. Black eyes seared into her skin, charring it with hatred. "You steal strength with soft flesh. Beckoning eyes." The Indian eased down onto his haunches, his expression deadly. "Comanche no take squaw on raid. Rob power. White eyes no think with heads—only manhood." He slid his hand to the scabbard at his side and withdrew a long, lethal-looking knife.

Brianne screeched and shrank away. She clutched the shirt to her throat. "What are you d-doing?"

Half Bear's attention slid to the weapon he held. Slowly, he ran a thumb along the edge of the sharp blade, then gripped the handle. "Woman make Navaja weak. Half Bear return strength." He raised the knife.

"No!" Brianne wrenched frantically at the rope.

"Do it, and you'll join your ancestors, Comanche."

Brianne's gaze flew to the doorway, and she nearly collapsed with relief when she saw Malo standing there—his Colt pointed at Half Bear's head.

"Lower the blade, Indian—and stand up real slow."

Half Bear's muscles bunched. Cautiously, he rose to his feet and faced Malo.

For a long, silent moment, the two men stared at each other. Finally, Malo stepped to the side, leaving a path open. He flicked his gun toward the entrance. "Outside."

With his head held at a defiantly proud angle, Half Bear marched from the room, the knife still in his hand.

Navaja watched him exit then turned to her. "You okay?"

Unable to speak through the quivering knot in her throat, she nodded, trying not to think about what would have happened if Malo had been a second later.

Concern darkened his gaze. "I'll be back in a minute."

Brianne slumped against the center pole. Dear God. What next? Crossing her arms over her belly, she bent forward, trying to stop her body's wild trembling. She couldn't take any more of this.

Without considering the consequences, she brought her bound wrist to her mouth. Frantically she tore at the knot with her teeth and fingers. The tough hemp hurt her jaw. The nails on her free hand snapped mercilessly. But she couldn't stop. She had to get away.

It seemed like forever before the bindings loosened enough for her to slip her hand free. Instantly, she jumped to her feet and raced to the rear window. Without hesitation, she climbed out and ran wildly toward the mountains.

The hills loomed in the distance. Thorns and weeds stabbed her legs and feet. Hard baked earth seared her tender soles. But she couldn't stop. Not now.

On and on she ran. Pain cut into her side, but she didn't slow up. She pressed her hand to the stitch, but the movement caused her to lose her balance and stumble forward, landing on her injured knee. Blackness exploded in a burst of swirling lights. She shook her head and frantically willed her eyes to focus.

Slowly, hazily, her vision cleared, and she scrambled to her feet. Spotting a small row of trees near the base of the mountain, she sent up a silent prayer of thanks and stumbled into the concealing foliage.

Beneath the shade of a mesquite, she collapsed, the pain in her side and knee nearly unbearable. She hugged the scraggly tree trunk, trying to catch her breath and slow her racing heartbeat.

Every muscle in her body throbbed, and the dry desertlike heat thickened her breath. But nothing could have stopped her smile.

Exhausted, she leaned on a boulder. Her pulse was finally, slowly, returning to normal, but with tranquility came the unsettling truth of her situation. Now that she'd gotten away from the outlaws, where could she go? She had no water, no way to earn—or even *steal* food. For goodness sakes, she didn't even have any shoes.

She glanced down at her dirty bare toes in disgust, then lifted her gaze to the sun. Before long, that blazing yellow ball would snatch her shade—and her senses. She needed to move while the temperature was still cool enough.

Determinedly, she staggered to her feet. Pain nearly blinded her, and she buckled to the ground, clutching an injured foot with one hand and her aching knee with the other. Her throat contracted unbearably as she fought a surge of tears. Curse it. She *had* to walk.

She tried again, only to land in a heap. Angrily, she slammed her hand down on the rocky ground and was promptly rewarded with a stinging palm to go with her other aches.

Her temper climbed another notch, and she curled her fingers into the gritty dirt—only to receive another jolt of discomfort.

Taking a deep breath, she pushed up and looked around. Okay, she conceded. She couldn't leave yet. But it wasn't the end of the world. She'd merely have to stay hidden while she tended her wounds and regained her strength.

Surely in that span of time—and if she stayed well hidden—Malo wouldn't find her.

But what if one of the others did?

Don't be ridiculous, she consoled herself. If Malo couldn't find her, no one could. It wasn't hard to tell that he was by far the most intelligent man in the group. Too bad he hadn't used his intellect for a better cause.

She glanced around for somewhere to hide until she was sure the outlaws—especially Malo—had given up their search for her. A space behind the boulder caught her eye. She was certain she could squeeze herself in between the rock and trees.

After gingerly wedging herself into the tight space, she realized there was a larger area just beyond the narrow passage. Satisfied, she wriggled on through.

"That should do it." She warily examined the shady cocoon. "I hope."

71

10

*H*ayden cast one last glare at the retreating Comanche, then headed back to the hut. His pulse still pounded when he thought of the scene he'd witnessed. He'd only left the girl for a few minutes to relieve himself, but he'd never once imagined the Indian would try to kill her. He should have, though. The Comanche had made his feelings pretty clear. And if Hayden had been just a moment longer . . . He clenched his fists, not wanting to think about what might have happened—or why it concerned him so much.

Ducking beneath the low doorway, he stepped into the shadowed room and halted abruptly. He swung his gaze from one side of the room to the other. The girl was gone. He scanned the area again and noticed the limp rope, one end still tied to the pole. "Sonofabitch." Wheeling around, he bounded for his horse.

Fleetingly he gave thought to letting her go. The girl had caused him nothing but problems since they left Wichita Falls. Hell, he'd had run-ins with every one of the Hawkins Gang over her. If he kept it up much longer, there wouldn't be anyone left to lead him to Logan. But the idea of releasing her didn't sit well with him, and he couldn't explain or understand the reason why.

He rubbed at a tight muscle in his neck. Indecision conflicted with his need to see Billy Wayne avenged. Then he recalled the look in Kathy's eyes the day Hayden told her his brother had been killed, and the battle ended. His gaze rose to the distant hills. He *had* to find the girl.

Still, he couldn't help being concerned over Half Bear's threat to Brianne. He smiled wryly. After his little "talk" with the Comanche . . . He glanced down at the razor protruding from his belt, and his grin widened. He didn't even have *that* to worry about now. Satisfied that things would stay fairly quiet until Pedro's return, Hayden mounted his horse.

The hot midday sun had settled over the area by the time he returned to camp, his shirt sticking to his skin, his face streaked with dirt and sweat, and his temper at the boiling point. Where the hell was she? How far could one scrawny little girl make it on foot? He'd followed her footprints to the mountain range, but lost them in the rocks. For the last two hours, he hadn't found a sign of her.

Swearing beneath his breath, and wondering if he was losing his touch, he reined his palomino to a halt and dismounted. *Or maybe you don't really want to find her,* a little voice intruded. "The hell if I don't," he muttered, slapping his sweat-stained hat against his dusty jeans. When he got his hands on the little witch, he'd tie her to his damned horse!

After unsaddling his animal, he headed for Lou and Frank's hut. If he was lucky, the older outlaw would be dead by now—leaving him one less criminal to deal with when the time came. Damn that woman. She had him so muddled he couldn't think straight.

When he stepped into the stuffy, sun-brightened room, he found Lou sitting up, braced by the wall.

Frank sat next to his father while Half Bear stood by the window, his arm braced on the lower frame. Cold black eyes glared their hatred—and revenge—but Hayden ignored the threat.

"Goll dang it, Navaja. Where ya been?" Lou grumbled in a weak, but much healthier voice.

Maintaining his facade, Hayden raked the recovering man with a cold sneer. "Out." Without another word, he turned to leave.

The sound of thundering hooves stopped him dead.

"Where's my gun!" Lou bellowed.

Frank scrambled to his feet.

Half Bear unsheathed his blade.

An uneasy thought hit Hayden. Had the woman run across someone to help her? A sheriff? A cavalry patrol? Shit!

Drawing his gun, praying he wouldn't have to use it on an innocent man, Hayden charged out the door and dodged to the side. He crouched down by a broken bench and waited.

A flash of familiar silver caught his eye. Pedro. Straightening, Hayden holstered his Peacemaker and stepped into the open.

The short outlaw lifted a hand in greeting. *"Ola, amigo. Pedro, he make good time, no?"*

"Ya goll dang fool," Lou spat from the doorway. "Ya dang near got yerself kilt. We wasn't 'spectin' ya till tomorry."

"Yeah, Mex. What happened? Couldn't ya git ahold a El Hefty? That why yer back so soon?" Frank added.

Pedro spit out a piece of candy. *"El jefe."*

Half Bear brushed past the two men, thrusting his knife back into its scabbard as he walked forward. "Chief tell of more gold?" He glared at Pedro as if to say he damn well better have.

Pedro didn't waver under the savage's stare. "Ah, no. *El jefe*, he has special mission for *mi amigos*."

What about the girl? Hayden wanted to bellow. Surely Pedro mentioned her. Didn't Logan want her back? Damn it, Hayden couldn't have been wrong.

The Indian's nostrils flared. "Comanche want money buy rifles, not give to mission."

Pedro rolled his eyes, obviously realizing that Half Bear thought a "special mission" was a place of worship.

But Hayden wasn't in any mood for nonsense. "All right, Mex. Spit it out. What's the big boss's plan this time?"

A line of teeth flashed beneath a thin black mustache, and a satisfied smirk crinkled the corners of his eyes. "Navaja, he is eager, no? Ah, but you will be pleased. *El jefe,* he say is good Navaja take *senorita.* She bring *mucho dinero.* He say take to arroyo near Santa Fe. *El jefe,* he will arrange ransom with *la nina's padre,* then meet us in de Pajarito Canyons."

The little Mex dismounted, and glanced around. "Where is your pretty *querida?*" He eyed the hut where Hayden had held the girl. "Ah," Pedro said, nodding. *"La senorita,* she is tired, hmm? Maybe sleeping, no?" He strode toward the mud house.

But Hayden was barely aware of his departure. His thoughts were too full of Logan. He'd done it. He'd drawn the bastard out.

His conscience nagged. But at what cost? Not liking the sick feeling in his gut, Hayden watched the Mexican enter the building.

Pedro emerged a moment later, his features tightly controlled. "The *senorita,* she is gone?"

Off balance, Hayden stared, suddenly aware that Pedro possessed an icy restraint Hayden hadn't suspected. A danger.

Lou mumbled something low and Frank led him back inside.

Half Bear edged closer to Pedro.

Hayden watched the squat Mexican approach. In that instant, he knew that Pedro Torres, for all his smiling, camaraderie, posed the biggest threat of all. Hayden met the man's gaze head-on. "Yeah. She's gone."

For a moment Pedro appeared startled, then horrified. *"Amigo,* no! Navaja, he no kill Brianne."

Hayden fought to keep his surprise under control. He hadn't even thought of that. The real Navaja probably would have killed her, and Hayden wasn't about to tell them she'd escaped him. He opened his mouth to spout a lie, but a rush of caution changed his mind. What if the girl showed up again?

Meeting the slight man's gaze, Hayden shook his head. "No. But she's good as dead. After I finished with her, I left her in the hills. Got tired of the extra baggage." He twisted his mouth into a smirk. "She won't last long without food or water."

Pedro seemed relieved at first, then a tiny spark of suspicion entered those obsidian eyes. "Why? Navaja, he no longer want ransom?"

"Yeah, I wanted it. But I figured the girl was more trouble'n she was worth." He met the Comanche's hostile gaze. "Now we all know different."

"Then we must find her, no?"

"That's right, Mex. No."

The outlaw's hand moved dangerously close to the weapon at his side. "Pedro, he insist. The woman, she be found, quick. *El jefe,* he no like Navaja to lose the little *querida. Comprende?*"

"Yeah, I understand, Torres. But *I'll* go after her, not *we.*" Turning, he headed for the livery. Though he deliberately kept his pace at a slow swagger, he felt like kicking up his heels. Logan had fallen into the trap—and the bastard was as good as caught.

Hayden's satisfaction sagged just a little when he remembered his immediate problem, but he brushed it off with a confident shrug.

He'd find the girl. Somehow.

Swiping at the tears trailing her cheeks, Brianne stared down at her rolled-up trouser leg. Her knee throbbed like the dickens, and the piece of material she'd torn from her shirttail hadn't done a thing to ease the sting. Come to think of it, it wasn't even much good for keeping the injury clean, since a layer of grime coated the fabric.

Trying not to think about the infection causing her knee to swell, she pressed her spine to the boulder. Her head ached like the devil, and she couldn't stop shaking. What was the matter with her? It must be a hundred degrees out. May wasn't supposed to be this hot—or was it this cold?

She blinked rapidly, trying to clear her vision and

thoughts. What she'd give for a bath, a soft bed, and a healing poultice about now. Not to mention a drink of water. She licked her parched lips and was surprised to find that they felt puffy, her tongue fat.

A shiver took her, and she curled up into a ball. Tiny pricks of pain tingled across her skin. She rubbed her upper arms trying to instill warmth into her flesh. Perhaps she shouldn't have hidden so well from her kidnapper, she mused foggily.

A tiny smile pulled at the corner of her mouth. For such a savage killer, Malo Navaja didn't track worth beans. Chills racked her, and she tightened her grip on her arms. Swallowing became a chore. Her throat felt so dry. Her thoughts spun . . . then scattered.

Why didn't the maid bring her something to drink? "Mother? Where's Maria? Tell her to bring a pitcher of lemonade, will you? The heat in this place is stifling. I can hardly breathe."

Through a hazy vapor, she saw her mother's pretty face waver, then ebb into cloudy swirls.

Maria shook a scolding finger at her. Out of nowhere, her father's cold blue eyes glared at her, then narrowed menacingly. He raised his hand to strike her. "No!" she screamed. She ran wildly. But the ground tilted. She felt as if she were sliding . . . falling.

Pain exploded in her head, then blessed numbing emptiness. . . .

"Shit," Hayden swore again as he rounded another pile of rocks and found nothing. "She's got to be out here somewhere."

Disgusted, he brought a hand up to shade his eyes and scanned the area. Rolling hills, mesquite, rocks, tumbleweeds, and sagebrush—but no woman.

Reining his horse toward the next cluster of boulders, Hayden released a frustrated snort. The girl couldn't have walked the three-mile distance to Lake Arrowhead. Not in this heat. Besides, he'd already gone that way.

"So where the hell is she?" he grumbled as he pulled the

bandanna from around his neck and wiped it over his sweaty face. The little fool was going to fry if he didn't find her soon.

"No."

Hayden whipped his head to the side, listening.

"No. Go away."

Grinning, he spurred his palomino toward a mound of stone backed by a cluster of trees. When he spied a bare foot and leg protruding from between them, his smile widened. "Well, *chica,* seems like you're as bad at hiding as you are at stealing."

Swinging down from the saddle, he sauntered toward her, surprised that she hadn't come back with some smart remark. But as he drew closer, saw her rolled-up pant leg, the rag tied around her knee, and her flushed face, apprehension replaced any sign of humor. She was unconscious—and ill. *Really* ill.

"Chica?" he called softly as he knelt beside her. "What's wrong?"

"Mama? Tell Maria."

He placed a hand on her forehead and brushed her hair away from her face. Fever radiated from her smooth brow. Concern jarred him. He pulled her up into a sitting position and shook her. Her head lolled to one side, and he saw red staining her golden curls. His gaze moved to a blunt rock smeared with blood, and he closed his eyes. "Sonofabitch."

He lowered her to the ground, torn between worry and wanting to strangle the woman for her stupidity. She'd apparently fallen and knocked herself out.

Then he remembered the bandage on her knee. Frowning, he carefully untied it.

Grotesquely swollen flesh surrounded an ugly gash matted with dried blood, dirt, and bits of rock. Damn her, why hadn't she told him?

Because of his arrogance, she'd kept the injury from him, probably because she thought he would scorn her.

Plagued by feelings of shame, he straightened and glanced at the southern horizon. The town of Henrietta was bound to have at least one sawbones.

Making an instant decision, he lifted the girl into his arms and mounted his horse, the slight burden held close to his chest. The rest of the gang wasn't going to like it, he mused. But they were in for a short layover.

He examined the woman's bleeding head nestled to his shoulder. Or maybe a *long* one.

11

Climbing up through layers of black fog, she groped blindly. It hurt to breathe. Her eyelids felt heavy. Her head ached, and every muscle in her body throbbed. Then the pain slipped away in a swirling mist, and a tall, broodingly handsome man stood in front of her, laughing, mocking. She shouted at him. *"Brianne! My name is Brianne."*

The man's image faded, and heat surrounded her, restrained her. She struggled to free herself from the ropes that bound her arms. Leather snapped, and pain sliced across her spine. *"No. Oh, please. No."* She tried to lift a hand to ward off another blow but it wouldn't respond. *"Mama, help me. Oh, God. Someone help me."*

A cool cloth glided across her brow, and a warm voice rumbled softly. "Easy, *chica*. Easy."

She tried to identify the voice, the name he'd spoken. But for the life of her, she couldn't.

Her head started to clear, and she concentrated hard on prying open an eyelid. When she managed, bright light nearly blinded her, and she quickly shut it again. "Oh."

The soft thud of footsteps sounded nearby, then a rustle

of material—and that rich voice. "You can open your eyes now, *chica*. I closed the curtains."

That name again.

She forced her lashes up. It took a second for her vision to clear, but when she was able to focus, she found herself staring into a pair of wickedly beautiful steel blue eyes.

Startled, she pressed back into the pillow, enabling her to view the man's face. Her heart tripped over itself. Good heavens. The man was breathtaking. So *male*.

Her gaze moved down the straight length of a perfectly shaped nose, over warm golden skin shadowed by a few days' growth of beard. The dark hairs shaded his smooth flesh and framed a deliciously male mouth that was so attractive it made her insides flutter. She had the ungodly urge to touch his slightly pouting lower lip and trace the mysterious scar along his lean jaw.

Dreamily, she lifted her gaze up to his and offered an unsteady smile. "Hello."

That gorgeous mouth widened, dazzling her with a display of straight white teeth. "Hello, yourself."

The sound of his voice penetrated her thoughts. She swallowed. "Do I know you?" Frowning, she tried to bring a hand to her forehead, but her arm wouldn't move. She glanced down to find her limbs tucked under a blanket. Alarmed, she found, too, that a bandage was wrapped around her knee—and she was naked beneath the covers. Completely disoriented, she blurted, "Where are my clothes? Where am I?"

"You don't know?"

She perused the small, neat chamber, then returned her attention to the man sitting on her bed. "No. And why are you in my room? *On my bed?*"

He seemed surprised. Leaning forward, he inspected her closely, then lightly gripped her chin and stared directly into her eyes. His own darkened, and he turned her head from side to side as if searching for an answer to some question.

It was terribly unsettling. "What are you doing?"

He eased away, his puzzled gaze still locked on hers. "Don't you know who I am?"

"No."

He swore beneath his breath and rose.

She watched him pace and rub the back of his neck. It was an incredible sight. Broad shoulders and lean hips moved with a dangerous, almost animalistic grace as he walked away from her, then a tight flat stomach and muscular chest were presented when he turned around.

Her concentration drifted to the open collar of his light gray shirt, to the fine swirl of dark hairs that stirred when he breathed. Maybe this was a dream, she mused. He was certainly the stuff fantasies were made of.

He stopped suddenly and placed his hands on his hips. The very masculine, spread-legged stance robbed her of breath and emphasized hard thighs and the snug fit of his jeans. Realizing where she stared, she brought her gaze upward.

"What's the last thing you remember?" he demanded.

The question surprised her. She tugged one of her hands out from beneath the cover and tried to think. She massaged her forehead in an attempt to look into her thoughts. But it was like staring at a black wall. "I-I don't know."

"You don't remember anything?"

She concentrated harder. "No."

"Shit."

"I beg your pardon?"

He nearly pounced at her. "Tell me your name."

"You don't know it?" She snatched the blanket to her chin. "Then why are you in my room?"

He sent a frustrated glance toward the ceiling. "I damn well do know who . . ." he hesitated, ". . . you are, but I don't think *you* do."

"Don't be absurd. Of course I know my own name."

"Fine. What is it?"

"Why, it's . . . it's . . ." Panic threatened. "Oh . . ." She tightened her grip on the blanket. "God . . ."

"Unless I'm sorely mistaken, that is *not* your name." He expelled a heavy sigh and turned for the door.

"Where are you going?"

"To get the doc."

"What doctor?"

"The one who's been tending you for the past four days, *chica.*"

"Four days!" She buckled into a sitting position, then winced in pain. The blanket slipped and she snatched it up. "And who's Chica? Is that my name? Why has a doctor been seeing me? Good heavens. What's happening?"

The man simply stared. "Yes, four days. *Chica* is what I call you, but your name is Brianne. As for the sawbones, he's been tending you because you've been ill." He lifted a black brow. *"That's* what's happening."

Wildly, she realized that she couldn't recall a thing. "None of this sounds familiar. What do you mean ill?"

"You came down with the fever because of an infection in your knee. A bump on your head complicated matters."

"But how—"

"I don't know all the hows. Now settle down while I fetch Doc Crawford. Maybe he can answer your questions."

"You still haven't told me who you are."

He stared hard at her, then to the door and back again. Those magnificent eyes took on a mischievous glint. "You really don't remember?"

She shook her head.

His lips drew into a slow smile. *"Chica,* I'm your husband."

"My h-husband?"

Hayden watched the woman sputter in surprise and felt a rush of guilt. But when he'd left the others at the abandoned village and brought the woman into a hotel, he'd told the proprietor and the doc that he was her husband. He'd even purchased a ring to put on her finger to make his tale appear authentic. Shit. What was he supposed to have done, told them he kidnapped her?

Concerned about her head injury, yet relieved that he wouldn't have to worry about her blabbing to the doc about being abducted, Hayden turned for the door. "Yeah, *chica.* I'm your husband. Now lay down while I fetch Crawford."

The door shut softly behind him, but she couldn't move. She felt paralyzed. Husband? She had a husband? Lowering the blanket to her chest, she stared at the well-mended cover. She didn't *feel* married—and, though she felt she knew him, she sure didn't remember anything. Good heavens. How could she possibly forget something like her own wedding? She glanced at the closed door. Forget someone like *him?*

Yet, on the third finger on her left hand, was an intricately carved gold ring—proof of their union. Thin swirls accentuated by tiny etched flowers surrounded the band. Instinctively, she knew it was the kind she would have chosen for herself. Vaguely, a man's voice penetrated her brain. *You're tied to me for better or worse, chica.*

The ache throbbing through her head grew, and she closed her eyes, wishing she could recall at least one small moment of anything—of her life, her wedding. Wedding. How strange that sounded, but she knew there had to have been one. The familiar feeling she sensed when she looked at him, the ring, his concern, the vague words she remembered, all pointed to the truth of his claim.

The door creaked, and she opened her eyes to see a scrawny man with gold-rimmed glasses perched on a pointed nose. He stepped into the room, followed by her husband.

"Howdy, Miz Caldwell. How are you feelin' today?" He squinted down at her through swirls of smoke rising from a cigar he held clenched between his teeth. "I'm Doc Crawford. Remember me?"

She shook her head and directed her gaze to the man standing across the room. Like a blow, it hit her. She didn't even know her husband's name. Swinging on the doctor, she grabbed his hand. "What happened to me? I mean, why can't I remember anything?"

Doc Crawford placed his fingers over hers and patted gently. "Don't you fret now, child. You'll get your memory back soon enough. Best I can figure, when the fever took you, you passed out and hit your head." He gestured toward her left temple. "If that there bump means anything. Besides, it isn't so unusual what's happened to you. I've heard before of folks forgettin' everything when they busted their head. Not to mention what a high fever can do to your senses. But they usually get over it before long."

He glanced at her husband. "And your fever was sure 'nough high. Why, Hayden here didn't leave your side for four whole days, he was so worried. He just kept washin' your face and coolin' you, and talkin' to you real low."

Brianne peeked up at her husband. Hayden.

He turned away, suddenly appearing quite interested in the far wall. But she didn't miss the flush of red that darkened his throat, or the warmth that cupped her heart. No wonder she'd fallen in love with this man.

And married him.

Hayden Caldwell. Brianne Caldwell. She mentally tested the names, wishing she could remember even a tiny piece of their life together. If this recent display of consideration was an example of how he treated her, then she must be a very happy bride. Bride? Was she a bride, or had they been married for years? Did they have children? Good heavens. Why couldn't she remember? "Is there anything you can do—*I* can do—to regain my memory now?" *At least the part that remembered my husband.*

"I'm afraid not. From the cases I know of, it just takes time. It can return all at once, or in pieces." He frowned. "Course I have heard tell that another blow to the head sometimes jars the memory back. But I'm not too sure about it. Seems a bit risky, if you asked me."

It might be worth it, though, Brianne thought hopefully. But *how* did one go about acquiring such a knock? Surely it wasn't self-inflicted.

". . . rest for a few more days, then you can take your missus and be on your way."

Brianne blinked, having only caught the tail end of the physician's words as he spoke to her husband. But it was enough. In just a few days this man she barely knew would take her . . . where? Then what? She tightened her hold on the blanket.

Hayden watched the play of emotions flicker over the

girl's face, and again he felt a pang of guilt. She looked so confused, so damned scared. Christ. He really did hate this job.

"Yeah, Doc. We'll hole up a few more days." He slipped the physician some coins. "Thanks for your help."

"My pleasure, son." The sawbones tipped his head at Hayden, then to Brianne. "Miz Caldwell."

Hayden closed the door behind the thin man, then turned to the girl. "Better get all the rest you can. Once we leave here, it's going to be hard going for the next few weeks."

She bit her lower lip, her expression uncertain, frightened. "W-where do we live?"

Her question caught him off guard. He hadn't even considered that. Or of all the other questions she'd undoubtedly want answered sooner or later. "We, er, live in Texas, but we're heading for Santa Fe."

She frowned slightly, as if trying to think, then lifted her chin. The action made her appear to be in control, but he could see by the way she worried the blanket between her slim fingers that she was far from it. "D-do we have children?"

The breath whooshed from his lungs. Where in the hell did she come up with these questions? Just the thought of her carrying his child hit a soft spot in his gut. Why the hell hadn't he said she was his sister instead of his wife? Yet, somehow, the thought of calling her his sister turned his stomach sour. Not liking the way this woman twisted his innards, he spun toward the door, feeling the urge to unsettle her like she had him. "No, *chica*. You said you didn't want my babies."

Ignoring her sharp gasp, he left the room and trudged down the stairs, not even glancing at the saloon on the lower level as he passed through. All his thoughts were concentrated on the sickening feeling in the pit of his stomach. He shouldn't have said that to her. Shouldn't have hurt her—and instinctively, he knew he had. But, damn it, she'd caught him off guard, and she *had* told him that—in a manner of speaking.

Disgusted, he glanced down the wide, hard-packed main

road through Henrietta. Only a half mile long, it was dissected in the middle by a crossroad and littered in both directions with wood frame houses, making it appear bigger than it actually was. He could hardly believe that it had only been three years since settlers had returned to the area after being run out by hostile Indians.

He glanced across at the sheriff's office and the church that stood side by side, then to Smith's Mercantile at the corner, knowing he needed to get supplies there before he left.

Turning down the boardwalk, he passed the courthouse near another saloon, then headed for the livery at the end of the street. As he fronted the telegraph office, he made a mental promise to send McNelly a wire, updating him on the Logan situation.

Laughter erupted from the doorway of a third saloon but Hayden ignored the beckoning sound and continued on. Before he could even think about pleasure, he wanted to find where the Hawkinses had made camp. When he'd left them in the deserted village, he'd been in a hurry to get Brianne into town and hadn't had time to wait for them. But they assured him they'd follow. Which he didn't doubt in the least. Not with Logan's treasure in Hayden's possession.

He scanned the miles of flatlands to the west and the occasional grove of mesquite, knowing they were out there somewhere. He wanted to tell them the doc's verdict—and, hopefully, send them on ahead to Santa Fe. If he could manage that, then, at least, he wouldn't have to worry over the girl's safety for the rest of the trip.

Although he didn't think Pedro would be easy to convince. The Mex had been pretty upset over Hayden taking the girl into town. Probably afraid someone would recognize her—possibly another politician who knew Logan—which would be damned hard to explain since she was supposed to be dead.

For nearly an hour, Hayden searched the thick trees for the gang's camp unsuccessfully. When he finally did locate the hideout on the open range, he was surprised to find that they'd hidden inside a cowboy's prairie castle, a small wooden shack set down in a gorge that was just deep enough to hide the hut and horses from passing riders.

He shook his head. Half Bear, who had undoubtedly led the group there, was either extremely shrewd or extremely stupid to hide out in a place where anyone could happen by. Hayden smiled. Somehow, the word *stupid* just didn't fit the Comanche. Besides, it had taken Hayden forever to find it, and he was *looking* for it.

Reining his palomino to a halt, he dismounted and started for the door, but before his hand touched the latch, the barrel of a Winchester appeared from a side window. Hayden froze. "Put that damn thing down."

Frank's scarred features appeared behind the rifle. "Christ, Navaja, I didn't recognize ya with all them whiskers on yer face."

Hayden raised a hand to his jaw, realizing for the first time that he'd forgotten to shave. Since he'd been with the Hawkinses, he'd made a show of swiping off his whiskers with Navaja's menacing razor every morning. But lately, he'd been so wrapped up in the girl he'd completely forgotten. Glaring at the younger man, he shoved open the door.

Sweat, stale smoke, and the smell of rotgut nearly gagged him. Too tall to stand because of the low roof, he felt sure he'd puke if he didn't sit down. Snagging a broken bench by the wall, he straddled it.

"'Bout damned time," Lou snapped. Obviously the man had nearly recovered from his wound.

"*La senorita,* she is good?" Pedro asked, straightening from his sprawled position in a corner.

"She'll live."

The Comanche, sitting cross-legged in the center of the floor, gave a disgusted snort.

Frank squatted down next to Hayden and pulled out a tobacco pouch. "She gonna be able ta travel soon?"

"A few days."

"That long?" Frank spat before licking the edge of a paper and rolling it over a line of tobacco. "I don't know 'bout the others, but I'm plumb sick a bein' cramped up in this cracker box where the whole dang town can find us."

Half Bear scowled at the scarred man. "Lodge good. White man no see under nose."

Hayden ignored the Indian. "No need for you to stay here till she's ready." He eyed the others. "You can head on out. I'll bring the girl and meet up with you in the Pajarito Canyons beyond Santa Fe."

"I'm fer that," Lou rasped. "Cain't breathe in this stinkin' shack."

"Yeah," Frank seconded quickly, then lit his cigarette. "That'll give us a chance ta stop off at a cantina." He blew a stream of smoke. "Ain't had a piece a tail in so long my rod's 'bout ta fall off."

Pedro watched Hayden, but he said nothing.

Half Bear grunted. "Navaja weak. White squaw evil. Take power."

"I can handle her, Comanche."

"The Indian, he is right, *amigo. La senorita,* she give Navaja much trouble. Maybe too much. *El jefe,* he no like for *muchacha* to escape."

"You let me worry about that, Mex."

Pedro eyed him, then shot a glance at Half Bear. A secret look passed between the two men, then the Mexican grinned and took a swig from the bottle before passing it to Lou. *"Si, amigo.* You worry. We leave first light for de Pajarito."

12

*W*here is my husband?" *And where had he slept? Why haven't I seen him since yesterday?*

A maid with an overly ripe figure set a tray on a table by the bed, her dark eyes flashing distastefully in Brianne's direction.

Wondering at the servant's obvious disapproval, Brianne cleared her throat and tried again. "Um, my *espouso?*" At least she hoped that was how it was said.

The woman's full lips spread into a wicked smile. "Carlotta, she no see *senor* since he leave her roo— saloon —little after dawn."

The insinuation couldn't have been clearer. The woman hinted that Hayden had left her *room*. Her bed? Both shocked and hurt, Brianne clenched her hands on the covers. What kind of heartless man had she married? Perhaps it was a good thing she had lost her memory. "I see." *All too well.* "And did he say when he'd return?"

"No." She rubbed a hand down over the curve of her hip. "But *senor,* he no stay away long."

Brianne quelled the urge to scratch the woman's eyes out.

"When he does get back," she said through tight lips, "tell him I'd like to see him."

The maid smiled slyly. *"Sí.* Carlotta, she will tell."

After the witch left, Brianne simmered slowly. Her husband's obvious infidelity could quite possibly be the reason for her loss of memory. She could instinctively be trying to protect herself from pain. That might even be why she told him she didn't want his babies. To hurt him.

She frowned in concentration. If what the maid insinuated was true, this could be typical behavior for her husband.

Brianne brought her palm to her forehead, wondering if she was letting her imagination get the better of her. Curses. Why couldn't she remember anything? She rapped her knuckles on her skull hoping to jar her memory, then winced at the pain.

She glowered at the door, wishing thoughts of Hayden Caldwell lying in the arms of the sultry maid didn't twist her insides. Don't be a dolt, she mentally scolded. Any wife would feel that way over her husband sharing another woman's bed.

Closing her eyes, she tried desperately to see into her mind. *Brianne. My name is Bree-ann,* she remembered shouting at someone. Then a gray-haired man's image flashed. Her eyes snapped open. Who was tha—

"Good morning, *chica.*"

She swung around to find her husband standing beneath the arch of the door, looking disgustingly attractive, a large package tucked under one muscular arm. Her hand flew to her chest to still the sudden pounding of her heart. "Good heavens, you startled the life out of me. Didn't anyone ever teach you to knock?"

His blue eyes traveled over her face and down her body. "Not at my wife's door."

She simmered. "Forgive me. I seem to have trouble remembering that we're married." Her mouth thinned as she recalled the maid's words. "Much like you do."

"What are you talking about?"

Oh, such innocence. "Carlotta."

"Who?"

Brianne wasn't fooled for a minute by his confused act. "The maid you spent the night with."

He just stared at her, his expression at first shocked, then unreadable. "I see. And did I have fun with this Carlotta?"

"I wouldn't know."

"Why not? You seem to know everything else."

"Only because your *friend* has a loose tongue and let it slip—rather purposefully—that you'd been together." Good heavens, that couldn't really be her talking. She sounded like a shrew. So jealous. It must be the illness.

"She said I took her to my room?" He sounded baffled.

So he *did* have a separate one. "Not exactly. She merely hinted that you'd left hers."

"I did," he stated arrogantly. "This morning. *After* I stopped by to instruct her to bring you a late breakfast. I wanted you to get some rest." He tossed the package on the bed. "And I went to get you some clothes so you could take a short walk today. *If* you were up to it."

Brianne felt sick. She shouldn't have accused him without first hearing an explanation. Rubbing her temple, she sighed. "Am I always so quick to jump to the wrong conclusion?"

His eyes crinkled at the corners, and he flashed her a gorgeous smile. "Yeah, *chica*. You are."

Her heart did a funny flip, and heat singed her cheeks. Unable to meet his eyes, she turned her head and spotted the package at the foot of the bed. "Clothes?"

He retrieved the paper-wrapped parcel and placed it across her knees. "According to the mercantile."

She caught sight of the closet, its door ajar. No garments hung inside. As a matter of fact, not one shred of clothing lay anywhere in sight. "Where are the rest of my things?"

Hayden started in surprise. What was he supposed to tell her? He grasped the first idea that came to mind. "You, er, don't remember the robbery, either?"

"What robbery?"

"The one where you, er, cut your knee trying to stop the outlaws from taking our trunks."

"So *that's* what happened."

He seemed awfully interested in the curtains. "Yeah." He nodded to the package. "You gonna open that?"

She attempted to untie the tightly knotted string, but couldn't.

Shaking his head, he reached into the waistband of his jeans and withdrew a straight razor.

A vision flickered through her mind of a gleaming blade pressed to a man's throat, then another of a shadowy figure holding a razor strap, striking out at her. "Oh, God."

Hayden's head came up. "What's wrong?"

Brianne jolted back to her senses, but she couldn't stop trembling. She eyed her husband, and her shivering increased. Had Hayden used a strap on her?

No. She knew he hadn't. She didn't understand how, but she *knew* Hayden didn't do it. "Nothing. I thought I remembered an incident from my childhood, but the memory vanished before I could grasp it." *Now why did I say childhood?* But, for some reason, she knew it was true.

He studied her curiously, then slid the razor beneath the string on the package. When the twine snapped, he quickly folded the lethal-looking instrument and replaced it in his waistband. "Think you can manage the rest?"

Relieved that the blade was out of sight, yet not sure why, she nodded and unwrapped the paper. A pair of soft, kidskin boots lay atop a gray riding skirt and an embroidered white blouse with a low-cut scooped neckline. It was very similar to the one Carlotta had worn.

Brianne cringed at the idea of wearing such a revealing garment but appreciated her husband's thoughtfulness nonetheless. "They're lovely."

He reached out and traced a long tanned finger over the embroidered trim. "I'm not sure they'll fit, but it's all the town of Henrietta had to offer on such short notice. Personally, I would have preferred something a little more conservative." He inspected her curves outlined beneath the blanket. "A lot more conservative."

He strode to the window and stood with his back to her. "Try them on."

Touched by his concern for her modesty, Brianne quickly slipped into the outfit, using the bedcover as a screen. After tucking the blouse into the waistband of the skirt, she pushed aside the blanket and rose. The soles of her feet stung as she rose, and she winced. How had she hurt them?

Immediately the answer came to her. The outlaws that had taken their clothes must have confiscated her shoes, too. She'd probably had to walk barefooted into town.

Satisfied with her summation, she changed position to inspect the discomfort, and a board creaked beneath her.

Hayden spun around. "Do they fit?" His gaze darted down her figure, then slowly drifted back up. With each inch he gained, he seemed to grow paler, then his gaze stopped at her breast, and a muscle began to tick in his jaw. "Sonofabitch."

"What?"

He turned abruptly for the door. "I'll be back in a minute."

Confused by Hayden's odd behavior, Brianne shakily walked across the plank floor until she stood before an oak-framed looking glass. What had her husband so disgruntled?

She glanced in the mirror and inhaled sharply at the image. The skirt clung to her hips and thighs very nicely, but the blouse fit too snugly. The daringly scooped neckline barely concealed the tips of her breasts—and the material was so *thin*.

Heat gushed to her face, and she turned away, but as she did, another thought occurred to her. Why had her husband been so upset by the display? Unless . . .

Her illness must have taken its toll on him. They probably hadn't been able to—Good heavens. When she'd recovered he would expect her to—

Crossing her arms protectively over her chest, she sat down on the bed. She couldn't think about what he might expect of her. Wanting to keep her thoughts occupied, she reached for her boots and gingerly slipped them on.

The door swung open and Hayden strode purposefully into the room. He tossed her a wrinkled gray shirt that looked like it had been crammed in his saddlebags.

"What's this?"

"Just put it on."

His arrogant male stance jarred her memory. She could see him in the moonlight, his powerful, naked length bathed in silver shadows. Her heart picked up speed. She recalled the musky scent of his skin, the firm strength in his muscles. A warmth spread through her lower belly. She could vividly recall the weight of his bare body pressing down on hers, the gentleness of his mouth. . . .

"Put the damn thing on."

Brianne came to her senses. But as she pulled on the shirt, she hid a small smile. She may not remember her wedding, but she most certainly knew that she'd been intimate with this man.

Intimate with him? Placing a hand to her flushed cheek, she glanced away, not understanding the awful embarrassment she felt. Uncomfortable and wanting to busy herself, she gathered the paper that had wrapped her garments. But as she picked it up, a small bottle dropped out onto the mattress. Curious, she retrieved the vial and read the label. Mrs. Addington's Rosewater.

Her heart melted. How sweet. Hayden had bought this for her. She peeked up at her husband and felt another sudden warming. He might look stern and unapproachable, but he obviously possessed a great deal of depth beneath that harsh exterior. The doc's words echoed in her mind: *Hayden didn't leave your side for four whole days, he was so worried. He just kept washin' your face and coolin' you, and talkin' to you real low.*

She slid her tongue along her lower lip and smiled. "Thank you, Hayden. I love roses." She felt a moment's confusion and touched her temple. "At least I'm pretty sure I do." She popped the cork out of the bottle and sniffed. Instantly, the face of a beautiful woman wavered in her thoughts. Fair skin. Dark hair. Sad violet eyes.

Hayden watched Brianne. She stared thoughtfully, the bottle held just below her nose. He could almost feel her confusion, her frustration, and he wished to hell he could help her—without telling her the truth.

Knowing he was nearly as helpless as she, he pulled his gaze from her face and let it wander over her outfit. Those clothes didn't flatter her gorgeous figure at all, but *he* felt a hell of a lot better.

Why hadn't he realized the blouse would be too tight? True, there hadn't been much of a choice, but he'd never misjudged a woman's size before. Of course, beneath her baggy man's shirt he hadn't really been able to tell.

Hell. Even when she'd been racked with fever, he'd had the maid undress her. He'd been obsessed with keeping the covers pulled up to her chin, not wanting to be tempted by Logan's daughter—or his whore. Neither identity sat well with him. He couldn't imagine desiring a woman who carried Art Logan's blood. The man he thought responsible for his brother's death. And if she wasn't his daughter, Hayden damned sure wouldn't take the bastard's leavings.

He glanced again at his shirt draped over her too-small blouse and relaxed. At least now he didn't have to watch the thin material expose her charms.

But even in those clothes she bothered him, and he tried his damnedest not to notice how innocent she looked with that milky complexion and those big dove gray eyes. Or the way all that wedding-band-gold hair curled around her face.

He still didn't understand, either, what had compelled him to buy that damned rose stuff. But something about the woman reminded him of flowers. Sweet. Heady. Petal soft. Uncomfortable with the turn of his thoughts, he tried for distance. "You feeling up to that walk?"

Brianne stared up into the achingly handsome face, her thoughts on how it would feel to be kissed by this man. Even though she couldn't recall their life together, Hayden sparked a need—a craving—deep within her. Instinctively, she knew she could trust him. Wanting more than anything to remember the love they shared, the happy times, the sad ones, she cast her doubts—and pride—to the wind. "Are we in love? I-I mean, *really* in love? Or did we marry for some other reason?"

Trying to hide his shock at her bold question, and the warmth suddenly seeping into his chest, he simply stared. Finally, he answered truthfully. *"Chica, I wouldn't marry a woman I didn't love."* *And the last time nearly cost me my sanity.*

Her eyes locked on his, and in their depths, she could see he sincerely meant the words. He wouldn't have married for any reason other than love. The urge to know this man, *really* know him, overwhelmed her. "Would you kiss me?"

How he kept his mouth from gaping, Hayden didn't know. And why the hell did his body go crazy at the thought of doing just that? Hadn't he learned his lesson, yet? He cleared his throat. "Why?"

"I want to remember."

What could he say? *No you don't?* Knowing it would be a big mistake, but unable—or unwilling—to come up with a reason to deny her request, he slid his arms around her waist and pulled her up against him. Just a quick kiss to ease some of his own frustration wouldn't hurt.

But the slightest contact with her sweet curves stole his breath away. Damn. "I think this should wait for another time. When you're feeling stronger."

She raised up on her toes and pressed her mouth to his. "I feel fine."

The moist heat of her breath and the softness of her lips sent a stab of desire straight to his jeans. His blood pumped furiously, numbing his brain, clouding his memory. He drew her closer, suddenly hungry for the gift she offered. Like a starving man, he feasted on her delicious mouth, on the honeyed warmth he found beyond her parted lips.

Brianne's insides went soft. Chills, then fever, raced through her limbs. *This man's a stranger,* a part of her warned. Desire curled in her belly. *This man's your husband,* the other countered. Flames seared her lower belly, and the battle ended. "Oh, yes," she whispered, spreading feathery kisses across his lips. "Make me remember."

Hayden jerked away from her so fast she nearly fell, his chest heaving, his eyes blazing with fury. "Stop acting like a whore."

13

*E*mbarrassment nearly choked her. How could he say such a thing to her? She was only trying to let him know she was willing to accept their marriage. "I-I'm sorry. I just wanted to—"

"I know what you wanted." He grabbed her hand. "Let's get out of here."

Hayden was angry enough to spit rocks. Damn it. How could he possibly want her? Forget who she was? Even if she did have the softest skin he'd ever felt.

Disgusted, more with himself than anyone, he stalked down the stairs and through the saloon, dragging the girl behind him. They'd be a helluva lot better off out in the open, around people.

Hot liquid sunlight poured over him as he stepped onto the wooden walkway. His stomach rebelled at the mustiness of the cotton yard on the south end of town, and he turned in the opposite direction, his hand in a death hold around Brianne's.

As he passed the second saloon, he glanced in at the display of scantily dressed women plying their wares. He fought the urge to leave the girl standing on the boardwalk and race inside to relieve himself in one of those well-used bodies. Bodies that had nothing to do with Art Logan.

His gaze flicked to Brianne, and felt a wave of shame. *Shit.* What was the matter with him? He strode briskly toward the center of town. He needed to change his train of thought— at least get it above his belt. But even the feel of her small hand curled in his sent tingles up his arm.

"I thought you said we were going to walk," Brianne huffed feebly from behind him.

Realizing the girl was still weak, and nearly running to keep up with him, Hayden quickly slowed his stride and damned his callousness. This wasn't entirely her fault. "You hungry?"

She took a couple of rapid breaths and nodded. "Very. You hauled me out the door before I had a chance to eat."

Hayden clenched his teeth. Glancing across the street at the cafe, he steered her in that direction. At least this problem could be easily solved.

A few tables covered in red and white checked cloths, centered by a vase of white flowers, sat on the walk, while several others lined the inner walls. "In or out?" Hayden asked, gesturing toward the tables.

"Inside."

When they entered the somewhat cooler interior, Hayden automatically took a seat with his back to the wall, enabling him to view the entire room. Then he noticed Brianne standing by her chair. Waiting. What the hell? When it hit him, he felt humiliated. He could almost hear his mother scolding him for his lack of manners. Not looking at Brianne, he rose and snagged the chair for her to sit in. The woman was starting to annoy the hell out of him.

"Thank you," she said primly as she sat down.

He scooted the chair in. *Thank you,* he mimicked silently to her slim back, brushing aside the fact that it was his own failing that caused his discomfort. If she hadn't gotten him so agitated, it wouldn't have happened. Damn her troublesome hide.

After resuming his seat, he scowled at the flowers on the table, not wanting to watch the girl. But when his gaze focused on the vase, he felt another burst of frustration. Roses again.

Brianne fiddled with the napkin in her lap, wondering at her husband's testy mood. Why was he staring holes in those roses? Resisting the urge to crack the vase over his contrary head, she turned and waited for the pudgy, aproned woman who waddled in their direction.

"Howdy, folks. Right hot day, ain't it?" The older woman, wearing a dust cap that hid most of her reddish gray hair, set a tin pitcher filled with liquid on the table. "Got roast beef and cabbage fer yer bellies"—she tapped the tin container—"and chilled rose-hip tea fer yer thirst."

Hayden groaned.

Brianne frowned. Now what? "That's fine with me," she answered warily.

"Just great," her husband grumbled.

When the woman left, Brianne leaned forward and filled her glass, then gestured with the pitcher. "Would you like some tea?"

"I've had enough roses for one day."

"What?"

"Never mind. And, no, I don't want any damned tea."

"Well, fine." She set the pitcher down with a clank. "Excuse me for offering."

"Listen—" A shadow passed in front of the door, and he whipped his head in that direction. He gaped in surprise, then he smiled and sprang to his feet. "I'll be right back."

Brianne turned to see what had his attention. Her eyes widened. The man speaking to Hayden was stunning. Brianne had never seen a more perfectly formed male. Every inch of him, from his silky raven hair to his shiny black boots, was heartstopping. Even his black clothes and the evil-looking guns strapped to his hips enhanced his intriguing appeal. He was every inch a wickedly dangerous gunman.

From beneath the low brim of his hat, he sneaked a glance at her, and she blushed under the impact of those silver-blue eyes.

Appalled by her own boldness, and how she stared,

Brianne wrenched her gaze away. She was married, for goodness sakes. Besides, she cared a great deal for her husband. Didn't she? She snatched a quick peek at Hayden as he shook hands with the newcomer. Seeing the two towering men side by side, she knew that she did. Though her husband's features weren't quite as perfect as the other man's, she preferred Hayden's earthy, masculine appeal.

Her husband moved and began speaking hurriedly to the man in a hushed voice.

The stranger's eyes grew wide as he obviously listened. He shot Hayden a quizzical glance, then Brianne. To her everlasting mortification, the stranger burst out laughing.

Hayden clenched his jaw.

Still chuckling, the man raised a hand in departure and sauntered on down the boardwalk.

His face grim, her husband returned to the table.

"Who was he?" she asked, praying she never saw the rude man again.

"No one."

"But—"

"It wasn't anyone, woman. Now drink your damned tea!"

"I married an ogre," Brianne mumbled testily two days later when she mounted the little mare Hayden had purchased for her. He wouldn't tell her about their home, the robbery except to say they were on the way to her folks or even their wedding. She peered over at her sullen husband. In fact, he'd hardly said a word since they'd eaten at the cafe, and he hadn't ventured from the hotel room since . . . except at night to sleep—wherever.

Those sleeping arrangements made her feel very uneasy, too—that something wasn't quite right between herself and Hayden. He hadn't attempted to share her room, and, in truth, she didn't know whether to be pleased by his consideration or upset by his rejection.

Watching him covertly from the corner of her eye as they rode along a mesquite-lined path out of Henrietta, she felt a strange stirring. It really was hard to believe this magnificent man belonged to her; even if he did sulk—and wouldn't tell her who his friend was. Still, sitting astride a sleek golden palomino, his gray hat pulled low, those seductive gunmetal eyes narrowed against the sunlight, there was a dangerous, masculine beauty about him that made her pulse race.

She doubted the man had any idea how good he looked in that smoke-colored shirt or those dusty jeans that clung to his thighs, outlining a very generous display of his gender.

But she knew, and she couldn't turn away. She dug her nails into her palms. The rocking movement of the horse beneath him tightened then loosened the denim around that particular area, captivating her.

Shocked by her shameless ogling, she closed her eyes and turned her head, but as she did so, she could have sworn she heard a low chuckle rumble from her husband's throat.

Heat spread over her face. It was bad enough for *her* to realize she was gawking at him like that. But for him to catch her at it! Good heavens, he must think she's—

"Watch where you're going, *chica.*"

Brianne swung her head around just in time to see her mare wander toward a low-hanging branch. Wishing Hayden had kept his mouth shut and let her hit it—jarring her out of her wayward thoughts and possibly jolting her memory, she pulled on the reins, then guided the animal back onto the path. But she couldn't face her husband, see the amused grin she knew she would find. Curse him. He was a coldhearted snake.

Attempting to avoid his mockery, she set her gaze to the other side, only to hear another chuckle. Brianne thought she would die of shame right then and there.

Damn him to hell. She forced her eyes to a spot between the mare's ears, vowing they would stay there for the rest of the journey.

For several hours, she remained true to her oath, only occasionally allowing her attention to wander to the now barren landscape as they traveled west along a trail just south of Wichita Falls. Fleetingly, she wondered why they didn't ride through the small settlement, perhaps stop for refreshments, but she wasn't about to ask. Instead, she concentrated on the stiffness of her posture, on the throbbing ache in her spine from being held so rigid.

They stopped for the noon meal, which passed in complete silence, then mounted up again shortly afterward. When Hayden had said they'd be in for some hard riding, he'd apparently meant it.

Finally, when dusk darkened the sky, he stopped for the night. Brianne was so exhausted she didn't even care that they were on the open range, amid the sand and sagebrush.

Wrapped in her own blanket, and unsure of her position with Hayden, she made her bed near the low fire, a good distance from where her husband had spread his bedroll. Yet, he didn't lie down. Instead, he grabbed his rifle and disappeared for the better part of an hour. Then, when he returned, he stationed himself in the shadows near the edge of their camp. What he was watching for—or guarding them from—she didn't know, and she didn't think she wanted to. And, at the moment, she was too tired to care.

His odd behavior set a pattern for the days that followed. Hayden completely ignored her.

Nearly a week into their journey, they came across a group of cowboys moving a large herd of longhorns.

"Howdy, folks," a large man standing before a chuck wagon greeted, waving a tin ladle. "Rest a spell. Eat."

For the first time in days, Hayden relaxed his stiff demeanor and smiled. "This Charlie Goodnight's drive?"

"Hayden?" a bearded bull of a man called out, riding toward them.

Her husband swung around in his saddle, and his whole face brightened. "Charlie? Charlie Goodnight! Well, I'll be damned."

The older man drew his mount to a halt and dismounted. When Hayden had done the same, they shook hands heartily. "What are you doing in these parts?" Hayden asked.

"Been lookin'—and found—the great valley a Mexican friend of mine told me about. Soon as I get rid of the beeves I'm herdin', I'm goin' back. Gonna make it mine."

"Where is it?"

"'Bout twenty miles west of here. But enough about me, boy. You're forgettin' your manners." He glanced up at Brianne. "Introduce me to the little lady."

Hayden had the grace to look uncomfortable. "Um, Charlie, I'd like you to meet Brianne, my, uh . . . wife."

Charlie's gray beard stretched wide with his smile. "Hot damn!" He swung toward a group of men who were just riding up. "The kid's been lassoed and hog-tied tighter'n a steer at brandin' time!" he shouted.

A round of whoops and congratulations burst from the men. But when Brianne peeked at Hayden, she saw red staining his neck. He was embarrassed. By her? Or was it just the cowboy's boisterous banter? Somehow, she didn't think it was the latter. And it hurt.

"Josh, help Hayden's missus down, will you?" Charlie boomed, then swung on the cook. "We're gonna celebrate, Barnie. See if you cain't find some fat steaks in that mangy wagon." Slapping a meaty arm around Hayden's shoulders, he nudged him toward the other men. "Come on, kid. I think I know where to find a full bottle."

Calloused fingers touched Brianne's hand. "Miz Caldwell?"

Startled, she looked down to see a tall, lanky cowboy about her own age offering his assistance. Awkwardly, she accepted his help in dismounting.

"Name's Josh Walker," he greeted. The sparse beard he sported wasn't able to hide his youth or boyish charm.

"Call me Brianne," she said, feeling a little shy. Why had her husband all but deserted her?

The drover grinned deeply, then looped her hand through his arm. "My pleasure, ma'am."

As they approached the group of men Hayden had joined, his gaze slid from her to Josh, to their linked arms. For the barest instant, his eyes hardened, then he abruptly returned his attention to the man beside him.

Even though she still wore Hayden's shirt over her skimpy blouse, that dark look made her feel exposed. Cheap. He'd shown her at every opportunity that he didn't want her, yet it was obvious he disapproved of anyone else paying her a little notice. Sighing, and wishing she could understand her unpredictable husband, Brianne gently removed her arm from Josh's. "Do you think I might have a drink of water?"

Several men in Hayden's group spun around. "I'll get it!" they all said at the same time.

Brianne winced at their eagerness.

Josh stood with his mouth open as if he'd also been about to respond.

Hayden narrowed his eyes and stepped forward. "I'll get my wife's drink."

Feeling chastised for some unearthly reason, she eased as far away from the men as she could get without appearing rude and awaited her husband's return.

Only moments had passed before he thrust a tin cup in her hand. "Stop enticing the drovers," he said gratingly. "They don't need your kind of temptation with twelve hundred head of cattle to guard." Without another word, he walked off.

Her mouth nearly dropped open. *Enticing the drovers? How? Anger mounted. The beast. She hadn't done one thing to warrant that remark. Throwing the cup down, she stormed to her horse and mounted. "To hell with you, Caldwell. I'm leaving."

Hayden cast a not-so-surprised glance in her direction, then called to Charlie. "Sorry we can't stay, but the little woman's got her dander up over something. Guess I'll have to take you up on your offer to celebrate next time."

A chorus of groans followed his announcement.

Brianne fumed. How dare he make the cowboys think it was her fault they were going. Furious, and embarrassed to the toes, she kicked her horse into a gallop.

By the time Hayden had caught up with her, she'd had time to think about what he'd said, and her fury subsided. Perhaps she had unconsciously been flirting. But for the life of her, she couldn't recall doing so. Still, Hayden wouldn't get so angry over nothing, would he? She must have done *something*. Her father had accused her a thousand times of doing the same thing.

Shocked by the brief flash of memory, she tightened her hold on the reins, trying to grasp more information from the black depths of her mind. Nothing surfaced, but the realization that she'd apparently behaved unacceptably in the past caused her uncertainty over Hayden's actions to grow.

Hating the way her stomach knotted when she thought of how she must have embarrassed him in front of his friends, she promptly decided to apologize for—whatever. Resolutely, she veered her horse closer to his. "I'm sorry for . . . upsetting you. I didn't realize I'd done anything wrong. . . ."

"You didn't," her husband countered uninterestedly. "I just didn't feel like lording over a bunch of sex-starved cowboys who haven't seen a woman in months. Making you angry was the quickest way out of there."

Stunned, and not knowing how to respond, Brianne clamped her mouth shut. Anything she said was bound to get her into trouble. But she couldn't help wanting to put a lump on the top of that arrogant head.

Yet, at the same time, she felt just the tiniest bit pleased. Though he hadn't said as much, she was sure Hayden had been jealous. Otherwise, why would he have cared if she was the center of the cowboys' attention? It would have kept her out of his hair. Her spirits brightened. If he was jealous, then he most definitely cared.

As they rode deeper into the panhandle of northwestern Texas, Hayden's stoic demeanor didn't change. If anything, he became more subdued, more watchful. Several times, he left her to retrace their path, yet never said why.

But his sullen mood didn't upset her. She was too happy over his reaction at Goodnight's camp to care, and the idle hours on the trail had been spent daydreaming about Hayden, and the kiss they'd shared in Henrietta.

"We'll stop here for dinner," her husband commanded, drawing his horse to a halt in a rocky area that offered shade from the blistering sun.

Standing near a pile of sandstone, Brianne arched her spine, stretching her tired, aching muscles, and watched Hayden gather tumbleweeds and dried cow chips to start a fire.

Out of nowhere, a whirring sound pierced the air, followed by a heavy thud.

Brianne turned, confused.

"Get down!" Hayden shouted. He dove at her, knocking her to the ground. Her back hit the sand hard, then Hayden fell on top of her, covering her with his body. He snapped his Colt from its holster and fired toward the hill of boulders just behind her.

Arrows thwacked all around them. War hoops and savage shouts echoed through the rocks. Hayden's gun exploded again and again.

Oh, dear God, Brianne thought wildly. *Indians!*

14

Hayden!" Brianne screamed in terror.

"Stay down," he ordered, then shoved himself off her and crouched low, still firing his weapon repeatedly.

A man cried out in the distance. Then another. And another.

Arrows hissed like vipers. The smell of gunpowder filled the air. The sounds! Oh, God, the sounds reminded her. Brianne fought a rush of terrifying memories as some unseen force jerked her back in time to another place. "No!" she moaned, curling into a ball, shaking uncontrollably.

Whir! Crack!

Her thoughts spun crazily. The image of a man wavered and grew. *"Bitch! Slut!"* he spat.

Whir.

He swung the razor strap.

Crack.

It tore into her flesh. Oh, God. The pain.

Whir! Crack! Whir! Crack!

"No. Oh please, no more. Make him stop."

"Brianne! Damn it, Brianne. Snap out of it!"

Hard hands shook her. "We've got to get out of here before they regain their courage."

Hayden yanked her to her feet. "Get a move on." He shoved her to the mare, then tossed her up.

Numbly, she turned to see him mounting his own horse.

Appearing strained, he slumped over his mount for a moment as if to catch his breath, then lifted the reins and nodded to her.

Then she saw it—blood oozing from an arrow imbedded in his shoulder. "Hayden! Oh, God! You're hurt."

Ignoring his injury, he quickly scanned her. "You okay?"

"Yes, but—"

"Keep up." He kicked his stallion into a gallop.

Their horses' hooves pounded the dry earth, stirring up thick clouds of dust as they rode wildly across the flatlands. She tried not to think about Hayden's wound, in fact, she did everything to avoid it. But even the meaning of that last distorted memory wouldn't stick with her long enough to figure it out. Nothing could ease her concern or stop her from shooting nervous glances at her husband and checking to see if the Indians were following. Miraculously they weren't.

Her attention returned to her husband.

Blood dripped from the hand clutching his shoulder, and he was deathly pale. With every jolt of the horse, she feared he might fall. She turned away, praying he wouldn't, yet too afraid to keep watching in case he did.

Hot sun beat down on her head. Sweat beaded beneath her clothes. What she'd give for a drink, for a shade tree, she thought numbly. Just a breath of fresh air would help. And how much worse Hayden must be faring. Curse him. Why didn't he stop?

Finally, after what seemed like hours, he halted his horse at the edge of a ravine where the valley cut into the arid flatland like a dark slash, then dropped a good seven hundred feet to a river surrounded by acres of rolling grassland. Cedar and china trees lined the bottom along the water's edge, while apple trees jutted from the sloping sides.

It had to be the valley Charlie Goodnight spoke about—and the most beautiful sight she'd ever seen.

Unfortunately, seeing the lush bottom of the enormous gorge and getting to it were two different things. They had to weave their way down an incredibly steep, impossibly narrow path. One slip of the mare's hooves . . . "Hayden, I don't think this is such a good idea."

"Keep your eyes on me, *chica*. If you look down, it only makes it worse."

Brianne lifted her gaze abruptly. "Isn't there a safer way down?"

"Probably. But this one's closest."

She noticed the way his head drooped slightly, and how sweat and blood plastered his shirt to his skin. Then she saw his hands. They were shaking.

Concern jolted her. "Are you all right?"

Hayden lifted his uninjured shoulder in nonchalance, but she could see the lines of strain around his mouth. He was hurting.

"Come on," he commanded and urged his horse forward.

Too worried to argue, she followed as he guided his palomino down the steep path.

It was a horribly frightening descent, but not so much because of the danger to herself as the way Hayden began to sink lower and lower over the saddle. Wanting to take his mind off his pain and ease her own fears, she searched for something to talk about. "How long have we been married?"

He seemed to shift uncomfortably as he turned his horse into a final bend in the path. It brought them at last to level ground. "Not long."

His voice sounded unsteady, and her worry over him doubled. Nervously, she babbled, "A week? A month? How long?"

He opened his mouth as if to speak, but the words never came out. As if in slow motion, he closed his eyes, slumped over the saddle, then slid to the ground.

Brianne was off her mount with a speed she hadn't believed humanly possible. She fell to her knees beside him. "Hayden? Oh, God. Hayden, wake up!"

When he didn't respond, she glanced wildly around the rocky, thickly bushed gully. Not far away, two towering boulders stood about ten feet apart. Matted grass covered the ground between them, offering a bed of sorts.

But she didn't try to fool herself. There was no way she could drag him to that spot. Hayden was a very big man. Too big, at the moment. Helplessness engulfed her. "Damn you, Hayden. Wake up. I can't do this alone."

As if he'd heard her words, his eyes fluttered open and he stared groggily into her face.

"Oh, thank God," she breathed. "Can you move? I've got to get you over there." She gestured to the space between the boulders.

He nodded slowly. "Get . . . the bedroll."

Brianne sprang to her feet and quickly untied the blankets from the saddle of his mount. When she turned, she saw that Hayden had managed to get to his feet and was staggering toward the grass.

"Wait, I'll help you." She raced to his side and wedged her shoulder under his uninjured arm.

Defiantly, he shook his head, but was too weak to do anything about it.

When they reached the rocks, he leaned tiredly against one while she quickly spread the bedroll. The instant she was done, he collapsed on the pallet.

Relieved that they'd accomplished this one small feat, but knowing there was a much bigger one yet to face, she sank down beside him. "You've got to get that arrow out."

He met her eyes. "I can't. You'll have to do it."

"What?"

Unaffected, he pushed himself up into a sitting position, his arms quivering with the effort. "Get behind me."

Nervously eyeing her husband, she scooted around him, then cringed at the sight of the bloody arrowhead protruding out of his shoulder. Her voice shook. "What am I supposed to do?"

Hayden was silent for a moment, then expelled a breath. "Might be better if you don't know till it happens."

Now why did that scare the stuffing out of her? Her breath

stilled. Surely he didn't expect her to use that awful razor he carried. She knew she'd never be able to.

A snap jerked her attention upward. She smothered a gasp of surprise when she realized that Hayden had broken off the feathered end of the arrow. "What are you doing?"

"Chica, now isn't the time for questions," he grumbled shakily. "Now, grab your end of the arrow with both hands."

"Why?"

"Just do it."

Struggling to keep her hands from trembling, Brianne curled her fingers around the smooth wood, praying that Hayden didn't expect her to pull the arrow out. She just couldn't.

She felt more than saw him drag in a long breath, then suddenly, he lurched forward. Shocked, Brianne stared down in horror at the bloody arrow she still clutched. "Dear heaven." She dropped it as if it burned.

Standing on wobbly legs, she moved around in front of him. He looked ready to pass out, and she was sure he remained conscious by sheer force of will.

He drew in a breath. "Give me the shirt you're wearing." His voice was heavy with pain.

She glanced down to see him trying to stem the flow of blood seeping from the wound. Immediately, she tore the garment off and gave it to him.

His gaze flicked to her chest, and his mouth clamped into a grim line, but he took the shirt and pressed it to his wound.

"Can I help?" she offered.

He nodded. "Find something to tie this in place."

Her mind spun crazily for something to use, then she thought of the blouse she wore. Quickly, she pulled the lower hem out of her waistband.

"What the hell are you doing?" Hayden demanded in a strangled voice.

Confused by his anger, she blinked. "I was just going to tear off a strip to use—"

"Get a piece of leather," he nearly shouted.

When Hayden's makeshift bandage was in place, he eased

112

down onto his side and closed his eyes. Then, to Brianne's relief, he quickly drifted into a deep sleep.

She sat quietly for a long time, watching him, trying to understand this complicated man, and why, obviously, the sight of her unclothed upset him so. Reaching no reasonable conclusion, she finally cast the thoughts aside and decided she'd better do something about shelter.

Scanning the tall boulders overhead, she rose and got one of the blankets from her own bedroll to use as a canopy, then deftly—if nervously—climbed to the top ledge of the first one.

Of course, once she got there, she realized she'd need something to weigh the blanket down to keep it from falling, so she scampered down and gathered several smaller rocks. Ruefully perceiving that she couldn't carry them and climb at the same time, she set them aside long enough to tuck in her blouse again, then shoved them down the front.

Securing the first side was the easy part. But there was still the second. After several attempts using a long branch to drag the other end of the blanket across the chasm, she finally resorted to tying a small rock to one corner and tossing it over. When it caught, and the lopsided blanket flapped in the slight breeze, she let out a sigh, then in a matter of moments had the canopy secured and drawn tight.

That done, she set out to gather branches for a fire. It took nearly an hour before she got it started, but finally, the warm yellow glow flickered over their little haven, and she felt immensely satisfied with herself. Now all she had to do was fix supper. She frowned at that thought and was suddenly filled with a feeling of inadequacy. Shaking her head, she headed for Hayden's saddlebags.

She removed a packet containing freshly baked corn cakes, canned beans, and a thick knife, then carried them to a circular clearing around the fire. It took her a while to clumsily open the beans, but she soon had them nestled in the white coals, steam rising from beneath the mangled lid.

Hating to wake Hayden when he was resting so well, but knowing he needed food to regain his strength, she carried a plate over to him.

He woke with a start when she touched his cheek. "What?"

"You've got to eat something," she said, handing him the metal plate.

Wincing, he turned on his side and set the plate on the blanket beside him. As he ate, his gaze drifted around their camp, from the fire, to the meal, to the canopy overhead. "You do all this?"

Feeling a surge of accomplishment, she nodded.

A smile pulled at the corners of his mouth, then his eyes lowered to her chest. Immediately, his expression turned grim.

Rejection hit her swift and hard. She stared down at her plate, wondering what he found so detestable about her. And the thought stayed with her, even after she'd cleaned the dishes in the river and went for a walk to relieve herself.

On the way back, her thoughts tumbled. *What does he find so offensive about me?*

She examined the revealing blouse she wore. Surely he wasn't upset by her somewhat undignified display. It wasn't her fault the clothes didn't fit.

Her thoughts drifted to the incident in the hotel, when he'd stomped out of the room swearing, then returned with the wrinkled shirt, demanding she put it on. Did the sight of her nearly naked breasts appall him? She slid her hand over one mound, pleased to note that it felt firm and full, its center thrusting upward. Definitely not flabby or offensive. So what did he find so objectionable?

"Sonofabitch."

Brianne snapped her head up to find Hayden leaning heavily against a tree in front of her, his eyes fastened on the hand at her breast. She blushed to her toes. "Why are you out of bed?" she managed awkwardly, unable to keep the humiliation out of her tone.

Ignoring her question, his eyes remained on her breast, and she heard his breath hiss. "What are you doing?"

"T-trying to see what you find so repulsive about my body."

"Repul— There's not a damn thing repulsive about you."

114

"Then why do you find it so hard to look at me?"

"I find it hard because every time I do, I want to *touch* you."

Brianne's vanity took flight. "Is that so bad?"

He lifted his hand, then slid it over her breast. "I don't know. Is it?" He brushed her nipple with his thumb, watching it stiffen and thrust forward. His hot gaze met hers.

Tingling heat skittered through her body, but she couldn't move. Didn't want to. This man was her husband, and she wanted him.

He jerked his hand away and stepped back, his anger clearly visible. "Get out of here."

Shivering, as much from his sensual overture as from his unjustified rage, she quickly raced toward their camp. She would never understand this man. One minute he acted as if he desired her, yet in the next, he seemed repelled at the idea of touching her.

Hayden staggered through the bushes, willing his flaming body to cool. Even the pain in his shoulder hadn't damp-ened his desire for her. Damn the woman. Every time she looked at him she made him ache to possess her. She must know what her questions—*actions*—did to him. Shit. The way she'd cupped her breast in front of him had nearly sent him to his knees, and no force on earth could have pre-vented him from touching her. Just once.

Bent on changing his course of thought, he scanned his surroundings. They'd be stuck in this miserable gorge for the next few days—at least he *hoped* it would only be a few days—until he recovered. Thank God, the wound had been clean, that the arrow hadn't hit anything vital. At thirty, Hayden just wasn't ready to die.

Tiredly, he brushed a wayward lock of hair off his forehead and started weaving his way toward camp—and Brianne. He dragged in a breath. Damn. He had to stop thinking about her. He had enough to worry about right now—his recovery, the plan for Logan . . . and the un-known man who'd been following them since they left Henrietta, something he had yet to tell Brianne.

Hell, he'd just discovered it himself a few days ago, that's why he'd kept backtracking, hoping to spot the scum. But he hadn't. The culprit was good, Hayden would give him that. Maybe too good. And it was time Brianne knew.

Hayden made for camp.

He'd just entered the last of the trees when her small body plowed into him with such force, they both fell.

He hit the ground hard, Brianne sprawled on top of him.

"What's wrong?" he demanded, clutching her shoulders.

Breathlessly, she stared at him, her eyes flashing, her chest thudding against his with her labored breathing. "My memory's returned!"

15

*H*ayden tensed, his heart thundering nearly as hard as hers. And he waited for the inevitable outburst of fury.

But it didn't come.

He cleared his throat. "Your memory?"

Brianne nodded, her silky hair falling around them like a shimmering gold waterfall. "Not all of it, but some." Her eyes flashed like an excited child's. "I remember Santa Fe, and the house I grew up in, and my horse, Chester, and my mother, and Maria, and—"

"Whoa. Slow down. And get off me so we can talk." Not that he really wanted her to, but the heat radiating from those sweet curves was driving him crazy.

She sprang to her feet.

He followed quite a bit slower, his shoulder pumping with a flood of pain. "Now," he said, trying not to wince as he guided her into camp, "settle down and catch your breath. I'll make coffee, then you can tell me what you remember."

A hundred thoughts chased through his head as he threw a handful of grounds into the tin pot. Did she remember the jailbreak? That he was taking her to Logan? Would he have to tie her up again? He frowned at the idea. Damn it, he didn't want to do that. His chest suddenly felt tight. Did she now know they weren't married?

"Hurry, Hayden."

He sent her a sideways glance.

She sat on a dead log, her hands fidgeting anxiously, her lovely gray eyes sparkling, expectant. Jesus, did she know how beautiful she was?

Joining her on the log, he watched her warily. "Okay, *chica.* Start at the beginning."

She shoved the hair away from her face. "Well, I ran to camp, because I was so upset after . . . what happened. And I sat down." She patted the log. "Right here. I was feeling sorry for myself, I guess, and cursing you, then all of a sudden, the memories started rushing in . . . out of nowhere.

"I remembered my mother first." She gripped his hand. "Oh, Hayden. She's so beautiful. Her hair is the color of dark whiskey, and her eyes remind you of velvet, so soft, such a rich violet color. And her voice, when you hear it, it's like someone poured warm oil down your spine. So soothing, so comforting."

He smiled, knowing that she didn't even realize her own voice sounded the same way, though he would have said husky rather than soothing. It was the kind of voice that made a man's insides tingle. *As well he knew.*

"Anyway," she continued brightly. "Once I remembered Mama, it was as if everything else just tumbled into place." She tightened her hold. "Did you know that I was born in Santa Fe? And that I'm the daughter of an assemblyman? My parents are wealthy and I live in a lovely hacienda, and . . ."

Hayden felt his guts clench. She *was* Art Logan's daughter. Sonofabitch! The mangy bastard had killed another woman—and buried her—to cover Brianne's disappearance. But why, damn it? Was his reputation that important? Hayden's eyes narrowed. Or did Brianne know something that could cause Logan serious damage?

". . . and that's all I remember," Brianne finished on a whispery breath.

"What? I mean, *what* was the last thing you recall?" Hayden asked, having only caught the tail end of her story.

"My birthday. Didn't you hear me? I said the last thing I remembered was my eighteenth birthday party just three months ago. On February twenty-eighth."

Hayden felt the tension in his muscles ease. "Nothing after that?"

"Not a thing." She searched his eyes, her own tinged with sadness. "I still don't recall our wedding." She smiled tremulously. "But at least I know who I am and where I came from."

Hayden stood up. "Yes." *Now we both know.*

"How's your shoulder?" she asked, looking at him, her face still glowing with newfound discovery.

"I've had worse."

"By Indians?"

"Sometimes." He turned to face her. *"Chica,* apologizing doesn't come easy for me, but I'm sorry I've been so testy. I've just had a lot on my mind."

"About us?"

He shrugged. "Some, but mostly Char Daniels, the man you saw me talking to in Henrietta. He came for me."

"Why?"

He wished she wouldn't ask so many questions. "Because I'm a Texas Ranger, and while I've been spending time with you . . . taking you back to your parents, McNelly, my captain, was in bad need of help down on the Nueces Strip. Gangs of outlaws have been killing and terrorizing folks along the border, and McNelly's Rangers were sent there to stop them. Things are about to come to a head, and he needs every available man. That's why he sent Char after me. I'm supposed to turn the . . . current situation I've been working on over to Captain Coldwell, head of the northern region."

Hayden bristled, thinking of Char's message. He didn't want to go back. Not yet. Besides, Captain Coldwell and his

Rangers had their hands full with renegades. They didn't have time or manpower for tracking a gang of outlaws, or their illustrious boss. Hayden curled his fingers into the log. Besides, he couldn't go back now. He was too close. "We're supposed to meet Char at Fort Craig."

"How long will it take us?"

"A couple weeks."

"That doesn't leave much time," Brianne mumbled distractedly, then rose and walked toward the trees, her expression thoughtful.

"What are you talking about? Where are you going?"

She ignored his first question. "To wash up."

Hayden watched her disappear, wondering at her sudden preoccupation. Then, deciding he was too tired and sore to try and figure her out, he eased down onto the pallet, flinching in pain, and determined to get some rest.

Unfortunately, his mind wasn't cooperative. Brianne recalled everything up until her birthday three months ago, but nothing more. Three months, he mused, realizing it was just a few weeks before her mother disappeared.

He smiled, remembering how Brianne had described Suzanne Logan. Except for the hair and eye color, Brianne could have been describing herself. But Hayden would have added a few more adjectives, like beautiful beyond words, seductive, soft, tempting, compassionate, captivating, and so . . .

When he woke up an hour or so later, Brianne still hadn't returned. Instantly, Hayden became alarmed. Grabbing his shoulder, he staggered to his feet. Anything could have happened to her. She could have fallen, hit her head, drowned, been taken by the Hawkins Gang. Captured or killed by the bastard following them. Anything . . .

His heart pounding, Hayden started for the trees. He stopped short, when a shadowy figure darted behind a tree halfway down the path leading from the rim.

Glimpsing the man spurred Hayden into action. Fear raced through him. Brianne. God, what if he has Brianne! A hundred thoughts chased through his head as he scrambled up the incline. Brianne, dressed in baggy men's clothes, her eyes defiant. Her saw her again tending the outlaw who'd tried to attack her, the compassion she'd shown, the deep inner goodness that couldn't be squelched even in the face of danger.

He remembered how helpless she'd been, lying in that hotel bed, raging with fever . . . and how frightened he'd been. And how he'd nearly lost control when she kissed him the morning after she recovered, how good she'd felt in his arms, how soft her lips were, how he'd nearly forgotten himself and taken what she offered—and damn his quest for revenge.

In Goodnight's camp, Hayden had almost shown his true side. When the drovers swooped down on Brianne like vultures out for a feast, Hayden saw red. He'd have done anything to get her out of there, away from those hungry-eyed wranglers who were looking at her like she was a loaf of fresh baked bread. And he knew just how they felt. He experienced the same sensation each time he saw her. Though he'd tried his best to remain coldhearted and distant, one saucy flick of her lashes made his insides crumble, and he knew she was getting under his skin. The very thing he'd vowed would never happen.

When he came to the spot where he'd seen the shadow, Hayden snapped out of his reverie and quickly searched the area for signs of a struggle or footprints.

A piece of cloth caught his attention, and when he fixed on it, an icy chill slithered up his spine. Not ten feet from where he stood, a shirtless man lay facedown in the weeds, a bloody knife protruding from his back. "Jesus," Hayden whispered, anxiously scanning the brush and trees nearby.

There was no sign of the attacker.

Edging closer to the body, he rolled it over with his foot. It was Half Bear. His fear for Brianne becoming explosive, Hayden whirled around, desperate to locate tracks, broken branches, anything that would lead him to her.

A flash of yellow fluttered in the creek below.

Hayden bolted in that direction, unmindful of the pain in

his shoulder, or the terror squeezing his chest. But when he reached the water's edge, he skidded to a halt.

Just yards away, Brianne stood ankle-deep in the middle of the stream—stripped to the skin. "Christ!" Hayden bellowed, torn between paralyzing relief and blinding fury.

Brianne heard Hayden's shout and had scrambled out onto the bank by the time he stormed to her. Clutching her blouse close to her bare body, she waited for him to speak, praying he wasn't as furious as he appeared.

"Just what do you think you're doing?" her husband snarled. He yanked the blouse from her hands and quickly wrapped it around her shoulders, then drew it closed beneath her chin.

"Washing?" she answered warily.

His hand shook. "In broad daylight? Where anyone could see you?"

"It's dusk, Hayden," she said as patiently as possible. "You're the only one who saw me, and we *are* married."

"How about the man tailing us?"

"What man?"

Hayden released her and stepped away. "I wish to hell I knew. But for the life of me I can't figure it out—or catch a glimpse of the sneaky bastard."

"What does he want?" Her eyes grew wide. "I-is he dangerous?"

Wishing he didn't have to tell her, but knowing her safety could depend on it, he nodded. "At first I thought it was . . . er, one of the outlaws I'd been tracking, one called Half Bear, but I was wrong." He cleared his throat. "I found Half Bear a few minutes ago. Whoever's tracking us put a knife in the Indian's back." Hayden now understood that look that had passed between Pedro and the Comanche. Half Bear had been sent to watch them.

Brianne clamped a hand to her throat. "He's going to kill us!" Her gaze flittered nervously around.

"I don't think that's his intention, *chica.* At least I hope not. Besides, he's had plenty of opportunities, all ready, if that was his goal."

Her shoulders lost some of their tenseness. "Maybe it's your friend, the one you saw in Henrietta."

Hayden shook his head, wishing to hell it was. "Char left the day before we did."

Anxiously, she explored the upper rim. Then her expression suddenly changed to one of mortification. Her cheeks glowed pink. "Oh, God, he saw me nak—"

"I know," Hayden growled. Frustrated, not to mention jealous as hell, he grabbed up her skirt, then gripping her roughly by the arm, he hauled her to a heavily bushed area and pushed her into it. "Now, get dressed." He tossed her garment over the hedge.

Brianne gritted her teeth as she quickly pulled on her clothes. Hayden was impossible. His concern for her was obvious, yet it always held an undercurrent of anger. *Unjustified anger.* And bullheaded bossiness. He'd even called her a whore back in the hotel, for no reason at all.

She stilled. Or was there? Was she being too brazen? Perhaps Hayden wasn't raised the way she had been. Her mother had always told her that folks who really loved each other didn't have secrets or modesty between them.

Battling the urge to shout obscenities over the one part of her memory she couldn't reach, she stepped from the bushes and plodded along behind her husband.

Once in camp, Hayden tossed a piece of wood onto the dying fire, then knelt before it, doggedly stoking it to a higher flame. The fine sprinkling of hair on the back of his long-fingered hands moved with the effort. A yellow glow danced over the shiny black lock of hair brushing his forehead and the soft swirls darkening his chest. The man was impossibly rude, overbearing, arrogant, and damned bossy, she fumed. But still, she couldn't keep from appreciating his magnificent form. His masculine beauty was both dangerous and appealing.

When he'd gotten the fire burning to his satisfaction, he tossed aside the stick. "This should be enough to last the night," he clipped in a harsher tone than usual. "Get some sleep."

Frustration galled her. She wished she could keep up with the man's mercurial moods. Or at least understand why he felt it necessary to keep distance between them. "What about you—"

"Don't argue."

Brianne heaved a sigh, fighting the urge to jab a finger into his sore shoulder. "At least let me give you one of the blankets."

"Keep it." Rising unsteadily, he removed his rifle from the scabbard on his saddle and sat down in front of one of the tall boulders, dismissing her as if she'd never been there in the first place.

Gnashing her teeth, Brianne flounced down on the pallet and turned her rump to him. Bossy bastard.

She woke up the next morning to the sound of Hayden's voice.

"I've been up all night, and I wanna get some sleep. So quit playing possum and fix breakfast."

Brianne's eyes sprang wide open. *Possum*. Why that— Then an even more upsetting thought hit her. Breakfast? She didn't know how to cook. A flicker of a conversation she'd once heard popped in her mind. *Maybe if I gave it a try I'd manage to poison the bastards.* Who in the world had she been talking about? She narrowed her gaze suspiciously on her husband. And why didn't Hayden know she couldn't cook?

Brianne pulled the blanket around her and sat up. She brushed a heavy lock of hair out of her face and tried to think. Hayden had to know about her lack of culinary skills, didn't he? Unless . . . He did say they hadn't been married very long—and she knew from what she could remember, the wedding had to have taken place sometime in the last three months. Good heavens. What a shock for a bride-groom. She closed her eyes, wondering how in the world she would break it to him.

"Get to it, *chica*."

Her lashes flicked upward. "But—"

"I've got a hankering for hot biscuits this morning." Hayden gestured toward a dented tin pan he'd apparently taken from his saddlebags and a small white muslin sack that had FLOUR printed on it.

Brianne bit her lip to keep from asking who was going to make them. She coughed lightly. "Um, sure." Well, she'd give it a try, anyway.

Hayden nodded, then rubbed his stubbled jaw. "I'll go clean up. Call me when it's ready." Without waiting for a reply, he turned and stalked away.

Not sure where—or how—to begin, she straightened her clothes, then carefully folded the blanket and set it down neatly atop a flat rock. She dusted off her skirt, finger-combed her hair, then doggedly swiped the dust off her boots.

"All that stalling isn't gonna help you learn to make biscuits."

She whirled around to find Hayden standing there, towel in hand. "How did you know?"

His mouth curved into a lazy smile. "It wasn't hard to figure. Only a woman who doesn't know how to cook would turn pale when her husband asks for breakfast."

"Oh."

"Luckily, I do know how."

"You do?"

Hayden retrieved a bar of soap out of his saddlebags, apparently the reason he returned, then strode over to her. "You're gonna need some water and more ingredients," he offered. "There's a canteen hanging on my saddle horn. You'll find salt and baking powder in the supply sack. Get them."

After gathering the items, Brianne sat down and stared helplessly at the dented metal. "Now what?"

"Just slop some flour in the pan and toss in a couple pinches of salt and baking powder. Add water till it's good and tacky, then shape it into fat balls inside the pan."

That didn't sound too difficult. Brianne did as instructed, then wiped a floured hand across her cheek. "What next?"

He brushed his finger over the floury spot on her jaw, his hand lingering for just a moment. "Set it on the coals near the edge of the fire."

She felt as if the fire were inside her. Quickly, she did as he said, then remained on her knees, avoiding his gaze and staring at the ugly, sticky balls. "Am I finished?"

"For now."

His voice, she noticed, had suddenly grown cooler.

"I should be back by the time they're done." Turning, he again headed into the trees.

Brianne felt ill, and totally incompetent. What kind of wife was she? She annoyed her husband at every turn, nagged him, and she didn't even know how to cook. Hurting from the blow of her own thoughts, she sprang to her feet and raced away from the camp. From her humiliation. Her own wretched misery.

Thrashing her way through the underbrush, cursing her ineptness with every breath, she tripped and fell. Pain shot through her newly healed knee. But with it came a burst of undisclosed memory. She was running frantically. *Help! Help me!* Then an arm came out of nowhere to grab her.

Shaken, she rubbed her temples, trying to see more. But it was gone.

She sat down, massaging her knee. Who had she been running from? Why would she need help? Who had grabbed her? There were still so many unanswered questions.

The sting of tears filled her eyes, but she quickly brushed them away. Curse it. She wouldn't cry. She wouldn't. She'd find the answers.

Filled with a new determination, and a few thousand questions to ask her husband, she started toward their camp.

A twig snapped on the cliff above her.

Terror skipped up her spine. Nervously, she lifted her gaze.

16

Nothing moved on the cliff overhead. Not even a slight breeze stirred. Knowing the man following them was still out there, yet relieved that she hadn't actually seen him, Brianne continued on to camp, wishing Hayden had never told her about the stranger.

She found Hayden sleeping, his gun by his side within easy reach, and the pan of biscuits nearly empty.

Resigned, she picked up one of the remaining buns and nibbled it, tying to decide what to attempt for the next meal, and praying *their friend* didn't show his face while Hayden was so defenseless.

It took her the better part of an hour to decide that a handful of flour and a few strips of beef jerky would make a fair meal. She dumped both into a boiling pot, praying for the best.

Sitting on the log, idly weaving pieces of grass together, she glanced again at her dozing husband. He'd turned over, his face to her, and she gazed longingly at him.

The harsh lines of his face had softened with sleep, and he seemed younger, more approachable. She wanted to reach down inside him and free the man he kept from her, the man she so desperately wanted to know—the one she fell in love with and married.

As if her thoughts had been spoken aloud, he opened his eyes and stared directly into hers.

Their gazes locked for a long, breathless moment, and she felt herself grow warm all over.

Only half-awake, and not yet completely in control, Hayden explored her somber gray eyes, detecting the tension that swirled inside her, and knowing he was experiencing the same sensation. He ached to touch her, to run his fingers through that silky gold hair, to fully taste those luscious pink lips . . . and what lay beyond. The need was so powerful, it staggered him. Damning himself for letting his guard down, he gathered his senses and sat up. "Isn't dinner ready yet?"

Brianne fought to regain her balance. "No." Not that she was really sure. But she needed a few minutes to compose herself.

Leaning on a boulder, he rubbed his bandaged shoulder. The movement drew her gaze to his open shirt and a forest of curling black hairs.

"How long till it's done?"

She forced her attention away. "Not much longer."

Hayden rolled his head as if the muscles in his neck were stiff, and she appreciated the way the cords in his throat worked, the creases in his cheeks deepened.

"How about some water?" Nodding toward the canteen, a raven lock fell forward on his brow, causing her pulse to skip. "My windpipe feels like a dusty grain chute."

He had to be one of the most appealing men she'd ever seen, she decided as she rose and got the canteen. She also knew that if it wasn't for his rigid control in their awkward situation, she'd be hard-pressed not to throw herself at his feet.

"Would you like some berries, too?" She flicked a hand toward the flour sack that now contained the gooseberries she'd picked earlier. "They might soothe your throat."

"Just water."

She handed him the canteen.

His fingers covered hers.

Startled by the contact, her belly gave a tiny lurch. She tugged against his hold, but he didn't release her.

Gunmetal eyes held hers. "Thank you."

She didn't know how to respond. This was a side of Hayden that unnerved her. He could melt her with a single look—an instant before he mentally froze her out, leaving her rejected. Completely vulnerable. She swallowed. "You're welcome."

Taking a healthy drink, he set the canteen down and rose, still maintaining his hold on her hand. He stared at their entwined fingers as if he didn't know who they belonged to, then slowly met her eyes. For an eternity, he held her captive with a look that curled her toes. Then inch by frightening inch, he moved closer. "Damn you," he breathed softly. "You're destroying me, *chica.*" He leaned nearer still, his lips a heartbeat from hers. "And I can't stop you."

Icy hot flames swept through her belly, and she shivered. "I—"

Her words died beneath the sweet pressure of his mouth. Cold and heat chased up her spine, and her world spun out of control. She had wanted this for so long, needed it so desperately. Her lips parted, and she willingly accepted the gentle thrust of his tongue.

But she wasn't prepared for the warmth of his mouth, the lazy exploration, or the explosion of desire that rocked her. It thrilled her. It terrified her. Suddenly fearful, she pulled away. "No!"

Eyes that had only moments ago been bright with hunger were now glazed over with frost. She could feel him retreating into an impenetrable shell. "Why stop, *chica?* You were enjoying the hell out of it."

"I was not!"

"Liar."

Brianne whirled away from him and crossed her arms over her stomach. "What kind of man are you? How can you kiss me in one second, then say such cruel things in the next?" She glared at him. "Don't you have any sense of decency?"

"Not a shred."

The very trait she'd admired in him, his honesty, was beginning to grate.

His gaze traveled over her body. "But you're blaming the wrong person for what just happened. You've been begging to be kissed for days."

Unable to deny it, or understand why she'd been so afraid of his passion, she stepped away. "Leave me alone. I'm tired of the games you play at my expense. You've shown me often enough how much you despise me, maybe it's time I start believing it."

"I don't despise you."

Suddenly feeling defeated, she brought a hand to her brow. "Hayden, what's wrong with our marriage? Why are we so . . . distant from each other? So at odds?"

What could he say? Because we're not married? Because we don't belong together? Because our association will end the minute we arrive in Santa Fe? *Because your father's responsible for my brother's death?* He took a breath. "We just don't get along, *chica*. We haven't for some time." He hated to have to say the next words but knew they were necessary to ease some of her confusion . . . and for his own piece of mind. "Before your accident, we were about to split up."

He felt her gasp all the way to his soul.

"Why didn't you tell me?"

"Because you had enough problems," he ground out, loathing himself for the lie. "I didn't want to add to them." He stared at the grass, unable to bear the hurt expression on her face. "I figured you'd remember sooner or later."

"I see."

Her voice sounded small, shaky, and he ached to take her in his arms, to soothe away the pain. Cursing himself for his weakness, he clenched his fist.

"Then why'd you kiss me if you don't care anymore?"

Hayden closed his eyes, detesting the way she made him feel like such a bastard—and why did she assume *he* was the one who didn't care? "It just happened. We always were physically attracted to each other." Well, that much was true.

"But not in love? What happened? I mean, you must have loved me once."

"We just have differences that can't be resolved."

"Is that the reason I didn't want your baby?"

Hayden felt sick. "Yes."

"But—"

He'd taken all he could. "Brianne, I'm taking you home to your parents and that's the end of it."

"But what if I'm pregnant now!" she blurted, angry that he'd be so callous as to return her to her vicious father. "We must have made love before the accident."

Just the thought of her carrying his child warmed him. Of course, *he* knew it wasn't possible since they'd never . . . He shoved his hands into his pockets and glared at her, strangely unwilling to set her straight. "If you are, then we'll just have to work things out."

"If we can do that for the sake of a babe, couldn't we do it for our marriage?"

He wanted to shake her. If they kept up this conversation much longer, he would start believing they *were* married. "For the welfare of a child, a man can force himself to endure most anything." He laughed harshly. "But if you think I'll put myself through hell again for any other reason, then your brain has suffered worse than your memory."

The instant the words were out, he regretted them—felt them tear out a chunk of his heart. They were words from his past, meant for someone else. They'd just slipped out in the heat of argument, the same way they had that day so long ago. . . .

He shook his head and faced her. "Listen, Brianne. I didn't mean—"

She was gone.

Despair tightened his stomach. He hadn't wanted to hurt

her, hadn't meant the things he said. But, damn it, she had to stop harboring plans for their future. There just wasn't one.

Tears streaming down her cheeks, Brianne ran, ignoring the sting of branches and thorns that tore at her flesh and clothing. She hated him. Never wanted to see him again. She just couldn't take any more of this pain and horrible confusion.

Feeling as if she were dying inside, she threw herself down onto the rocky ground, her fist plummeting the sparse grass. He was a beast. A bastard. Only Father had ever said such vile things to her, and she loathed him!

Shocked by the thought of her father, she sat up, dragging her hand across her eyes. Yes, she did loathe him, she recalled vividly. With good reason.

The overpowering odor of roses assaulted her nose, and she blinked, looking around in bewilderment. Then she felt it, the dampness on her leg. Her hand automatically covered the pocket of her skirt and broken glass moved beneath her palm.

It was stupid, she knew, but the bottle seemed to represent how she felt about her entire life. Shattered.

A new torrent of tears erupted, and she curled forward, cradling her stomach. Everything was falling apart around her, and she didn't know how to stop it, didn't know how to save her marriage . . . or even if it was worth saving.

If only he'd tell her what went wrong, perhaps they could work it out. Or, at the very least, maybe she could accept it and get on with her life.

Drawing in a shaky breath, she lifted her chin. She needed to talk to Hayden, get him to open up and tell her exactly why their marriage had failed. Only then would she know if it was salvageable.

Rising, she brushed the tears from her face, then emptied the glass out of her pocket, wishing she didn't feel as if a part of her heart lay among the jagged pieces. Her thoughts more stable now, she headed back to camp. Tonight, come hell or high water, she'd have a long overdue conversation with Hayden Caldwell.

From behind a row of evergreens, Hayden watched Brianne. He had followed her, intending to apologize, but when he'd seen her crying as if her heart were crushed, he couldn't do it. Anything he said would only make matters worse. He couldn't reassure her, couldn't explain, couldn't hold her like he wanted, make love to her, or take away her hurt. Too many things stood between them. His past, his job, his brother's corpse . . . and her father.

Feeling hollow inside, he rubbed the ache in his shoulder, then headed for the path that led to the rim. As much as the wound pained him, he needed to bury Half Bear. He'd put it off too long, already.

After completing the gruesome task and washing up in the creek, he returned to find that Brianne had dished him up a plate of stew—which had grown cold. Too tired and sore to care, he suffered the searing throb in his shoulder and ate in silence.

Brianne watched her husband with concern. She didn't know where he'd gone after she'd run off in tears, but whatever he'd done, it had taken its toll on him. His skin had grown ashen, his features drawn, and she could tell he was in a lot of pain. "Is there anything I can do to help?" she asked, gesturing to his shoulder.

"No." Hayden set his half-full plate aside and settled against the log behind him. While he'd dug Half Bear's grave, he'd done some thinking, and he wanted to know what Brianne's life had been like with Logan. "Tell me what it was like when you were living at home."

Brianne looked surprised, and Hayden instantly realized his mistake. A husband would know all about his wife. He thought quickly. "You know, you've never told me much about yourself."

She gave him a halfhearted smile. "I could say the same about you." Twisting some dead grass between her fingers, she lifted a slim shoulder. "I told you, I was raised in Santa

Fe—in a hacienda just five miles from town, though I didn't get to go there much." Her mouth pulled down at the corners. "You'd have to know my father to really understand, but he had lived in fear his whole life that I would do something to bring scandal to the Logan name, so I was pretty much confined to the house."

Nudging a stone with her toe, she stared at the ground. "My days were mostly spent with tutors, daydreaming on the terrace, or riding my horse, Chester."

"What did you daydream about?"

"A prince. Mama once told me a story about a beautiful princess hidden away in a cellar by an evil stepmother, and how she was saved by a dashing prince. I guess I saw myself as that princess and spent a lot of time waiting for my knightly savior."

Hayden propped an elbow on the log, imagining the unhappy young girl with a wistful smile. "It sounds like a lonely existence. Didn't you ever go anywhere?"

"A couple times. Mama convinced Father to let me attend parties his friends gave to help raise money for his campaign. When he ran for assemblyman," she clarified. "Unfortunately, both were disasters."

"Why?" he asked, knowing she must have been breathtaking in a fancy dress with her hair all done up.

"The gentlemen. The first time, Father caught me talking to a boy and accused me of making plans to meet him later. The second, a gentleman wanted to dance with me." She took an unsteady breath. "On both occasions, Father punished me when we got home. He called me horrible names, most of which I didn't know the meaning of, and he accused me of trying to ruin him like Grandma did Grandpa."

Hatred for Art Logan grew, and Hayden had to force the bitterness from his voice. "What happened to your grandfather?"

Her hand trembled as she brought it to her temple. "He was a politician like Father. But the face he put on for the public and the real one at home were very different. He used to beat my grandmother—and my father. One time, I guess Grandpa went too far. Grandma left him—and she told everyone in town why she'd done it. She destroyed his career."

"So your father fears the same thing will happen to him?" She nodded.

"I see," Hayden barely kept from snarling. "And does he beat your mother?"

She wouldn't meet his eyes. "Sometimes."

"And you?"

She sprang to her feet, a hand pressed to her stomach. "I don't want to talk about this anymore."

The frightened look on her face gave him the answer. Fury pumped through his veins so hard his hands shook. The marks on her back had been put there by that lowlife bastard, Logan. He was almost sure of it. Hayden uncurled his fingers. "What do you want to talk about then?"

Her shoulders sagged with relief, and she resumed her seat. "Chester."

"Your horse?"

"Uh-huh. He was so beautiful and smart. All glossy black with a white spot right here." She pointed to the area just above her nose. "Mama gave him to me for my thirteenth birthday, even though Father had forbidden it." She grinned. "Chester could race the wind—and win. I rode him everyday."

"Did you ride into town?"

"No. I wasn't allowed to leave the property, but there was a stand of juniper trees near the back fence. I used to pretend the grove was my palace, and each tree was a different room." She grinned. "Beneath the biggest one, I'd dance in my grand ballroom."

"And you waited for your prince," Hayden finished, hoping the sadness and outrage he felt didn't seep through.

"Yes."

Hayden's chest twisted at that simple comment. Logan had kept her a virtual prisoner her entire life. Shit. No wonder she'd run away. "Do you still have Chester?"

"No."

"What happened to him?"

"Father sold him."

"Why, for God's sake?" Hayden's anger knew no bounds. The one thing she'd loved above all else, that bastard had taken from her.

"I tried to run away on Chester, and Father caught me."

"What did the bas— your father do to you?"

"Told me he'd kill me if I ever tried to leave again."

Fear for Brianne spun through Hayden like a whirlwind. No wonder she'd been so afraid of going back. He tightened his fists, knowing he'd kill Logan if it was the last thing he ever did.

Brianne watched the anger flicker over her husband's taut features and wanted desperately to change the subject. She hated thinking about her father . . . about returning home. Only knowing she'd see her mother and Maria again made it bearable.

An uneasiness moved through her, but she didn't understand why. Perhaps it was because she knew how volatile her father's wrath would be when he learned her marriage had failed. "Hayden? You insinuated that I'd made your life hell. Would you tell me what I did?"

He remained silent.

Stunned by the grief darkening his eyes, she got up and knelt beside him, touching his arm. "Hayden?"

He pulled away. "Those words weren't meant for you, *chica.* I said them to my first wife."

"First wife?" She couldn't keep the shocked surprise out of her voice. "Why didn't you tell me? You know I don't remember." She wanted to kick her infuriating husband. "Why didn't you mention it before?"

"It's not something I like to talk about."

"Not even to me?" Her indignation rose. "And just where is she now? Did you toss her aside like you plan to do me?"

Hayden shoved a hand through his thick hair and stared into the fire, his features twisted with sorrow. "Carmen is dead, *chica.*" His throat knotted. "She and my son are both dead."

── *17* ──

Dead?" Brianne whispered. "How?"

"Comancheros."

Horrified, she tried not to visualize the atrocities done to his loved ones. After a moment, when he said nothing else, she peeked at him. There had to be more that he wasn't saying. She could feel it. Moving into his line of vision, she forced him to acknowledge her. "Tell me all of it."

"*Chica,* I told you, it's not something I—"

"Please."

He studied her, then sighed and propped his foot on a small rock. "About a year after the war, when I got out of the army, I met Carmen Delgado, a little Spanish gal down in Galveston. She was so beautiful, so fiery, hell, I couldn't wait to tie the knot, and it was plain to anyone who had eyes that Carmen cared for me." Hayden shook his head. "But the bliss didn't last long. My job caused us a lot of problems. Being alone so much of the time while I was off chasing outlaws was real hard on Carmen. You couldn't really blame her, though. She worried a lot."

His mouth twisted with regret. "I should have quit. My

place was at home with my family. If a man's going to make that kind of commitment, the least he should do is see it through. Especially when children come along."

"Why didn't you?"

"Because I'm a lawman first. I'm from a line of lawmen that goes clear back to my great-grandfather. Some say even farther." His eyes met hers, silently urging her to understand. "It's not just a job to me, it's a part of who I am. It's in my blood like a disease. I don't think there's a force on this earth strong enough to separate me from it . . . not even a family."

The heavy weight of loss pressed down on her. "Is that part of our problem?"

Hayden seemed to choose his words carefully. "My job is definitely at the root of our difficulties."

"Was it the same with Carmen?"

He nodded. "The night she was killed, we'd had a big row about me being gone so much, and I stormed out. I'd had a hell of a day. I'd been tracking a gang of comancheros since dawn, nearly been killed, and in the end, had to shoot down two of them. The others got away."

He rubbed his shoulder. "Having to kill someone always grieves me. Hell, no man with a shred of decency can kill another without feeling like he's eaten bad pork."

"What did you do when you left Carmen?"

"Went to the local saloon." He took a deep, unsteady breath. "But later, when I rode back into the yard at home, I noticed the sound of receding horses, and the strange stillness about the house." He closed his eyes as if to blot out the memory. "That's when I found Carmen and Joey. Those filthy comanchero bastards had taken their vengeance out on my family."

Brianne felt his agony and fury as if they were her own. How he must have suffered. "They murdered them because you were doing your job?"

"Murdered is too mild a word," he grated with unconcealed hatred. "They mutilated Carmen. And Joey . . ." A muscle worked in his throat, and his voice grew raspy. "My son was just a baby, and those vermin carved him up like a butchered animal."

Closing her eyes against the horrifying image, she curled her fingers into her palms. "You must have been devastated."

"I was more than that, *chica*," his voice rang with self-loathing. "I was to blame." He lifted his chin, his face etched with agony. "I was the one who left them."

His guilt, consuming, destroying, blew around her like an icy winter wind . . . taking him farther from her. "But it wasn't your faul—"

"Yes, it was," he countered hostilely.

In his state of mind, she knew it wouldn't do any good to argue with him. "Did you ever catch the men who did it?"

"Every last one of them. And believe me, when I got through, the slaughter I'd left behind was enough to make the devil cringe. But killing them wasn't enough. Not nearly enough."

Brianne sat down, her knees weak with sorrow. She felt sick inside. Hayden had been through so much. "When you told me tonight that we were going to split up before I had my accident, I was devastated. Now I don't even understand why you married me in the first place. And to think I was going to try to hold our marriage together by any means possible." Her belly quivered in defeat. "But now I understand. You're afraid the same thing will happen again." A tear slid down her cheek. "If only you could have loved me enough to—"

"Brianne, don't."

"I should be in bed," she blurted and scrambled for her pallet. She couldn't talk to him about this any more tonight. Maybe never.

The next day passed with very little said between them, yet they seemed to have reached a silent agreement to avoid subjects of the past while Hayden recuperated.

After the dishes from the evening meal were cleaned and put away, Brianne knelt down to stoke the fire.

"I'm bored as hell," Hayden mumbled. Sitting Indian fashion on his pallet beneath the shelter, he braced an elbow on his knee then propped his chin on a closed hand. "Do you know how to play any games?"

Brianne thought of a game she used to play with her mother, but she couldn't imagine herself and Hayden doing it. "One."

He brightened. "What?"

"I believe it was called Pat-a-cake."

A low groan left his throat. "Don't you know any card games?"

She shook her head.

"Chess? Checkers? Dominoes?"

"I'm sorry." She rose. "But I'd be willing to learn if you wanted to teach me."

He considered her proposal, then nodded to his saddlebags. "Get a deck of cards. We'll try a hand at blackjack."

With the cards wrapped in her fingers, she took a seat across from him on the blanket. "What do I do first?"

He took the cards and began shuffling. "I'll deal you two cards, facedown, and myself the same, with one up. The idea is for you to beat me by getting as close as you can to twenty-one without going over. The cards all count at face value except the king, queen, and jack. They count as ten. And the ace can be eleven or one, whichever you choose. Any questions?"

"Why's it called blackjack?"

A slow, beautiful smile stretched his provocative mouth, and Brianne clutched the blanket to keep from reeling from the impact. It was the first genuine smile he'd ever given her—and it was breathtaking. His teeth were strong and straight, their whiteness nearly blinding. Masculine softness claimed his whole face, making him look years younger. "It's called blackjack," he answered, "because an ace with a jack not only counts as twenty-one but it pays double, as well. It's what you hope for with each hand."

Her thoughts scattered like dandelion puffs in the wind. "Pays?"

"Yes. We bet on each deal."

"Bet what?"

"Usually money."

She shrugged. "I don't have any."

"Okay, we'll think of something else." He drew his straight brows together in concentration, then eyed her clothing. His gaze caught hers, then quickly escaped. "How about . . . beans? There's a sack in with the supplies. We can use them like money."

After placing an equal pile of pintos before each of them, Brianne sat back and awaited the first deal of the cards.

She lost the first four hands, but quickly grasped the objective and won several.

"Shit," Hayden grumbled as she raked in another pile of beans—the last of his. Either he'd lost his touch or she was a damned quick learner.

He eyed her suspiciously, but as he'd been doing for the last couple hours, he couldn't remain focused on his thoughts. Her hair, touched by firelight, gleamed like newly minted gold, and he wanted to toss down the cards and run his fingers through the thick masses, feel its silkiness, inhale the sweet lingering scent of soap and clean mountain water.

Her breasts, full and firm, were outlined by the blouse with brazen accuracy, leaving nothing to his imagination—unless it was how good they would feel in his palm.

And that voice. Every time she spoke, her velvety tone rippled over his flesh like the soothing waters of a hot spring, making him feeble with desire. His male instincts bellowed at him to throw her down and take her right there on the blanket, to enjoy again the feel of her womanly curves squirming beneath him like he had that night in the outlaw camp. How the hell was a man supposed to pay attention to cards with all of that to distract him?

"Does this mean I won?" Brianne asked innocently, staring at the huge pile of pintos in front of her.

He couldn't help smiling. "Unless you want to play a different game."

"What?"

The expectant rise of her chest drew him. "Strip Poker."

A frown creased her smooth forehead. "Is it hard to learn?"

Hayden couldn't do it to her. He may be a heartless bastard who'd exploit her to avenge his brother, but he wouldn't take advantage of an innocent. And the more time he spent with her, the more he detested himself for using her at all. "Never mind. I'm too tired to play more tonight anyway." He stacked the cards. "You get some rest, too, *chica*. We're leaving early in the morning."

When Hayden roused her, dawn hadn't yet lightened the Texas sky. But he was anxious to be on his way—and as brooding as she'd ever seen him, as if last night's companionship had never taken place.

Dew still clung to the leaves and grass. The late spring chill forced her to clutch the blankets he'd insisted she make tighter around her as she hung onto her horse's reins.

He must be so cold wearing just his shirt, she thought. But what could she do? He refused to accept one of the covers.

But by midday, beneath the molten sun, she was so hot that she'd discarded the blankets and ached to remove her sticky blouse.

When they came to a small trading post that offered a long, shaded front porch and tall glasses of lemonade, she wanted to kiss the ground.

Returning from the convenience of an outhouse and holding tightly to the cool drink she'd just procured, she walked up beside Hayden as he strapped on the fresh supplies he'd purchased. "May I buy another blouse?" she asked timidly. "One that fits me better?"

He kept working. "No."

Brianne opened her mouth to protest, but before she could say anything, he gestured to a package sitting on the porch. "But those might work."

Her eyes grew wide, then, unable to hide her delight, she thrust her drink in his hand and hurried to retrieve the bundle. She glanced over her shoulder to see Hayden down her lemonade, his strong throat working as he swallowed.

There was something so intimate about him placing his mouth on the rim her lips had touched. Gripping the package tighter, she quickly rounded the trading post and again headed for the outhouse.

In record time, she'd changed into the snug jeans and yellow shirt. At her feet lay a tan leather coat that she'd surely need this evening. She couldn't suppress a happy grin as she tucked her hair under the band of the cream-colored hat that Hayden had bought for her. She felt wonderful. For the first time in months, she wore clothing that fit. Her smile faded. Months? Hayden said the robbery where they'd stolen her things had only happened a couple of weeks ago. So, where in the world had that notion come from?

Shrugging, she hurriedly gathered the wrappings, automatically checking for another bottle of rose water as she did. When she didn't find one, she tried not to let her disappointment spoil her happy mood. Discarding the paper, she picked up her smelly soiled clothes and new coat, then raced to show her husband how well the garments fit.

Hayden was still having trouble dealing with the conversation they'd had the night before. He shouldn't have pried into Brianne's life with Logan. As long as he thought of her as a tool to reach an end, he could convince himself that using her was right. He didn't want to know her as a person, one with hopes and dreams . . . and fears. It was damned hard to keep his distance as it was.

And why in the hell had he told her about Carmen? Other than Char and his old friend Colonel Modock, he'd never told anyone what happened *before* the raid . . . or how he felt. His brain must have been muddled from the wound he decided as he tugged on the new sack of supplies, making sure they were securely in place.

"How do I look?"

Hayden swung around to see Brianne, a totally new Brianne, standing in front of him, her face flushed, excited. Wayward gold curls peeked out from below the brim of her hat, and her gray eyes glinted like silver. Her breasts rose and fell enticingly beneath the tailored man's shirt, the open neckline revealing the pulsing hollow at the base of her throat. Unable—or unwilling—to stop his exploration, his gaze slid lower to inspect the boy's jeans that buttoned down the front. He nearly groaned out loud when he saw how they molded to every curve of her shapely hips.

He brought his gaze back to her face. It was safer. His damned body still acted crazy around hers—especially after the other night. "You look—" He'd started to say something smart to ease his own discomfort, but the expectant expression on her face killed the words. "You look good, *chica*. Real good." The second the words were said, he wanted to bite his tongue. *Distance, you fool. Keep your distance.*

"Thank you." Brianne turned away to hide her blush and busied herself with rolling her belongings in one of the blankets behind her saddle. But she was very pleased, and she could say the same thing about him. He, too, wore new jeans and shirt; he was wickedly handsome. Smiling happily to herself, she patted her mare's rump, then glanced up.

A man darted behind a building.

Her smile died. They were still being followed.

The next two weeks passed in a blur of hard riding, short rests, tasteless food, and freezing nights. They had crossed the Pecos River two days ago, and, thank goodness, Brianne had at last been able to wash her not-so-new-anymore clothes.

That Hayden pretended she wasn't there grated on her nerves. She couldn't understand what had changed him. Before they'd stopped at the trading post, he had been almost friendly. Now, he merely barked orders, rode hard, and refused to meet her eyes. He spent a lot of time backtracking, completely unconcerned with how nervous she felt while he was gone.

Brianne shifted against her damp saddle and flicked a wayward curl out of her eyes. She was still chilled from crossing the Rio Grande and could only pray they'd reach their destination soon. Wiggling uncomfortably, she pulled at a leg of her jeans. They were beginning to chafe.

Up ahead, she spied the distinct outline of a tall, spiked fence. "Is that Fort Craig?"

"Yes."

"For a while there, I'd begun to wonder if it really did exist." Staring at the large compound, she didn't think she'd ever seen a lovelier sight. The rectangular adobe and brick buildings surrounded by a high wall, stood amid rolling tree-covered hills with a tall mesa rising in the background. To her tired eyes, it was as beautiful as the palace grounds she'd envisioned as a child.

Hayden nudged his stallion into a faster trot. He was anxious to get inside the fort. He'd once been stationed there for several years—and visited as often as he could. He needed a friend, preferably Char, to talk to. The effort he'd put forth in the last weeks to keep some space between himself and Brianne had worn on his nerves. If only he'd stop noticing her . . . everything.

When they reached the towering wooden gates, he signaled to a familiar guard on the parapet walk.

The infantryman smiled cheerfully and motioned them through the entryway as it opened.

The pungent smell of horse manure, hay, and woodsmoke clung to the still-warm evening air as they rode into the encampment. He hadn't realized how much he'd missed the sounds of civilization until now. And how much worse it must have been for Brianne—the girl—he corrected. After letting down his guard the way he had in the canyon, he'd reverted to calling her that again. It was less personal.

As Brianne nudged her horse to follow Hayden across the main grounds, she noticed a group of soldiers off to the left performing some sort of drill, their navy blue uniforms dusty as they stepped and turned, then marched in formation, rifles balanced on their shoulders. "What do they do here?"

"Protect travelers on the Rio Grande from Apache," Hayden offered almost reluctantly, as if it pained him to even speak to her. *As if she hadn't noticed for the last weeks.*

A horse whinnied from the other side, and she saw a dozen or more brown saddled mounts tied before a long stucco building with several windows. Apparently the soldiers' accommodations.

She stopped her mare beside Hayden before a neatly kept brick building fronted by a wooden porch. Above the door, a weathered sign read: COMPANY OFFICERS' QUARTERS, 3RD U.S. INFANTRY.

An older gentleman, dressed in an immaculate blue uniform, stepped out on the boardwalk. Beneath the brim of his hat, she could see thick gray curls that matched his neatly groomed mustache, and a friendly smile that belied his stern appearance.

"Hayden! By Jove, it's Hayden Caldwell." He hurried down the steps, his posture soldier-erect, his hand outstretched in greeting. "Char's here, too. Imagine the two of you showing up only a day apart."

"Colonel Modock," Hayden acknowledged as he dismounted and shook the man's hand. "It's good to see you again, sir."

"Now, now, boy. How many times do I have to tell you? There's no need for formalities. I'm not your commander anymore. Just call me Will." He smiled at Brianne. "And who's this pretty little gal? And what's she doing with a no-account like you?" He winked.

Hayden shifted uncomfortably. "She's, um . . ."

"Hayden's bride," a man announced from the colonel's doorway, grinning broadly.

It was the attractive man Brianne had seen talking to Hayden in Henrietta.

The younger man met her eyes and smiled. "Introduce me, Hayden."

She could have sworn Hayden cursed beneath his breath. "Brianne, this is Charleston Daniels, the friend I was telling you about."

"I'm pleased to meet you," she greeted warmly, instantly liking the Ranger—even if his laughter had embarrassed her in Henrietta. She just wished he hadn't come to summon Hayden back to McNelly's band on the Nueces Strip.

He brushed past the openmouthed colonel and took her hand. "My pleasure, beautiful."

Hayden gnashed his teeth. He hated that liquid voice Daniels always used on women, and the way his eyes gleamed when he took inventory of Brianne—*the girl's*—assets. And he still hadn't forgiven the fool for bursting into laughter when Hayden told him about his fake marriage and plans to take her to Santa Fe.

"Bride?" the colonel asked belatedly. "You don't say. After what happened last time I didn't think—er, I mean, ain't that nice. Glad to see you've come to your senses, Caldwell." He walked over to her, deftly nudging Char aside. "Pleased to meet you, Mrs. Caldwell. Real pleased." He gripped her hand firmly, his hazel eyes bright with genuine pleasure.

"It's nice to meet you, too, Colonel Modock," she said timidly.

"Will," he corrected. Releasing her, he turned back to her husband, who still frowned. "What brings you to these parts this time, Major—Hayden? Not that I'm complaining."

Char interrupted before Hayden had a chance to speak. "He's taking his new bride to Santa Fe."

Hayden shot him a dark look. "Yeah. We just stopped in for supplies and a night's rest before heading on up."

"You going to stay in Santa Fe long?" the colonel inquired.

Hayden massaged his bandaged shoulder but didn't respond. Not in front of Brian—the gir— Ah, hell. Brianne. He'd tell the colonel everything when they were alone.

Will frowned, watching Hayden worry his arm. "What happened?"

"Indians."

The colonel looked concerned. "Apache?"

"Kiowa. Over Texas way. Just a bunch of wild youngsters out for a good time."

"Y-youngsters?" Brianne sputtered.

"Yeah, *chica.* Youngsters. If it had been a raiding party they'd have had guns. The gunrunners in those parts are real accommodating. And the Kiowa would have followed us." He spoke again to the colonel. "The wound's nearly healed, but I'm looking forward to a decent bed for the night."

The officer frowned, then pointed to a row of covered wagons near the north gate. "See those settlers? With them holed up here for a couple of days, nearly all our extra beds are taken." He nodded to Hayden. "Best I can do is share my quarters with you and your missus." He smiled at the other man. "Unfortunately, Daniels, you'll have to bunk with the troops."

He pulled a face. "You always were partial to Hayden."

The colonel laughed, a full, warm sound. "Hell, Char, Hayden's heroics earned me most of my stripes during the war." His eyes glinted at the younger man. "Not that you didn't gain me a few, too. But unless things have changed, you don't have a wife, at least not one in tow, so you don't need special treatment."

Char scowled like a petulant child. "You have to be married to get a good bed?"

Will grinned and opened the door, then gestured for them to go inside. "Come on. Let's have a drink, then I'll have Corporal Walters show Char where to stow his gear."

Hayden swirled his drink. Brianne had entered the chamber Colonel Modock had so generously offered, and just watching her jaunty stride as she'd disappeared behind the door, sent Hayden's frustration soaring. He didn't want to share a bedroom with her. It was hard enough on the trail. He tightened his fingers on the glass. All these damned do-gooders like Modock, would be the death of him.

He took a swig of brandy and felt it burn a path to his stomach. The woman caused nothing but trouble. And he'd be glad to get rid of her.

"Stop glaring," Char taunted. "Much more of that and you'll burn the hinges off the door. If you want to be with your wife, just go on in there."

Heat climbed Hayden's neck, and he stared threateningly at his friend. Friend, hell. The skunk.

"Leave the boy alone, Daniels," Colonel Modock reprimanded. "If you'd ever been newly wed, you'd know what he's going through."

Char shuddered. "Heaven forbid."

Colonel Modock smiled warmly at Hayden. "But I do

148

think Char's right, Caldwell." He nodded toward the bedroom door. "Why don't you join your bride?"

And why don't you mind your own business? Hayden wanted to shout. He glanced at Daniels for support. Support? Ha!

Humor danced in Char's eyes, and Hayden felt the ungodly urge to blacken them. To keep from doing just that, he rose to his feet. "Any chance of getting a tub brought in? I'm sure she's gonna want a bath." Not that he gave a damn. She could drown for all he cared. But he'd say anything at this point to distract their attention. If he didn't, the next thing you know they'd be giving him instructions on how to bed her!

"There's already a tub in there," Modock answered. "Behind the dressing screen. I'll have Walters bring the water after he shows Char where to bunk."

"Thank you, Colonel. Now, if you'll excuse me, I'll see if Brianne needs anything." God, he hoped she'd finished freshening up. All this talk about wives and brides was playing hell with his baser instincts. Knowing she'd had more than enough time to splash water on her face, he forced his feet into motion.

When he opened the door, at first, he didn't see her, and when he did, he wished the hell he hadn't. She stood in a corner by the dressing screen, bent over a washbasin . . . stripped to the waist.

── 18──

*H*ot blood rushed to his loins. She was so beautiful it hurt to look at her, and he ached to bury his fingers in the mane of glistening hair rippling down her bare back, to stroke the smooth line of her porcelain jaw, to kiss that full ripe mouth.

Unable to drag his gaze away, he watched as she slowly, almost tauntingly, drew the washcloth down one arm, then the next, the damp material brushing across her nipples as she did so, causing them to pebble into hard little peaks.

Hayden felt the pressure of his shaft against his jeans, the pounding ache growing stronger with each swipe of the rag. When she finally dropped the blasted thing, he nearly collapsed with relief. But she chose that moment to face him fully.

"Oh, Hayden. I didn't hear you come in." She brought her hands up in a belated gesture of modesty, her tone entirely too innocent.

But Hayden had slipped beyond the bounds of rational thought. He wanted her as he'd never wanted anything in his life. Just the thought of her writhing beneath him, crying out her pleasure, sent a new leap of desire bouncing through his blood.

He took a step toward her.

Crying out her pleasure? He froze. She couldn't do that here. Not in an army post full of soldiers! *Shit.*

Sucking in a controlling breath, he hardened his features. "Cover yourself, *chica.* I'm not impressed." *Like hell.* "Just because lust got the better of me once, doesn't mean it'll happen again." He walked toward the window and stared out, hating the hurt on her face. But, damn it, she wasn't his wife. He wouldn't have another wife. Ever. And it's time she realized it. "Nothing's changed between us, *chica.* When we get to Santa Fe, we're still gonna split the sheets."

He heard her stifled whimper, but he didn't dare turn to face her. His resolve wasn't *that* strong. Besides, he spoke the truth. As soon as he confronted Logan with his living, breathing daughter, the man would be his, Billy Wayne would be avenged, and he and Brianne would go their separate ways.

And she'd despise him for deceiving her. For using her to draw her father out.

Disgustedly, he couldn't understand why that thought bothered him so much, but it did, and it crossed his mind to leave now. Leave her here. But he knew he couldn't. The Hawkins Gang was waiting in the canyons beyond Santa Fe, ready to introduce him to *el jefe.* Without Brianne, they wouldn't do that. Damn it, he'd made a vow to bring Billy Wayne's murderer to justice—any way he could, and he would. The "how" didn't matter as long as it happened. Hayden gripped one of the gingham curtains tied back at the side of the window. Nothing was more important than that.

Not even Brianne.

Feeling sick to his gut over his own despicable—if necessary—actions, he turned and left. Staying in the same room with her only caused more anguish.

As Hayden walked out, Brianne felt the weight of her husband's words all the way to her heart. He didn't want her. Though he'd married her, even after all his suffering, he couldn't accept the constriction. But, curse it all, he *must* have loved her. He said, himself, that he wouldn't have married her unless he did. How she wished she could recall their courtship where they'd met, where they'd gotten married. The love they'd shared.

Moving to the dressing table, she shoved her arms into the sleeves of her shirt and buttoned it. Had she made the same mistake Carmen had? Did she nag him about being gone so much? Worry excessively? Did she literally smother him with her love? She glanced into the mirror, but the woman who stared back didn't have the answers.

Then an even more startling thought hit her. Had Hayden told her about his past before that night on the trail? If not, that could explain a lot. If she hadn't known his deepest fears, she wouldn't have known how to ease them.

She tried to recall all the things she'd learned about him since their journey began. He wanted her physically, there was no doubt of that. She'd seen the longing in those steel blue eyes more than once, but he'd kept his distance. He'd protected her at all cost. Even at the risk of his own life, which was so like him. He's extremely jealous. And he hates roses. Her musings came to a jolting halt. *He's jealous.* If he didn't truly love her, then why would he be jealous? Surely he knew if he let her go there'd be other men, didn't he?

Concentrating harder, she recalled how resentful he'd been over Goodnight's drovers—over the attention they'd paid her, and how quickly he'd gotten her out of there. Those definitely weren't the actions of a man who wanted a divorce.

She smiled at her reflection. No. And she knew as surely as she breathed that their marriage could be saved. All she had to do was get Hayden to realize it. And what better way to convince a man than when sharing the most intimate of moments with him.

Humming softly to herself, she retrieved the hairbrush Hayden had bought her. With each stroke of the bristles, she planned the strategy that would rescue her marriage.

Her musings were interrupted momentarily when a soldier arrived at her door, then filled a brass tub behind the dressing screen, but once he'd retreated, she continued devising her course of action. Perhaps she could enlist Char,

Hayden's friend, in her plight. He seemed amicable enough. She grinned. Yes, maybe she could. But first, she needed to make herself more appealing.

Since she'd only washed up earlier, she decided to bathe fully, style her hair attractively, then do something about her clothes. She glanced down at the shirt she wore, and a wicked smile tilted her lips as she, slowly, deliberately, broke off two buttons.

Hayden stood with his back to the room, listening to Char and Modock's rowdy conversation. They sat by a low-burning fireplace, sipping brandy and joking over some of the more memorable mishaps during their military days. The smell of roasted chicken and steaming potatoes wafted from the table in the center of the room as they awaited Brianne. Hayden's stomach growled. What was taking her so long, anyway?

As if his thoughts had conjured her up, the bedroom door suddenly opened, and he turned around to see Brianne step into the room. His hand tightened around the glass he held. "Oh, shit."

"What?" Char raised his head, then swung his gaze to Brianne. His face paled. "God have mercy."

Modock seemed to be the only man in the room whose mouth worked. He stepped forward, his eyes bright with masculine appreciation. "Well, well, my dear. You are absolutely ravishing."

Ravishing was not the word Hayden would have used. More like breathtaking, heart-stopping, or sinfully beautiful. Was this really the same woman he'd spent the last three weeks with? The same one who'd been covered in chicken shit? Had her eyes always been that smokey gray, her lips that red, that full? When had her hair gotten so long, so thick and glossy? So . . . silvery? And when had it started curling around her face like a silky cloud?

His gaze drifted lower, and he forced himself to breathe. That shirt never gaped like that before, he was sure of it—and he knew damned well it never showed so much of her breasts. Blood galloped through his veins, racing to that part of him that refused to behave when she was around. She was trying to kill him. That was all there was to it.

"Here, Mrs. Caldwell," Modock invited, motioning her to a chair at the table on his right. "Sit here, next to Hayden." He winked. "And beside me. It does the old ticker good to look at such beauty."

Hayden ground his teeth. He didn't want to sit next to her! He didn't want to be within ten feet of her! How the hell could he eat with his eyes glued to her chest? Her throat? Her mouth? Her— Damn. Damn. Damn!

By the time Hayden came to his senses, he saw that Brianne had been seated, and Char, the grinning jackass, had plopped down on the other side of her.

"If you want to sit beside a beauty like this around here, Hayden, you're gonna have to be fast." Char scooted his chair closer to Brianne then winked over at Modock. "Ain't that right, Colonel?"

Modock just chuckled and shook his head.

Throwing himself into a chair across from them, Hayden jammed his elbows on the table and glared at his friend. "Pass the breasts—*biscuits.*"

Before Char could reach for the plate, Brianne grabbed it, then bent forward, leaning low over the table as she offered it to Hayden. Her shirt separated to reveal a brief glimpse of one rosy nipple to his stunned gaze, while her arms seemed to block the view from the other men. Moisture coated his brow, and he snatched the dish out of her hand. "Thanks."

"Some potatoes, Caldwell?" Modock asked reaching for a blue stoneware bowl on his right.

Brianne beat him to it and started to pass it across.

"No!" Hayden bellowed, then felt heat climb his neck. He cleared his throat. "No, thank you," he said in a more level tone. "I wouldn't care for any." He stared down at the single biscuit on his plate. "I'm . . . uh . . . not very hungry."

Char snickered.

Hayden glared.

Brianne smiled.

"How about some chicken?" the colonel offered.

Seeing the platter directly in front of him, Hayden lunged for it, picked it up, then glowered at Brianne as she eased back into her seat.

With the plate safely in his possession, Hayden smiled smugly. "Maybe I will have a little." He plopped two large pieces on top of his biscuit. But when he looked up, he found Char's gaze fixed on Brianne's gaping shirt. "Daniels!"

Everyone at the table jumped.

Blood rushed to Hayden's face, and he fought wildly for something to say. "Uh . . . you want some chicken?"

Char's eyes twinkled with laughter. "Yeah, sure."

Mentally promising his friend a few broken teeth, Hayden handed him the platter.

The meal seemed to last forever, at least to Hayden, especially when he watched Brianne carry on such an animated conversation with Char.

When they'd finally finished the meal, Hayden couldn't wait to get outside alone for a smoke—*and* a bottle of flesh-numbing whiskey. Anything to rid him of the vision of Brianne's tempting little body. God. He'd never gotten himself so worked up over a woman before, and he sure as hell didn't like it.

Standing on the porch, the colonel's quarters behind him, and the shadows of evening dancing around a beam from the open window on his left, Hayden lit a fat cigar he'd snagged from the colonel's desk and drew deeply. The tobacco burned his lungs, but he needed the jolt to clear his head. What ever happened to his firm control? His cool, unshakable composure? His Malo Navaja facade?

At that thought, he paused. Malo Navaja. In less than a week, he'd have to resume that role for the last time. After meeting with the illustrious boss man, there wouldn't be a need for it again. Thank Christ. Hayden's gaze drifted to the door, wondering how Brianne would react to the abrupt change in him. She was bound to see it when he joined the others in the canyons.

He slammed the cigar down onto the wood walkway and crushed it beneath his heel. He didn't give a shit what she

155

thought. He had a job to do—and that did not include sleeping in the colonel's bedroom with her! The soft lilt of her voice, the warmth in those beautiful, cat-shaped eyes, the scent that was hers alone touched every nerve in his body. Inflamed him. He'd be damned if he'd put himself through any more torture. He'd invent some lame excuse for the colonel and sleep in the barracks. Away from temptation. His resolution firm, he started inside.

The front door opened.

Brianne, smiling warmly, walked outside with Char, her slender arm looped through the younger man's. She halted when she saw Hayden. "Oh. I didn't realize you were out here."

Just where the hell did she think he was? China?

"Um, Mr. Daniels is just going to give me a tour of the fort."

"In the dark?"

Char cleared his throat. "Yeah, well, the moon's full. There's enough light for a quick . . . look."

"Seems to me you been doing a lot of that lately."

Char arched an amused brow. "You wanna do the honors?"

Hayden's gaze slid to Brianne's crestfallen expression, and he had the gut-awful feeling that she was taken with Daniels. Something ugly slithered through Hayden's stomach at the thought of Brianne panting beneath Char. He forced the image aside. He *did not* care what the woman did! Yet, knowing the skirt-chasing Daniels better than most, and damned unwilling to give his consent, Hayden didn't answer. He just brushed past them and headed indoors.

Relieved, Brianne turned away from the entrance. That was close. Hayden had nearly spoiled her plans. If he had taken her for a walk, how could she have made him jealous? And that was what this was all about. She'd deliberately weaseled an invitation out of Mr. Daniels.

"What's going on?"

Brianne swung her attention to Char. "What?"

"You heard me, darlin'. I want to know what you're up to."

She glanced toward the open window on the porch. "Um, can we go for a walk?"

Eyeing her curiously, he shrugged, then guided her off the sheltered walkway. He led her across the dusty grounds toward a row of stables, but stopped just outside. "Now, I repeat. What's going on? You all but wangled an invite out of me. Why?"

Her shoulders sagged. She withdrew her arm from his and leaned on a bale of hay. "I'm trying to make my husband jealous."

"I repeat, why?"

She couldn't just blurt out that she wanted Hayden to make love to her. "Because if he's jealous, then I know he cares. Regardless of what he says." She swallowed the half-lie and the sudden ache in her throat. "I love him," she said with all honesty. "And I just want to make our marriage work."

Char stared at her long and hard, seeming to war with himself. Finally, he turned away and shoved his hands into his pockets, almost as if to restrain himself from saying something he shouldn't. "Have you told him so?"

She thought about it for a second, then realized that she hadn't. "That I love him? No. But surely he knows that, and I think he loves me, too. He told me, himself, that he wouldn't marry a woman he didn't love. But he's too stubborn to admit it." She clenched her hands. "If only I could remember—knew what I'd done to change him."

"You didn't do anything," Char spat with such vehemence that she jumped. "It's Hayden. He's so damned thickheaded, he can't recognize a good thing when he sees it. If I wasn't such a confirmed bachelor, I'd give him a helluva fight over you myself." Char took hold of her arm. "And if making him jealous will help him see his mistake, then I'll be more than glad to help."

He looked toward the colonel's quarters and seemed to concentrate on something. Then his eyes crinkled, and he led her toward them. "I've got a plan, but you'll need to play along."

"I-I guess so. What are you going to do?"

157

Stepping up onto the porch, Char grinned. "You'll see." His gaze drifted to the open window, and he studied it for a minute, then guided her into the shadows beside it. His tone dropped to a whisper. "This may get me killed by my best friend, but let's give it a try."

Leaning against the outside wall, he turned his head toward the window, obviously so his voice would carry. "Jesus, Brianne," he said in a normal tone, "I can't take much more of this. You want me. I know you do. And so help me, darlin', I want you like I've never wanted another woman."

He sounded so sincere. Brianne clamped a hand over her mouth to hide a burst of laughter, then she cleared her throat. "Char, you mustn't. I'm Hayden's wife. I love my husband. If only things weren't so bad between us, I know I wouldn't even be tempted."

"To hell with Hayden. He doesn't give a damn about you. But I do. Feel me, Brianne. Give me your hand and feel how hard I am for you."

He was going to get *her* killed! Good heavens. Swallowing, she replied weakly, "Oh, Char, I mustn't. I'm certain it would be considered unfaithful."

Char rolled his eyes. "No it wouldn't, darlin'."

Warmed to the game, Brianne gave a small whimper. "I can't. I'm afraid."

He heaved a dramatic sigh. "All right. I understand. But at least let me hold you. Just for a minute." He paused briefly, then continued with the mock conversation. "Oh, sweetheart. God, you feel so good." He slurred his next words beneath his hand. "I'm going to die if I don't get you alone soon."

The door crashed open.

Brianne and Char jumped away from the wall.

Hayden, his fists bunched, pinned his friend with a murderous glare. "You're going to die if you even *attempt* it." Swinging on Brianne, he gripped her by the arm and hauled her inside. He stormed past the stunned colonel and shoved her into the bedroom, then slammed the door behind him.

The walls vibrated with the force, and Brianne felt the first stirring of real concern. She retreated a step and bumped into the bed.

His dark anger filled the room, his handsome features drawn tight, the corded muscles in his neck bulging. But when he spoke, his voice sounded deceptively soft, deadly calm. "Take off your clothes, *chica.*"

19

Take off your clothes. Her husband's form faded as the words echoed through her mind. Memory swirled into focus. Leering faces around a campfire. A horribly scarred man. Wet clothes. Fear. Then Hayden lying on top of her, the heat of his naked body pressing her down, his mouth on hers, almost brutal . . . then incredibly gentle.

She shivered at the vision, and her gaze cleared on Hayden. She didn't know what the images meant, but she had no trouble recognizing the expression on her husband's face. He looked angry enough to split wood with his bare hands.

"Get them off," he rasped again in that menacingly soft voice. "Or I'll do it for you."

"Hayden, please. Don't be angry with me. Let me explain."

"I'm not . . . angry."

And dust never blows in Texas. She edged along the side of the bed, trying to gain some distance between them. "I know what you're thinking about me and Char, b-but it isn't true. You see—"

"I passed angry five minutes ago," he continued as if she

160

hadn't spoken. He stepped closer, the muscles in his arms quivering as if he fought for control. "I think murderously insane more describes how I feel right now."

Brianne's knees went weak. Oh, Lord. She'd really done it this time. "Hayden, please. You've got to listen to me. What you overheard wasn't real. Honest. Char and I planned it. I knew if you got jealous then it meant you really did love me and didn't want our marriage to end. I only tried to make you want me."

His hot gaze raked her body. "Well, *chica,* it worked." Lashing out a hand, he caught her by the hair and pulled her against him. "I do want you." His warm breath teased her lips. "I want you naked and trembling beneath me. I want to hear your breathless little moans when I touch you, feel your long legs wrapped around mine, your body burning with need."

He shoved her from him. "But I wouldn't want you to get the wrong idea about our relationship." Coldly, he turned and walked out of the room.

The instant he was free of the building, Hayden found the nearest post and slammed his fist into it. The flesh over his knuckles gave beneath the contact, but he barely noticed the pain. In fact, he needed it to stop the wild thundering in his aroused body. Damn her. She had no right to turn him inside out like this. He was *not* her husband.

He took a steadying breath. The woman had no idea how near she'd come to being beaten. Yet he couldn't help the spark of pride he felt at her cleverness and daring. She wasn't some simpering female who would lamely accept her lot in life. She was a fighter, and he admired that trait. It was probably one of the many things that drew him to her. Even before her amnesia, he remembered how determined she'd been to escape. And she had escaped him—*a Texas Ranger* —twice.

Yeah, he praised her spunk all right, but when he'd heard that mock conversation, seen her with Char, Hayden's control had snapped. He closed his eyes and tightened his fists. God, how close he'd come to hurting her.

And Char.

Hayden's eyes shot open. Char? That sneaky bastard had better have a damn swift answer for his part in this. Swinging his gaze, Hayden searched the near-vacant compound but saw no sign of him. Hayden smiled slowly. "Come on out, Daniels. You can't hide forever."

"No, but I can stay outta your way until you calm down some."

"I'm not angry," Hayden lied quietly, hoping his friend would step within arms' reach.

"And I'm not stupid," Char's voice drifted from the mechanics' corral.

Hayden's gaze narrowed and moved along the perimeter of a horseshoe-shaped building, trying to make out a form. "Why'd you do it, Char?"

"Because I'm not blind, either. You're in love with her, Caldwell. Any fool can see that just by the way you look at her."

"You see lust."

"From me, that would be a possibility," Char admitted. "But not from you. Christ, Hayden, you never once devoured Carmen like that. You never looked at *any* woman like you wanted to strip her naked and attack her before a room full of people. Except Brianne."

The truth of Char's words hit Hayden's chest like a ball of cold steel. He wanted to deny his friend's words but knew he couldn't. Because that's exactly the way he felt. Sometimes worse. But love her? Not a chance.

Hayden raked his fingers through his hair and took a deep breath. "You're wrong, Daniels. But what I *am* doing is trying my best to catch the man who killed Billy Wayne."

"I understand that, Hayden. Yet, don't her feelings come into this at all?" Char asked softly. "Doesn't it matter that you're going to tear her heart out?"

"Of course it matters," Hayden snapped, staring at the darkness. "If there was anyway I could spare her, I would."

"You could let her go," Daniels's voice drifted closer.

"I can't," Hayden said tiredly. "I'm too close. And even if

I can't prove Logan killed Billy, I'll still have the bastard for the murder of an innocent woman—the one Logan buried as Brianne."

"And you'll destroy her."

Hayden felt the weight of his friend's words pressing in on his chest. Hayden knew that. He'd thought of little else. If only there was some way he could keep her out of it. Taking her into those canyons to meet up with the gang would be suicide. For all Hayden knew, Logan could have ordered Pedro or one of the others to kill her on sight. And why not? With all the caves and ravines in the Pajarito Canyons, her body would never be found, and no one would ever learn about the first woman.

Fear for Brianne skittered up his spine, and he wished to hell he could figure another way to nab Logan without involving her. But he couldn't. Brianne was his only hope. He'd just have to come up with a plan that would keep her safe. "I'll protect her every way I can," he vowed to his friend.

"But she'll still be hurt. And you'll still be in love with her."

Hayden's anger ignited. Char was overstepping the bounds of their friendship. "Stay the hell out of my business, Daniels. And you're dead wrong about my feelings for the girl."

Char emerged from the shadows, his black clothes blending with the darkness, only his face illuminated by moonlight. "You wouldn't want to make a little bet on that, would you?"

"On what?"

"That I'm not wrong, of course. I'll bet you a hundred dollars that you're married to the woman before the first day of summer."

Hayden couldn't believe what he'd heard. Char never made foolish bets. He did a lot of stupid things, but that wasn't one of them. "Did some injury addle your brain? You can't be serious. Shit, Char. It's nearly June now."

"Yep."

"You still want to bet?"

"And win."

Hayden smirked. "This time, you'll lose."

The younger man shrugged, the movement barely visible in the dim light. "There's always a first time for everything." His smile flashed. "Maybe."

"A fool and his money . . ." Hayden shook his head, then held out his hand. "So be it."

Char stepped up and gripped it.

Hayden snagged the front of his shirt. He brought Char's face close. "I'll win the bet, friend. But if you ever touch her again, your love life's gonna suffer a permanent setback."

Daniels tensed, and his eyes darkened for just an instant, then he relaxed. He flashed a mysterious smile and raised his hands in a gesture of surrender. "She's all yours, pardner."

Hayden released him and clenched his fists. "She's not mine!" But his words had no impact. The gunslinging Ranger had sauntered off.

"Hope you don't mind if I ride as far as Socorro with you," Char announced the next morning as they rode out.

Unconcerned, one way or another, Brianne shrugged.

Hayden looked murderous but didn't voice an objection.

She knew her husband was still miffed and wanted to punish her. Why else would he rise so early—from wherever he'd slept—and drag her from her warm bed? Then snap orders at her like he would a new recruit, barely give her time to dress and say good-bye to the colonel before tossing her into the saddle—without even as much as a cold biscuit?

Too, she couldn't help wondering why he wanted to reach Socorro in such a hurry. Or was it Santa Fe? Could he be that anxious to settle her in her parents' house and walk away? A ripple of uneasiness prickled over her forearms at the thought of returning. She just couldn't believe that Hayden would really leave her. Not after all they'd shared in the last weeks.

Feeling the heavy weight of loss, she kept her eyes

downcast as they rode along the Rio Grande's western bank toward Socorro. She wouldn't let him see how much his distant attitude hurt. And, if he did try to leave, she damn sure wouldn't make his departure easy.

Wrapped up in her own misery, it took several hours of silent riding before she finally realized something was different—a coolness she hadn't experienced before. She peeked at Char from beneath lowered lashes. He hadn't spoken to her once since they left the fort. Hadn't approached her, or even smiled.

Gripping the reins tighter, she slid a peek at Hayden. Come to think of it, Char hadn't said much to Hayden either. Had her husband and his friend had words over that little scheme last night? Remorse stung her. In her efforts to win Hayden, she prayed she hadn't destroyed the friendship he shared with Char.

She couldn't bear that kind of guilt, and in that instant, she knew she'd been wrong. No amount of scheming, planning, or strategy would make a man stay with a woman if he didn't want to. Hayden had made his feelings about their marriage perfectly clear. *She* kept reading other messages between the lines. False messages. And it was time she faced it. She had no hope of keeping her husband.

So why had he been jealous? She shifted against the leather when the obvious answer hit her. Pride. Hayden didn't want her, but he was too proud to watch another man trespass on his claim—even a worthless one.

Tears pooled in her eyes, and she wanted to cry out her frustration. She wanted her memory back. She needed to know the reason she still loved a man who despised her.

Filled with pain, she kicked her mare into a gallop, and leaned low as it charged past the men.

Hayden's angry shout faded as cool wind slapped her face and whipped the hat from her head, but she didn't care. It felt good. It helped loosen the ache in her chest. Recklessly, she pushed the horse harder, faster.

"What the hell do you think you're doing?" Hayden's voice erupted from behind her.

165

Shocked, she turned in the saddle to see him closing in on her mare, his powerful stallion eating up the sparse distance with ease.

When he came alongside, he reached out and grabbed her reins, then pulled back, slowing both animals to a halt. His chest heaved. His eyes sparked, and his furious expression made her cringe. "You little fool. Are you trying to kill yourself?"

Drumming up her own anger, she straightened her spine. "What do you care? If I did, it'd save you the trouble of getting a divorce."

Hayden swore. Damn it, he'd taken all he could. This pretense of marriage was killing him. He had to tell her the truth. "There won't be a divorce, *chica,* because—"

Her breath caught. *"No divorce?* You're not going to leave me?" She lunged forward, throwing her arms around his neck. "Oh, Hayden!"

Brianne was so happy, she thought her heart would explode. Suddenly, her horse sidestepped, and only her husband's quick reflexes kept her from falling. He jerked her from the saddle and pulled her onto his lap.

Too happy to be frightened by the near mishap, she burrowed against his chest and tightened her hold. She kissed his neck. His jaw. His chin, unable to get enough of the man who'd just made her so happy. But when she glanced up, she was stunned to see the shocked expression on his face. "What is it?"

"Brianne, that's not what I mean. . . ."

"Well, I see you two have finally made up," Char said mockingly as he rode toward them.

Hayden glared at his friend.

But Brianne was too content to care. "That's right. Hayden just told me we won't be getting a divorce. Isn't that wonderful?"

Hayden's hand at her waist clenched.

"No divorce? But you're not—" Char's eyes widened, and he stared incredulously at Hayden—then burst out laughing.

Hayden scowled. "Get the damned mare, Daniels."

His eyes bright with amusement, Char nodded. "Sure thing." He flicked his horse's reins and trotted after the grazing animal. But when he turned away, she noticed a definite quiver to his shoulders, as if he still chuckled silently.

Hayden must have seen it, too—and been irritated by his friend's humor.

Hayden made several stops that day during the long ride to Socorro to eat and rest the horses, and, by the time they reached the bustling silver-mining boomtown sprawled at the base of Socorro Mountain, it had grown dark. But it didn't matter to Brianne. Nothing mattered, not even the fact that she was weary to the bone, and cold and hungry again. Her joy couldn't be dampened by meaningless discomforts. Hayden was hers. That's what counted more than anything—and tonight, she'd prove it to him.

As her husband led the way down the only street, she glanced curiously at a tall, odd-shaped structure on her left.

"That's a smelter they use to separate the silver," Char supplied.

Brianne stared at the strange edifice. It looked like a three-story building that had half of the top level cut away.

Behind the smelter, several houses were nestled among the trees, while along the road, men wrapped in colorful striped serapes reclined against various wood or adobe buildings. Their heads, concealed by sombreros, were bent low over their chests.

Brianne smiled and glanced up the street, toward the music of strumming guitars that mingled with women's laughter and men's boisterous shouts. The sounds drifted from several lighted doorways on both sides. Above each glowing entry, a sign identified it as someone's cantina.

A strong gust of wind stung her cheek and caused a bell to clang above an old church near the end of town and echo the distant squeals and giggles of children. Dogs barked excitedly, adding to the rollicking cacophony.

Hayden drew his horse to a halt before a sand-colored

building with a freshly painted sign tacked above the door. TERESA'S CANTINA. On the wall between the window and entrance a poster announced: CLEAN ROOMS $1.00.

Reining up alongside them, Char stared thoughtfully at the lighted opening. He seemed to come to some conclusion. "Why don't you go ahead and get a room for you and the missus, Hayden?" He peered back down the street. "I'll, um, find my own bed for the night."

For the hundredth time that day, her husband scowled at his friend, but he didn't comment. He merely swung down from the saddle and reached to help Brianne as Char rode off.

Brianne happily leaned into Hayden's warm hands and slid down his length as he lowered her to the ground. For a heartbeat, she thought she felt a slight tremor pass through him when her thighs came in contact with the front of his jeans, but she couldn't be sure since he released her so quickly.

When they entered the rowdy, smoke-filled saloon, Hayden placed a protective hand at her spine and guided her toward the bar.

The musty scent of damp earth and whiskey combined with the odor of straw and unwashed bodies and the strong, syrupy-sweet smell of women's toilet water.

She turned her head in an effort to dispel the overpowering aromas and saw a short, round Mexican with a long mustache wiping the counter they'd just approached.

"Buenas noches, senor, senora."

"Two rooms," Hayden commanded rudely, slapping a pair of silver dollars down on the scratched surface.

Brianne's hopes sank. Two?

The cheerful proprietor's bright black eyes squinted above round cheeks, and a row of stained teeth flashed beneath the mustache. *"Si, senor, pronto."* He retrieved some keys from beneath the counter and handed them to her husband. *"Corredor fin."* He pointed to an arch across the room. "End of hall."

Hayden tossed another coin on the counter. "Water for our baths, too."

"Si, pronto."

Hayden nodded, then led Brianne through the crowd and down a narrow, dark hall. At the end, light from a hanging lantern flickered over two single doors that stood side by side.

Hayden's step faltered. "Shit."

"What now?"

He frowned down at her from his great height, then scowled at the two doors. "It seems we've been given adjoining rooms."

Trying not to smile, she watched him open one of them and motion her inside, then close it firmly behind her. Staring at the wood panel, she allowed herself a satisfied grin. Well, at least the fates were in her favor, if nothing else.

She eyed her dusty jeans and shirt. Now if she only had some appropriate clothes to give lady fortune a little hand. She considered the riding skirt and blouse rolled in her blanket, but quickly banished that idea. Hayden didn't like those at all.

Sighing, she inspected the small, sparse room as if it might hold the answer. But neither the brightly lit lantern on the dresser, the faded brown curtains, the iron bed covered by a tan quilt, nor the washstand with a tin pitcher and bowl were any help.

She stared thoughtfully into a tiny mirror that hung crookedly above the dresser. The women in the cantina flashed to mind. Could one of them help? At least with some decent clothes?

Not certain, but willing to find out, Brianne opened her door and peeked around the edge—just to make sure Hayden wasn't about. Seeing her way clear, she darted quickly down the hall. Hayden was going to be so surprised.

—— *20*——

*H*ayden patted the last of the lather from his clean face with a towel. God, he felt ten pounds lighter. Not to mention the inch he'd trimmed off his unruly hair. He smiled at his reflection in the cracked mirror. All he had to do now was feed Brianne, see her back to her room, then find himself a sweet diversion for the rest of the evening.

Smiling, he concluded that lack of sex had been his biggest problem over the last weeks. Once he'd taken care of that oversight, Brianne wouldn't tempt him again. Hell, that's why Char thought Hayden looked at her like he wanted to attack her. Because Hayden hadn't enjoyed female companionship since he met Brianne, and his body definitely felt the neglect.

For just a second, he paused, recalling what had happened earlier that morning. It wasn't in his nature to make instantaneous decisions like he had when he'd decided to tell Brianne the truth. And it showed. He'd muddled the whole business. But, as much as he hated the idea, he knew it still had to be done. It wasn't fair to her . . . or him, to continue this charade.

He flung the towel aside. But he had to get through

tonight, first. The sooner he fed the girl, the sooner he'd find a pretty *senorita*. Maybe even the lusty Lupe Montoya, if she was still around.

Setting his hat on his head at a rakish angle, he brushed at a wrinkle on his clean jeans, then whistling low, he picked up a shirt and pair of pants for Brianne. His smile grew, knowing how much she'd appreciate having fresh clothes after all this time. He'd bought them when he'd gotten her other ones at the trading post and had intended to give them to her at the fort. If things hadn't gotten so out of hand, he'd have done it sooner.

For a second, his thoughts drifted to Char and the bet. Again he was using Brianne. But Hayden just couldn't help wanting to best Daniels. It would serve the skirt-chasing sidewinder right to part with some of that money he hoarded so religiously. The only time he ever parted with any was for a bottle of whiskey and a woman—and most of the time he didn't have to pay for the latter.

Hayden snorted. Hell, Daniels was probably already in the sack with some obliging *senorita*. The bastard.

Feeling a heaviness in his own loins and vowing to be in a similar position very soon, Hayden sauntered to the door that connected his room to Brianne's.

When he knocked, he heard a faint rustle of clothing, a moment of silence, then a breathless voice. "Come in." Assuming that she had struggled into her dirty things, Hayden lifted the bundle of new garments he carried and smiled as he turned the knob.

But when he opened the door, he nearly dropped the clothes. "Jesus Christ."

Hayden's body surged to life when he saw Brianne. She stood in the center of the room with her shiny hair flowing down to her skirt-draped hips in gold waves.

Where the hell had she gotten that outfit? She looked like one of the whores in the cantina. His lungs struggled for air. Like one of the women he'd planned to spend the night with.

Torn between anger and desire, he slid his gaze to the blouse. It was wine colored and trimmed in gold braiding. The sleeves were short and puffy, and the front draped low over the rise of her breasts, revealing their firm upward thrust. Hayden curled his fingers into the clothes he held and forced his gaze from the tantalizing sight.

A matching, full skirt cinched in her waist, making it appear small enough to circle with his hands. And he ached to do just that: to slide his rough palms over the soft material that clung to her hips and thighs and flowed down to stop at a point just below her bare knees.

Bare? His gaze skipped to her long, slim legs and shapely porcelainlike feet, to the braiding bordering the hem, then returned to her face. "Just what do you think you're doing dressed like that?"

"Trying to entice my husband." She whirled around, the action lifting the skirt to show a brief glimpse of smooth white thighs. "Don't you like it?"

Like it? Hell. He wanted to rip it off her. "Where did you—" He cleared his throat, trying to get rid of the husky rasp. "—get them?"

"From one of the women waiting tables in the cantina. She . . ."

Listening to the warm lilt of her voice, Hayden closed his eyes, trying to rid himself of the burning need that shook his body. He could smell her scent from here. Could remember in vivid detail the taste of her mouth, the satiny texture of her skin, the way she made odd little noises in her throat when he touched her.

He opened his eyes. He couldn't take any more of this. Without giving her a chance to finish whatever she'd wanted to say, he tossed the bundle of clothes aside and grabbed her wrist. "Let's get out of here."

Stalking through the doorway, he dragged her behind him. If he didn't find relief soon, he'd shatter into a thousand pieces. He needed to get Brianne fed and back to her room. Quick.

When they reached the main part of the cantina, Hayden nearly shoved Brianne into a chair. He pounded his fist on the table and glanced around. "Where the hell's the service in here?"

Brianne jumped.

A young, wide-eyed Mexican woman hurried over to them. *"Buenas noches. Que' tomar la cena?"*

"Give us the fastest damned meal you have," Hayden snapped. "And rush it." He glanced at Brianne and found her smiling. "What's so damned funny?"

Her grin widened innocently. "Nothing. I just didn't expect you to be in such a hurry to . . . eat."

"I'm not in a hurry. Just hungry."

Her eyes met his, and she slid her tongue over her lips. "Me, too."

Hayden's blood started to pound. What the hell was she trying to do to him? His eyes fastened on her lips. On the sensuous movement of her small, pink tongue.

Suddenly music flooded the room, and Hayden swung around to see three men in black with tasseled hats and white shirts. Two played mandolins and the third a guitar.

The slow, choppy rhythm of the *Jarabe* dance evidently pleased the other patrons in the crowded room. Several individuals rose, then swirled onto the now cleared center of the floor. Along the sidelines, others clapped and stomped to the throbbing sounds.

For just an instant, Hayden allowed himself to imagine what it would be like to be out there with Brianne, her body brushing his as they danced. He felt himself stir and whipped back around.

"It looks like fun, doesn't it?" she said, tapping her fingers lightly on the table in time to the music.

"I wouldn't know. I don't dance." It wasn't exactly true, but he damned sure didn't want to do it with her.

"I could teach you. Mama and Maria and I used to hum and frolic around whenever Father was gone. Maria taught me the steps to the *Jarabe.*"

Hayden knew if he'd had anything in his mouth, he'd have choked on it. She didn't really expect him to . . . In *those* clothes? He wasn't about to touch her. He shook his head. "I don't want to dance. I just want to eat and, er, go to bed."

She opened her mouth to say something, but at that moment, the Mexican girl returned with two steaming plates of beans and tortillas, then quickly left.

For several long minutes, they ate in silence, but he couldn't miss the way her gaze kept slipping to the people dancing, and several times, he nearly relented. But with each dip in his resolve, he shoved another spoonful of beans into his mouth and chewed vigorously.

Finally, the meal was over, and Hayden congratulated himself on not staring at her chest even once. After wiping his mouth, he tossed his linen napkin down and rose, extending his hand to Brianne. "It's time for bed."

Hayden nearly groaned out loud when she placed her hand in his, her eyes bright with anticipation.

Not even wanting to consider the obvious direction of her thoughts, he ignored the strains of music and twirling bodies as he led her down the hall to her room.

At her door, he shoved it open and thrust her inside. "Good night, *chica.*" He nodded curtly and started to leave.

"Where are you going?"

Her pained look nearly cut him in two. What could he say? I'm going to buy some entertainment for the night? "I'm, um, going to play a few hands of poker before I turn in."

Relief—and something he couldn't name—softened her eyes, then she nodded. "Don't be long." Then in a swirl of wine material, she disappeared into her room.

A frustrated breath slid past his lips. Then, regaining his purpose, he whistled low as he headed out into the cool night. He spied Lupe's Cantina and smiled. He hadn't seen the sultry woman since he'd been here last year with Char, before Hayden knew anything about Art Logan. But he certainly hadn't forgotten their nights together or the hours of vigorous pleasure between her sheets.

Striding swiftly, he crossed the road and approached the lighted entrance. When he pushed through the swinging doors, he took a moment to adjust his eyes to the dim room and search out his quarry.

Leaning on the bar, her lace-front blouse gaping, the dark-eyed Lupe laughed huskily at something the thin man beside her said. She licked her lips, then pressed her full, bright red mouth into a pout. Slowly, she drew her fingers along the dipping neckline of her blouse, then glanced away. Her gaze came to rest on Hayden. Her eyes widened, then narrowed seductively as she stepped away from the counter.

Hayden watched her hips sway as she sauntered toward him, but for some odd reason, he wasn't particularly enticed by the display. He frowned, focusing on her well-developed body. She still possessed all the right tools in all the right places. So what was different? Why didn't he feel that same familiar tightening sensation he'd felt all night with Brianne?

Brianne? His blood started to pump. She didn't have to do anything to get a rise out of him. Just watching her, even when she didn't know it, made him ache, and when she played her games, like tonight . . . He felt himself harden. Hell, it was all he could do not to—

"Senor Hayden, *mi amour,"* Lupe said throatily, startling him. "Lupe, she is lonely long time." She slid her hand up his chest, then down over the bulge in his jeans and smiled. "You miss Lupe, too, no?"

For the first time in his life, Hayden felt repulsed by a woman's touch. Instinctively, he retreated a step, then cursed himself for doing so. "Um, I don't have time to stay right now, Lupe—much as I'd like to. I—" He searched for an excuse. "—just came to see if Char was here."

The woman's husky laugh grated on his nerves. *"Si, senor,* he is here. Magdalene, she win pleasure with *mucho hombre* whole night."

Hayden couldn't stop the smile. So the girls at Lupe's were now cutting the deck to see who got to bed the lusty bastard. "I won't bother him, then. But when—*if*—you see him, tell him I'm looking for him." Surprised at his urgent need to leave Lupe's, Hayden turned and walked out.

For the better part of an hour, he roamed the various cantinas, but nothing held his attention for long, not the women, not even the poker game at Rosa's. It was as if a vital part of him were missing. Nothing excited him, intrigued him, but thoughts of his curvy blonde lying in her bed back at Teresa's, snuggled down in the covers, her lips parted in sleep.

She had been through so much in the last months, first by escaping her father, then by trying to get to Fort Worth to find her mother. In order to eat, she'd even resorted to stealing, something that he knew intuitively went against her grain. But determination had carried her on.

He smiled. He'd never known anyone with more persistence than that little slip of a girl. She'd bucked him at every turn until she lost her memory—a feat very few *men* attempted. Then her tenacity had taken on a new direction —to save a marriage that didn't even exist. Not many women could lay claim to such dogged conviction.

Or stamina. Most females would have complained constantly over the way Hayden had pushed trying to get through Indian territory to Fort Craig. But not Brianne. She'd endured the journey without protest.

Oddly, Hayden realized he'd never admired a woman before, and it was unsettling as hell. Forcing his mind to the game at hand, yet still unable to concentrate, he folded his full house and left Rosa's. He needed to get some sleep if he planned to get an early start tomorrow. Not that he was thrilled about the next leg of the journey to Santa Fe. He damned sure wasn't. It meant being alone with Brianne again—totally alone—for nearly a week.

Disgusted with himself for letting the thought trouble him, he strode angrily into Teresa's and down the hall. But when he reached the end, he couldn't keep his gaze from Brianne's door. He could almost see himself walking toward it, opening it, and climbing into bed next to her warm body. Fearing he might do just that, he quickly unlocked his own and pressed down the latch.

He opened it a crack, then stood stock-still. An eerie sensation climbed his spine when he saw a low light burning in the bedside lantern. Someone was—or had been—in the room. He could feel it. Releasing the handle, Hayden reached for his gun. In one smooth movement, he drew the Colt and shoved open the door.

But the room was empty.

At least he thought it was until he saw a form on the bed. Stepping closer, he peered down into Brianne's beautiful sleeping face surrounded by a wealth of gleaming curls, then lower, to a sheer blue gauzy nightgown that hid nothing from view.

He stared at her. And stared. Then, inch by miserable inch, his resolve melted away. He'd fought her and his own urges long and hard. But he'd been in too many battles not to recognize defeat.

He wanted her.

And she wanted him.

Holstering his gun and removing the belt, he sighed, then tossed his hat on a chair. Filled with helpless need, a hunger he could no longer deny, he eased onto the bed beside her. "Damn you, Brianne." He bent over her, his lips a breath away from hers. "Damn us both."

—— 21 ——

*B*rianne felt a sweet warmth touch her lips, and for a moment, she allowed herself to believe it was Hayden kissing her, easing his tongue between her lips and stirring her senses with each gentle thrust. She could even smell his earthy scent, feel the brush of his hair on her brow, the heat of his palm cupping her breast, and the hot quivers that tingled through her body.

Her eyes flew open.

Hayden's smoldering blue gaze pinned hers. "You've won, *chica,*" he whispered, nibbling her lips. "I can't fight you anymore." Slowly, provocatively, he closed his mouth over hers.

Desire exploded under the delicious pressure. Hayden had never kissed her like this. Not with this earth-shaking tenderness, this intense, yet sensitive mastery. He lazily traced her lips, then parted them. The hand on her breast tightened, massaged, then moved back to allow gentle fingers to stroke the crest. Shivers shot through her, and she couldn't stop herself from arching into his hand, from whimpering beneath the sensual hunger of his mouth.

A tremor shook him, and he pressed down on top of her

with the full length of his body. He captured her hair in both hands, holding her head still while he took her lips again and again, each kiss becoming deeper, hotter.

She couldn't believe he was here, and she couldn't get enough of him. She wanted to cry out her joy, feel his smooth flesh beneath her palms, the silky hair covering his body. But his clothes got in the way. "Hayden, please. I-I need to touch you. The clothes."

With what seemed like reluctance, he left her and raised to his knees, pulling her up in front of him. Facing her on the bed, he lowered his arms. "Then remove them," he grated silkily, and waited, his eyes willing her to eliminate the obstacles between them.

As she reached for the buttons on his shirt with trembling hands, he brought his fingers up to rouse the tips of her breasts. She sucked in a breath and closed her eyes. But it only heightened her awareness. Made her shiver as he slid his palms up to cover them fully, then down, dragging his fingers over her sensitive peaks. Again and again he repeated the sweet torture as she fumbled with his buttons.

When the last one slipped free, she opened her eyes to enjoy the beauty of his golden chest, stroke the silky swirling black hairs that tickled her palms and set flame to her blood, to stare into those incredible blue eyes that said all the things she wanted to hear.

Trying to keep the urgency out of her movements, she edged the shirt off his shoulders, then down his arms until it dropped on the bed.

But as she did so, he slid his hands up to the laces of the sheer gown she wore and began pulling them free. With each inch of flesh he exposed, his eyes grew darker, his breath faster, his body tighter.

He eased the gown from her shoulders, letting it flutter to her waist. His gaze left hers to explore her bare flesh. A muscle in his throat moved. "I've never seen anything so beautiful . . . so perfect."

Brianne's heart began to pound wildly.

Hayden touched her with his hot gaze, then lowered his head and slid his lips along her shivering breast to its tip. He suckled gently, drawing her into his warm mouth, sending fiery ripples through her entire body.

"Hayden . . ." Her voice sounded heavy even to her own ears.

He lifted his head, and his gaze locked with hers. Both naked from the waist up, they stared into each other's eyes. "Take the rest of my clothes off," he whispered raggedly. "I need to feel your hands on me." He trailed his fingers up her bare spine. "And mine on you."

She had never seen him like this. Never imagined the way his features would tighten with need, his eyes intense, almost desperate. Shakily, she reached for the buttons on his jeans.

At the same time, he inched his fingers beneath the edge of the gown at her waist and pushed it down.

The hot, musky scent of their bodies mingled with the thick air in the room. Brianne felt dizzy and swayed against him when his palms curved over her bare bottom. With a strength she didn't know she possessed, she forced her fingers to complete their task, then sighed against his chest as the last button on his jeans opened.

As she shoved them down over his hips, she couldn't stop herself from sampling the smooth flesh covering his broad chest. She lovingly kissed his flat, male nipple.

"Jesus," he groaned. His fingers tightened, and he brushed his lips over her shoulder, then erotically nibbled her neck. He pulled her up and pressed her thighs into his, holding her close, letting her feel his strength, his power.

Her senses spiraled out of control, and she dug her nails into his back, her body aching for the fullness that strained between them.

Hayden lowered her onto the bed, then pulled her gown away. He left her long enough to rid himself of his boots and pants, then leaned over her, taking her lips with lazy expertise. After several pleasurable minutes, he kissed his way down her throat and chest, until he reclaimed a breast.

Brianne arched, her heart near bursting with love for this man. She wanted to tell him so, but her breath came in quick gasps, and her stomach constricted, but it didn't stop

Hayden's torment. He nursed hungrily, then gently teased each throbbing peak with the tip of his tongue.

Without warning, he turned over on his back, pulling her on top of him, his mouth still claiming its feast. First one breast, then the other.

Brianne grabbed the rails of the headboard as dizziness spun her senses. Did he know how good that felt, how devastatingly exciting?

Hayden's hands roamed up her spine, then down to cup her bottom. He urged her legs apart to straddle his stomach, then gently pulled her forward. He tasted the trembling flesh covering her rib cage, then lower to nibble her stomach.

White fire exploded from her nerve endings, effectively stilling the protest she'd been about to make. Nothing could compare with this feeling. Nothing.

Hayden's hands cupped her rear more fully, inching her higher. He kissed her navel, then wickedly thrust his tongue into the tiny recess.

Brianne's fingers tightened around the rail. Her head became too heavy to hold up, and she let it fall back.

He lifted her to her knees, his fingers gently stroking between her legs from behind, his tongue tracing sensual outlines on her lower abdomen, then down . . .

"Dear God," she moaned.

She felt the warmth of his breath as he kissed the inside of her thigh, inching his way upward until he nuzzled her curls.

Brianne gasped and arched back.

Hayden's mouth covered her. His fingers tightened on her bottom, drawing her closer. Then she felt it. His tongue, hot and wet, pressing into the folds of her need. Thrusting, withdrawing, swirling, then plunging hungrily.

This is indecent, her mind screamed, but she couldn't force words of objection past her lips. Her fingertips dug into the rail. Her insides tightened.

He tasted her lovingly, tauntingly, his tongue an instrument of torture as it stroked upward, then pressed slowly back. Again. Again.

Suddenly he quickened the pace.

Unprepared, her body exploded in a rush of sweet pain,

and she cried out. But he didn't stop. He drove her on and on, jabbing her with hot little thrusts, pushing her higher, faster, deeper into shuddering ecstasy. Her body convulsed. She pressed against his mouth. Beauty. Pain. Heat. . . . Delicious relief.

When the last spasm ceased, Hayden pulled her down full-length on top of him, then brushed his mouth over hers. The musky taste of herself on his lips, started new tingles racing through her blood.

"We're not through yet, *chica,*" he murmured huskily. He rolled her onto her back and covered her with his body. "We're just beginning."

Brianne knew if it got any better, she wouldn't live through it. But her body ignored the warning. Shivers skittered through her when he nibbled her ear, his breath hot as he whispered all the things he wanted to do to her.

Her senses went crazy. She clutched his back, digging her nails into the satin-tight flesh, urging him closer.

Hayden groaned low. He parted her thighs with his, then drove into her.

Pain flashed through her. She gasped.

"Sweet Christ," he whispered shakily. "Oh, Sweet Christ."

She kissed his neck, his shoulder, trying to reassure him it hadn't hurt that much, and the pain was almost gone now. Tauntingly, she urged him on. She gently bit his nipples and the firm muscles above them.

He burrowed into her hard, deep.

Her teeth sank into his flesh, and she trembled as another burst of fire ignited. She screamed into his chest. Her body shook. Flamed. Erupted. Molten lava poured from her center, trapping her in its fiery blaze.

She felt his stomach ripple. He plunged into her fiercely, savagely, harder, harder. His breath stopped. He tensed. His body jerked, then arched back, shuddering wildly. A low, hoarse cry rumbled from his chest. He thrust again, then dropped his head to her shoulder.

"Hayden?" Brianne whispered breathlessly from beneath him, her nails easing out of his back. "Why did it hurt?"

He tried his damnedest not to shout obscenities as he stared down into her wide, bewildered gray eyes.

"Then why—"

"Because it's been a long time, *chica*." Well, at least that was true. It had been a whole lifetime for her. God, he felt like a bastard.

She seemed to consider his words, then sighed. "Next time, could we maybe not wait so long? It hurt like blazes for a minute there."

Hayden wanted to smile, but the realization that he'd just made love to an innocent killed his humor. Shame consumed him. He'd violated her. Taken the one thing he could never return.

He lifted his head. "There won't be any more pain." He eased out of her body, immediately regretting the loss.

Leaving her now, like this, was the hardest thing he'd ever done. He wanted to stay with her, hold her, love her again and again, but he couldn't. There were too many conflicting emotions running around inside him. He needed to think.

Turning his back to her, he quickly dressed.

"Where are you going?"

Hayden didn't turn, but he didn't lie either. "I'm going to have a drink and think about what just happened. Whether you realize it or not, it changes things between us, and I need to know just how much."

He strapped on his gun, then jammed his hat onto his head. Yeah, he needed to think, all right. He'd just made sweet love to the daughter of a man he planned to kill. Too, Char's words about Hayden loving the girl kept ringing in his ears, demanding attention. He had to sort out his feelings, and he had to do it now.

When dawn lightened the room, Brianne opened her eyes. For a second, she felt disoriented, then memories of the night before rushed in, and she experienced a jolt of pleasure at the same moment she became aware of the warm flesh beneath her ear.

She lifted her cheek off Hayden's chest and rose up on one elbow to see his face, recalling how he'd returned to her in the middle of the night and reawakened all the desire he'd shown her earlier. The woman inside her melted a little. He seemed so young, so boyish with his hair all tumbled and his features relaxed in sleep. Nothing like the man who took her again and again until she'd collapsed in exhaustion. Heat singed her cheeks at the vivid memory—*and how it came about*—and she felt the need to bury her head in mortification. She'd virtually seduced the man.

Unsure of how he'd react this morning, and not wanting to find out just yet, she started to ease from the bed, but the arm around her waist tightened.

"I'm not ready to face the world, yet, *chica.*" He nuzzled her bare breast. "Not for another few years." He took her into his mouth.

Brianne's body leapt, and her hopes took flight. He wasn't angry over his loss of control last night. She'd feared he would be in the light of day. But he wasn't. In fact, he seemed quite content with their union.

Happiness cloaked her in warmth. She sighed and pressed into his searching mouth, her body coming alive with need.

He nursed lazily, then slowly drifted back to sleep.

Taking a stabling breath and forcing down the tingles, she again started to rise.

A movement off to the side caught her attention. She turned—just in time to see a man's shadow dart from the window. She sucked in sharply.

"What?" Hayden asked, snapping awake.

"N-nothing." She shook her head, trying not to be frightened. "Just a shadow."

"Where?"

She gestured toward the window facing the rear of the building.

"A man's?"

She nodded. "Probably just someone out for a stroll," she quipped, trying to lighten the moment, and soothe her own apprehension that it might still be *their friend.*

"A stroll?" Hayden glared at the clock on the dresser, then at the window. "Down a back alley at six in the morning? Like hell."

22

Oh, no," Brianne moaned.

Hayden set her away from him and tossed the covers back. Unconcerned with his nakedness, he stalked across the room and wrenched open the window, then ducked beneath the frame, searching in both directions for a moment before withdrawing and slamming it shut again. "He's gone."

"Have you figured out who it is?"

"No."

"But—"

"I still haven't gotten a look at him." He flung the curtain down. "Not that I haven't tried."

"I wish I knew what he wanted."

Her husband stared at her from across the room, looking entirely too desirable without his clothes. "So do I, *chica.* But I still say he's not out to do harm."

"I hope you're right."

Hayden shrugged his big shoulders and sauntered toward the bed, totally distracting her from the conversation. "If he'd wanted to shoot either of us, he could have done it several times over." Hayden's voice tugged her back to the

185

moment. But she couldn't remain focused on his words. Appreciatively, she watched him stretch out on the mattress and clasp his hands behind his neck.

He studied the ceiling. "But I don't like surprises."

Trying to ignore the appealing sight Hayden made, she cleared her throat. "Have you tried to follow him? Catch him?"

"Yep. But whoever he is, he's damned good—and he's not anyone I know." Hayden's eyes softened and lowered to her mouth. "Speaking of good . . ." He grabbed her hand and pulled her to him, cradling her against his chest. "Have I told you how good you make me feel? How alive?" He kissed her slowly, thoroughly. "How hungry . . . ?" His mouth claimed hers in a carnal feast.

A loud knock roused Brianne from sleep for the second time that day. But as she started to rise, she saw Hayden, fully dressed, striding toward the door. Burrowing under the covers, she anxiously peeked over the edge and waited.

A moment later, Char's large frame filled the opening. "'Bout damned time." His gaze flicked over the room, then stopped on Brianne. Surprise flashed in his eyes before he quickly averted his gaze and returned it to Hayden. "Well?"

Her husband stared at him. "Well what?"

"Lupe said you wanted to see me."

Hayden was momentarily dumfounded, then shifted uncomfortably. "Er, yeah. I'll meet you in the cantina. Five minutes."

Eyes twinkling with a mysterious light, Char nodded. "Sure."

As Char left the room, she glanced up to see Hayden strap on his gun. She wished he wouldn't leave just yet. She wanted to talk to him about last night. "Hayden?"

As if he'd read her thoughts, he shook his head. "Not now, *chica.*" He shoved the end of his hand-tooled belt into the buckle and tied the holster low on his thigh. Grabbing his hat, he planted a hard kiss on her lips. "We'll talk later."

When the door closed behind him, Brianne sighed, a

happy, contented sound that filled the room. Hayden's lovemaking, his tenderness and compassion, overwhelmed her. She couldn't imagine how she could have forgotten what it was like to make love to him.

Heaving another great sigh, she crept out of bed and went through the adjoining door into the other room. She washed up and dressed in the clean jeans and shirt Hayden had brought the night before.

Finding a strip of rawhide on the floor where the stack of clothes had been, she combed her hair and pulled it back away from her face.

Still feeling lazy euphoria, she collected her clothes and returned to her husband's room. She stopped abruptly.

Specks of blood stained the sheets where they'd slept.

Frowning, she tried to imagine where it might have come from. Her mother's subtle teachings concerning "the wedding night" came to mind, but, of course, that couldn't be it. She and Hayden had been married for months.

Clearing her throat and avoiding the bed, she noticed his overturned shaving cup and discarded clothes strewn about. Hurriedly, she began collecting the articles. But when she lifted his pants from the floor, sheets of papers fell out.

Curiously, she retrieved them and opened the folded leaflets. She scanned the first one. It identified Hayden as a Texas Ranger under Captain L. H. McNelly, which she supposed was necessary in case he was injured or . . . She didn't want to complete the thought. Instead, she touched the lettering with loving fingers, remembering the exhilarating night that had just passed.

Tingles skipped through her veins, and she quickly put a halt to her wanton musings. She examined the next page. It portrayed a drawing of a straggly haired man with wild, maniacal eyes and a thin sullen face. Below the picture, someone had printed the name Malo Navaja in bold letters. The man wasn't familiar, but there was something about the name . . .

The image of a coiled snake, etched in bone, teased her memory, then faded. Shuddering, and not certain why, she quickly replaced the documents in Hayden's pocket and finished gathering their gear.

Hayden stared at Char across a table in Teresa's, his hand gripping a glass of rotgut, a muscle jumping in his jaw. "What Brianne and I do is none of your business, Daniels."

Char twisted his mouth into a wry smile. "Yes, it is. We have a bet, remember?"

How could Hayden forget with Daniels pointing it out at every opportunity. Especially now. "That bet has nothing to do with how we spend our nights." Hayden downed his drink, wishing to hell Char hadn't seen Brianne in the bed. The skunk was mentally counting his winnings already.

Damn it. Just because Hayden hadn't been able to stay out of Brianne's bed, it didn't mean he'd lose the bet. And he wasn't going to. He smiled at that. He'd spent the night with her. So what? He planned to spend several more, too. But that didn't mean he had to *marry* her. His conscience tried to rear its head, but he reined it in. He would not feel guilty over the beautiful experience he and Brianne had shared. Would share again.

"What are you grinning at?" Char asked suspiciously.

"Nothing." Wanting to change the subject, Hayden directed his thoughts to his return trip. "You gonna stay at Lupe's till I get back?"

Char shook his head. "I'm going with you—just as soon as the telegraph office opens so I can send McNelly a wire."

"No, Daniels. This one's my fight."

"But—"

"I said no, and I meant it." Hayden softened his tone. "Now where're you gonna be?"

Char's expression became completely unreadable. "I won't be far."

Hayden stood. "Fine. I'll see you here on the twenty-eighth, then. If not before."

"With Brianne?"

Hayden smiled. "I doubt it."

Char didn't appear worried. In fact, he grinned. "In that case, I'd better say good-bye to her now."

Hayden bristled, but kept his mouth clamped tightly shut as he followed the younger Ranger down the hall. There wasn't anything he could say that wouldn't make him seem like a jealous fool.

Brianne sat on the bed, her hands folded and their gear packed when Hayden and Char strode into the room. She smiled warmly, and Hayden felt his blood heat. Her passion-swollen lips and heavy-lidded eyes called to mind the nearly sleepless night they'd spent in each other's arms. The hours of intense, exquisite pleasure. His gaze automatically went to the bed, and he was relieved to see the covers pulled up, concealing from Char the full extent of their union.

He focused his full attention on Char as the weasel crossed the room.

He held out his hand to help Brianne to her feet. "I came to say good-bye," Daniels said in that low, suggestive voice that curdled Hayden's blood.

Rising, Brianne went to shake his hand, but Char slipped an arm around her waist and pulled her to him.

"Char?" She stared at him nervously.

"Relax, darlin'. Hayden won't mind."

Like hell, Hayden thought blackly.

"Won't I see you again?"

Char cut a glance at Hayden, then back to the woman in his arms. "Oh, I don't know, darlin'. We'll just have to wait and see." Lowering his head, he pressed his mouth to Brianne's cheek. "Bye, beautiful."

Hayden smiled and quickly bustled Char to the door. *"Adios, amigo."*

Char grinned as he shook Hayden's hand. Then their eyes met, and the younger man's turned serious. "Sure you don't need an extra body along?"

"Not this time, Daniels. But I appreciate the offer."

Char tightened his grip. "Your hide ain't worth much, but I kinda like having it around. Be careful, pardner."

"I always am."

With a last wink at Brianne and another concerned look at Hayden, Char left the room.

"I hate to see him go," Brianne said quietly from beside the bed. "He's a nice man."

Nice? That's not exactly how Hayden would describe him. "He's okay."

She turned away thoughtfully, and Hayden wondered if she was thinking of Daniels, but when she turned around again, and he saw the warmth in her eyes, he knew he'd been wrong.

"Hayden? About last night . . ."

"Last night was a beginning, *chica*. Just a beginning. We still have a lot of things to work out between us." Remorse gouged him. *More than you can imagine.* For the first time, he truly wished she'd never lost her memory. That he'd never been forced to lie. That he didn't have to tell her the truth. "There's a lot that still needs to be said. Beyond that . . ." He shrugged. "We'll just have to wait and see."

She nodded. "I can't ask for more than that." She touched his cheek. "And this time, I won't mess it up. I won't give you any reason to hate me. To leave me."

Hayden turned toward the door to hide his discomfort. He wished to hell he could say the same. But there were too many lies hanging over his head. Too much deceit. Brianne might think she loved him now, but once she learned the truth, she'd hate him. And Hayden could only accept that, and enjoy her while he had her. He'd learned long ago that nothing was permanent. Nothing lasted.

Ignoring the sudden ache that clamped his chest, and vowing not to waste another minute of their time together, he swung back and pulled her into his arms. He nibbled her jaw. "I'm gonna love you till you wilt, *chica.*" He kissed her neck and the little place behind her ear. "Then we're gonna head out for some sweet days alone before we, uh . . . end our journey."

Brianne couldn't believe how much Hayden had changed toward her since they left Socorro. The whole day, he'd insisted she ride in front of him on his stallion and let her mare pack their gear.

And what a ride! Every time she moved, Hayden's hand touched a sensitive place on her body. He kissed her neck, nuzzled her hair, and murmured the most shocking things in her ear. Things that turned her bones to melted wax.

Near midday, after continually winding along the Rio Grande, he finally halted his horse in a grass-bordered area clustered with aspen trees.

Brianne thought she'd die from sheer relief. She couldn't stand any more. Hayden's caresses had completely unbalanced her. Her breath labored, and the craving in her lower belly made her weak.

Swinging out of the saddle, he reached up and gripped her around the waist, then lowered her down his length until her feet touched the ground. The sensuous contact buckled her legs, and he caught her against him.

"Easy, *chica*. My senses are as explosive as yours. Take it slow." He brushed his mouth over hers. "Very slow."

She tasted his breath on her lips, the moistness, the heat, the promise of pleasure, and pressed into him. "I'll try."

And she did. Unsuccessfully.

Several hours later, after they'd at last eaten and set up camp for the night, Hayden leaned against a tree trunk and pulled her to him. He seemed content just to hold her as they stared out at the sun slipping behind a distant rise, it's amber glow dancing on the river's surface.

"Was it like this for us before?" Brianne asked quietly, loving the feel of his warm chest touching her spine. "Before our problems?"

Hayden hesitated, then let out a slow breath. "No."

"Was it better?" Good heavens, it couldn't have been.

His arms tightened around her waist. "Leave the past behind us, Brianne. Just enjoy what we have."

A thrill shot through her at the sound of her name on his lips. It wasn't very often he used it. Not that she didn't like *chica*, but something about the way he said her given name stroked her heart. And since he obviously found discussing their marriage distasteful, she vowed to avoid the subject. Besides, she wanted to know more about him. All the things he surely told her before they were married that she couldn't remember. "Tell me what you were like as a child."

"According to my mother, I was hopeless."

She grinned. She could imagine he was. "That's not what I meant. I want to know about your family."

He rested his head on the tree trunk. "My pa was a sheriff down San Antonio way, in a small town to the southeast. It was near the Mexican border, so there was always horse thieves and outlaws keeping him busy. My brother, Billy Wayne, and I didn't see much of him. But we idolized the man. Wanted to be just like him."

She felt his smile against her temple. "When we were playing, we used to fight over which one would be the sheriff. Neither of us wanted to be the bad guy."

"What did you do?"

"Drew straws. But I always chose first, and *I* was the one who held them."

She chuckled. "Didn't your brother ever get wise to you?"

"No," he said, self-loathing lacing his tone. "Billy Wayne trusted me."

Seeing his eyes darken with sadness, she quickly turned the subject to safer ground. "What was your mother like?"

"Like most, I guess. She loved us and scolded us in turns. And she did her damnedest to steer us away from becoming lawmen. But she knew it was useless. Pa's adventurous lifestyle appealed to us in a way that's hard to explain. When he was home, we'd sit in front of the fire for hours, enraptured by the stories he'd tell. It was as natural as breathing that Billy Wayne and I would follow in his footsteps. Later, when I grew up and saw the world as it really was, I understood even more just how badly men like us were needed."

"Do you like what you do?"

"I don't think any man likes hunting down, sometimes killing, other men."

"Did you ever think about quitting?"

He massaged her palm with his thumb. "Yeah. Once or twice."

"What stopped you?"

"Men like Billy the Kid . . . the Hawkins Gang."

"Malo Navaja?"

Hayden tensed. "Where'd you hear that name?"

She rubbed her forehead against his chin. "I saw his Wanted Poster when it fell out of your jeans in the room at the cantina." She peeked up at him. "I wasn't snooping, either. I was just readying your gear."

He watched her but didn't speak.

Worried that he might take offense to her prying, she touched his cheek. "I didn't mean to make you angry."

"You didn't," he countered softly. Slowly, he took one of her fingers and ran it along the scar on his jaw. "Malo Navaja makes me angry every time I think of this."

"*He* did that?"

Hayden stared broodingly out at the dusky horizon. "Yeah."

"How? Why?"

"I tracked him down back in seventy-four after he pulled a stage holdup near Houston and caught up with him outside of El Paso. I was taking him into the sheriff's office, when the rest of his gang showed up." His voice turned bitter. "When they overpowered me, I thought they'd kill me, but Navaja had other plans. While his men held me down, he took the razor to my face. Then he mocked me, saying that he wanted me to live so everyone would know that Malo Navaja had marked one of the renowned Texas Rangers." Hayden fingered the ridge of flesh. "Fortunately, the scars faded. All except this one."

Brianne shuddered at the viciousness of the deed and the pain Hayden must have suffered. How *she* must have suffered with worry every time he left the house. She could almost visualize the lonely nights she endured while he was out chasing outlaws. "Did you ever catch him?"

"No. Another Ranger did. He's in jail, now."

"Well. Thank heavens for that." She relaxed her head on his shoulder. "Where are your parents now? Do you get to see them often?"

The muscles in Hayden's stomach grew taut. "No. My ma died from cholera a few years back, and Pa was killed trying to stop a bank robbery."

"I'm so sorry." She massaged the tight muscles in his forearm. "Do you see much of your brother?"

A moment passed before he answered. "No. He took an outlaw's bullet between the eyes three months ago."

"Oh, Hayden . . ." Her heart went out to him. Everyone he'd ever loved was gone. Most of them by vicious criminals. How could she blame him for fearing the same would happen to her? How he must live in constant terror of coming home to find her murdered—or worse.

Tears stung her eyes. There was no hope for their life together unless he gave up his profession—and he'd already told her he couldn't do that. She closed her eyes and felt dampness cling to her lashes. And she couldn't ask him to, not after what outlaws had done to his family. With a heavy heart, she realized that these few days were all they would have. Ever.

Suddenly desperate, she abruptly faced him. "Do we have to go to Santa Fe right now? I mean, couldn't I go to Texas with you first? You did say Captain McNelly was anxious for your return."

"No, *chica*. The Nueces Strip is no place for a woman." His voice turned bitter. "Besides, I've already wired your father. He's expecting us . . . and I wouldn't want to disappoint him."

23

*H*ayden stared through the darkness at the sheltering blanket above their heads—something Brianne had insisted on every night once she'd learned they were still being followed four days ago. Four glorious days, and so much closer to their destination.

He listened to the sound of her even breathing as he held her close, their naked bodies entwined and thoroughly sated, yet he couldn't find peace. In a few short days, she would learn the truth about their nonexistent marriage, if he didn't work up the courage to tell her before then. Up until now, he hadn't really dreaded her response, he'd just accepted it as a part of his job—and his due. But now he did. Damn it. He didn't want to see her hurt. But what could he do? He damn sure wouldn't marry her. He couldn't. Besides, once she found out the truth, she wouldn't accept if he asked.

The last weeks he'd spent with her, even before she'd lost her memory, played through his mind. He could again see her terror in the jail, then defiance when he forced her to go with him. He could still see the courage it took for her to face the others in the gang, hear her pleas when she thought he would assault her. Not to mention the nerve she revealed when she escaped him.

He brushed his lips over her hair, remembering her compassion toward Lou Hawkins. How she'd cared for the bastard, even though he'd once attempted to rape her.

The devotion she'd shown to their fabricated marriage had staggered Hayden. He'd never known anyone so committed. Despite the fact that she didn't remember him—hell, she didn't even *know* him—her determination to save the marriage had been near obsession.

Gently tracing his fingers up her arm, he recalled the extent she'd gone to in an effort to make him see how much he wanted her, to make him jealous—and, by God, it had worked. At Fort Craig, he'd wanted to kill her—and his closest friend.

That was when he realized he'd fallen in love with her—even though he'd refused to admit it back then—and just what his lies and deceit would do to her.

He eased away from her warmth and rose to his feet. For a long time, he stared at her sleeping form that was lighted by the campfire, at the gentle sweep of her lashes resting on her high cheekbones, the tiny up-tilt of her nose, the luscious red of her slightly parted lips. He ached to touch her again, bury himself inside her until the world went away.

Moving silently, he walked toward the edge of the trees and stood overlooking the river. Stars glinted in the black velvet sky. A soft breeze stroked his bare limbs and wafted earthy scents from the Rio Grande. Below, crickets and frogs chanted in unison, their serenade soothing in the darkness.

If only this one night could last forever, he thought. Then he'd never have to confront Art Logan. Brianne might never learn the truth, and Hayden wouldn't feel any more pain.

"Do you always stare at the stars in the raw?"

He turned around. "I thought you were sleeping."

Brianne yawned and stretched, her naked beauty cloaked in moonlight. "I was. But I got cold."

The sleepy lilt of her voice stroked him like a caress. She

looked so adorable standing there with liquid gold hair cascading down the length of her back, her arms stretched high, her round breasts thrusting upward.

Hayden's body erupted into flames. In two strides, he reached her and pressed her to his length. He burned where they touched, then shivered with need. She was his, damn it. *His.* He couldn't let her go. But even as the thought formed, he knew it was a lie.

Urgently, desperately, he took her lips, then lowered her to the grass. With primitive voracity, he implanted himself on her soul. Again and again, knowing their time together was almost over.

Brianne found herself alone the next morning, and quickly dressed. Where had Hayden gone? Why would he leave? Feeling an urgency, she rushed out of the shelter.

She didn't see him at first, but finally spotted him below where the horses were tethered at the edge of the river. He stood with his back to her, shaving. Relieved, she started toward him.

By the time she picked her way over the rocky distance between them, he'd finished and was shrugging into a blue shirt. "Good morning," she said quietly from behind him.

Hayden shoved his shirttail into his jeans but didn't turn. "I'm going into Isleta for supplies. We're camped just a few miles away."

Surprised by his cold tone, she stepped around to face him. "You mean *we*, don't you?"

"No."

"You're going to leave me out here alone?" Brianne puffed in shock, carefully hiding the hurt he'd inflicted by his coolness. "With that man watching me?"

"He won't bother you."

No one could bother me as much as you, Brianne thought angrily. "How do you know? That might just be what he's been waiting for. To get one of us alone."

Hayden's eyes softened just the tiniest bit. "No, *chica.* I've been alone several times when I went searching for him, and so were you while I was gone." His gaze drifted to the rocks surrounding them. "If he wanted to do anything, he could have done so at those times. Actually, I think I feel better knowing he's out there to watch over you. After all this time he's bound to have formed an attachment to you." His eyes swept her curves. "Unless the man's made of stone."

She wasn't appeased. "Why can't I go with you?"

"There are some things I need to ponder on the way in, and I won't accomplish anything with you jabbering all the time."

"Jabbering? Since when? I *do not* jabber. That's not fair. Just because I ask a few questions—"

"Just like now," he pointed out. Ignoring her sputter of indignation, he walked to his horse and withdrew something from one of the saddlebags, then placed the object in her palm and closed her fingers around it. "Keep this just in case our friend out there"—he nodded in the direction of the rocks—"isn't quite as harmless as I think."

Oh, well, that made her feel much better. The fool. Confused and hurt by his need to leave her—to think—yet touched by his thoughtfulness, she took the derringer. "Is it loaded?"

"Yeah, and there's no safety, so keep your finger away from the trigger. You do know how to use it, don't you?"

"Does it matter?" she said testily.

Shaking his head in a gesture of mild annoyance, he gave her a quick, hard kiss, then mounted up. "I won't be more than a couple hours."

Brianne was piqued as she watched her husband ride away, wishing she knew what was bothering him—and some problem obviously was.

Clutching the pistol, she tromped over the rocky ground to their camp, wondering if their relationship was the issue he needed to deliberate . . . without her input. She tossed the gun down on a grassy spot, then frowned at their messy campsite.

After she'd repacked their remaining supplies except for a couple of biscuits and jerked beef, she folded the blankets and cleaned the dented black coffeepot down at the river.

When she'd finished with the few chores, she sat down

and hungrily munched on the biscuits and beef and tried to think of a way to keep herself occupied until he returned.

As she popped the last bite into her mouth, she couldn't help wondering at her appetite. It seemed as if she stayed hungry all the time. Probably because she'd gone without food so many times in the last few months.

She nearly choked as she swallowed. Gone without food? Why? Where? Frantically, she searched her memory, but found it blank.

Frustrated and bored, she rose and glanced around for something to do. Absolutely nothing. Then she spied the pass that Hayden had said cut through the mountains and led to abandoned pueblos on the other side. It might be interesting to see those.

Trying not to think about the man who might be out there watching her—or what decisions Hayden might be making at this very moment—she started up the path. But as she climbed, she felt more and more unsure. Not only about Hayden and the man, but the pass as well. From camp, the trail that was carved into the side of the mountain hadn't seemed quite so narrow—or so high above the jagged ravine.

Deciding this wasn't such a good idea, after all, she turned to go back. Her foot hit a protruding stone. She jerked around to keep from pitching over the edge. Her head struck hard rock. White dots burst before her eyes. She blinked and felt herself sway. Frightened, she held her back pressed against the cliff wall and tried to reclaim her breath.

For several dizzy moments, she stood there, plastered to the fault-rock, inhaling slowly as she fought to clear the haze rolling through her mind. Finally, her senses steadied, and she carefully made her way to camp. That was definitely not a good idea, she mused, shaking her aching head.

When her nerves were again settled, she sat down and massaged the lump, then winced when fresh pain shot through her skull. "Ouch."

The sound of her own voice startled her. It was so familiar, so real.

How silly. Of course, it was familiar. She'd been listening

to it all of her life. Smokey meadowlark tones, Mama had always said.

Her mother's beautiful face, clear and sharp, came to mind. Wide, lonely violet eyes set in a porcelain face, drawn tight with despair. Thin veined hands that shook with nerves more often than not. Then she was gone.

Brianne gasped. "Mama!" Her memory exploded in a flash of light. Every moment, every detail of the last three months scrambled into place. Each minute after her mother disappeared. Every painful second spent with her father. Each hateful, vile word he'd ever bellowed at her, every beating.

Everything.

Hayden. Her heart thundered as each piece slid neatly into its slot. "The Hawkins Gang. Malo Navaja!" She drew in a sharp breath and frantically glanced around. She had to escape. Now!

Suddenly, the day at the cantina flashed to mind. The papers she found in Hayden's pocket leapt up to mock her. Malo Navaja's Wanted Poster. The papers identifying Hayden as a Texas Ranger.

Momentarily confused, she concentrated hard. Why would Hayden pretend to be an outlaw? Then the answer hit her. So he could infiltrate the gang—for whatever purpose. And scare the hell out of her in the process.

Then she recalled the last few weeks. "That bastard!" She dug her nails into her palms. "That rotten, conniving, no-good, deceitful, lying, lizard-bellied, son of a *snake.*"

Furious, she tromped down to the river, her fist periodically striking out at boulders and trees. "Oooo! You low-life weasel. You vermin. You'll pay for this. So help me, *you will pay.*"

For the barest instant, her anger lessened when she thought of all the things he'd done for her like buying her clothes and boots. And rose water. The concern he'd shown for her during her illness and the way he'd protected her when the Indians attacked. The agony he'd suffered over his loved ones. The total devotion he'd displayed during the last week.

Yet she couldn't understand why he'd taken her in the first place. Then she realized it must have something to do with his job. Maybe even with her villainous father.

Her memory drifted back to the first time she recalled seeing her father meet with disreputable looking men under the cover of darkness. Their low murmurs in the barn. And the bag of money she'd found in his study the next morning before he'd awakened. Though she'd been forbidden to enter that particular room, it had been Maria's birthday, and Brianne had needed some paper to cut out decorations.

Not fully understanding, she'd asked her mother about Father's friends that came in the night, and why they gave him money. But Suzanne had only looked frightened, and told her not to mention what she'd seen to anyone.

Brianne kicked a rock into the river. Yes. The dedicated lawman, Hayden Caldwell, was after her father. *And he must have known her identity from the start.* Perhaps even thought to use her to get to Father. For heaven's sake, he'd even lied to the members of the Hawkins Gang when he told them they'd get a ransom for her.

She remembered some of the other lies he'd told—mostly to her—and the way he'd seemed hesitant to do so. Lying obviously didn't sit well with him. She felt another slip in her anger, but forced her resolve to harden. He'd still spouted the untruths. Again and again. He made her believe they were married. *And he'd tried his best to avoid your bed,* her conscience defended.

His intentions didn't matter, she fumed. What did matter was the fact that he not only lied, but because of that, she'd let him. The deceitful bastard *stole* her innocence.

Her gaze wandered to her reflection in the water, and any leniency toward him vanished. That lying serpent wasn't entitled to compassion. He deserved punishment. And she'd make very sure he got what he deserved.

24

*N*othing can go wrong, Hayden consoled himself as he rode back toward camp. She had the damned derringer. Still, he couldn't shake the feeling that he shouldn't have left her. His only consolation was that he truly believed the man tracking them wasn't a threat. If he'd thought so for even an instant, he'd never have left. He hadn't wanted to, either, but he'd told her the truth when he said he needed time to think.

For the first time in years, he was seriously thinking about giving up his career. But being away from Brianne for only an hour or so had cleared his head. He'd never be able to stop. Being a lawman was as much a part of him as the heart beating within his chest.

Yet, he couldn't deny that he loved her. Nor could he denounce the glaring fact that he'd never be able to have a life with her. He'd never survive losing Brianne like he had Carmen. It would kill him.

And, as long as he was a Ranger, vengeful outlaws would be a threat to Brianne's life. No. He'd rather live without her, knowing she was safe, than risk her life—and his own sanity.

So where did that leave him?

In hell.

He didn't see Brianne when he stopped his horse at the river shortly after midday. Assuming she was resting, he tied the animal, then climbed the hill to their camp. He found it empty.

His muscles knotted in fear. If that bastard following them had touched her . . . Something moved at the edge of a tree. "Brianne?"

Her blond head popped out from behind a giant trunk. "Oh, Hayden. You nearly frightened me to death. I didn't expect you back until later." She stepped into the open, the derringer clutched tightly in her hands. "I thought you were *him*. Our 'friend.'"

Alarm raced through him. "Did he try to—"

"No." She shook her head briskly. "No. I'm just nervous, I guess."

Relieved, Hayden strode toward her. "It's a good thing he didn't show up, *chica*. If he had, that derringer wouldn't have done you much good." He glanced down meaningfully at her hand. "Your finger's supposed to be *on* the trigger, not over the loop surrounding it."

Brianne stared down at the gun. "Oh, you mean like this?" She placed her finger on the trigger and pulled.

A bullet exploded in the dirt between his feet.

"Shit!" Hayden yelped, jumping back. "Be careful!"

Brianne innocently held out the gun. "I'm sorry. I didn't realize . . ."

He snatched it away. "Yeah, well now you do." Shoving the derringer in the back of his waistband, he took a breath to slow his heartbeat, then slipped an arm around her waist, savoring the feel of her sweet curves. He was damn glad she was all right. "I thought you said you knew how to use a gun."

"Not exactly."

He drew her closer, and she leaned back in his embrace, a little stiff. Knowing she was probably still miffed over him leaving her, he sought to warm her up. He kissed her slowly, then nibbled a trail to her ear. "I got a present for my favorite girl."

She shivered, then pulled free of his arms. "What?"

"I don't know, I can't seem to remember."

"Hayden!"

He drew her to him again, enjoying the game, but hungry for the feel of her body next to his own. "Maybe a kiss or two would help my memory."

A wing-shaped brow shot up. "You think so?"

He traced her lower lip with his tongue. "Absolutely."

She seemed to consider it, then sighed. "Well . . . if that's the price I have to pay."

Hayden kissed her hard, then abruptly broke away. "Witch." He retrieved a small package from the supply sack he'd just gotten, then handed it to her. "Try not to break this one."

He watched Brianne carefully open the paper and remove the vial of rose water. She stared at it, her hands trembling, her head lowered as if she fought some emotion, then she lifted her lashes. Her cloud gray eyes met his, and he noticed they seemed brighter and clearer than they had before he left.

"Thank you, Hayden," she said in a soft, yet remote tone. "That was sweet."

Sweet? That's all? He cleared his throat. "You're welcome, *chica.*" He felt a swell of disappointment and turned away.

Brianne was torn between wanting to hug him and wanting to shoot him. How dare he bring her presents after all he'd done to her. If she wasn't so set on avenging herself, she'd break the thing over his head here and now. But she wanted revenge. God, did she ever. "Hayden? I . . . um, could we go someplace else besides Santa Fe? I really don't want to see my fa— parents just yet." *That was an understatement.* "I think we should go somewhere else."

"Where?"

You could go straight to hell, you serpent. "How about Fort Worth?"

"That's kinda far, isn't it?"

"El Paso?" *Anywhere away from here—and her father.*

204

Unexpectedly, Hayden wavered. If he did, she might never regain her memory. But what about his job? What about Billy Wayne? Picking his words carefully, he smiled. "After we see your folks, I'll take you anywhere you like—within reason." *Not that she'd want him within a hundred feet of her after she learned the truth.*

She appeared disturbed at first, then sighed. "Okay."

"Chica, what's wrong?"

"Um, nothing. I just have a bad feeling about going to Santa Fe."

He studied her, noticing for the first time that she really did seem edgy. "Did something happen while I was gone?"

"No! I mean, no, of course not. I just don't think I should see my, um, parents, yet. I can't explain it. Maybe a part of my memory trying to warn me. I don't know."

He wasn't convinced, but he sensed he wouldn't get any more out of her. At least, not now. "My pa always said that when you had to do something you dreaded, it was better to get it over with quick. I think he was right. The only way you're gonna stop worrying is when it's done."

Returning to the bag of supplies, he sorted through it until he found something to eat. He held out a chunk of cheese, a handful of shelled walnuts, and a piece of fresh baked bread. "Eat up. I wanna get a move on."

She started at the sound of his voice, then saw the food. "Oh. Thank you."

Taking the offering, she sat down and bit into a walnut. She chewed for a moment. "Hayden? Why were we splitting up? I mean, I know what you said about your job and all, but that can't be the only reason." She met his gaze squarely. "What was the real cause? Was I promiscuous?"

"No. You're not like that."

"How do you know? You can't have been with me every second. Maybe I—"

"No! Damn it, you're not that way."

She ducked her head and took a bite of cheese. "Then what's the reason?"

Hayden wanted to hit something. For the life of him, he couldn't come up with an answer. He knew full well, if he *had* married her, he'd never leave her. Ever. "We just didn't get along."

"We do now. What's different?"

"I told you. Before, you were alone too much. This time you're with me."

"If you were gone all the time, then how do you know I wasn't promisc—"

"Enough!" he roared swinging around on her. He couldn't bear the thought of her with other men—even if it was imaginary. He pulled her to her feet. "Come on, *chica*. It's time to go."

"Where do—did—we live?"

"In Texas. Now come on."

"But I haven't finished eating."

He took the small piece of cheese still clutched in her fingers and thrust it into her mouth. "Now you have."

"Mut," she tried to speak around the food. "What amout the mread?"

"You can chew on the bread while we're riding," he stated firmly as he nudged her toward their horses.

"Mut—" She swallowed. "But what about our gear?"

"I'll get it."

Hayden watched her walk dejectedly down the hill. He didn't know what had happened while he was gone, but he knew something had. Perhaps it was his sixth sense—or maybe the way Brianne avoided his eyes. He didn't know. But he'd damn sure find out.

By the time they stopped for the night in the sprawling town of Albuquerque and took a room above the White Elephant Saloon, Hayden wasn't any closer to understanding the change in Brianne. She'd been quiet, unnaturally so, and he'd caught a sadness in her eyes several times before she quickly hid it behind a false smile.

A thousand thoughts had entered his head during the long ride, uppermost, of course, was that she might have regained part of her memory—if not all. But he knew she couldn't have. She wasn't angry.

He considered, too, that she might have encountered the man following them and he frightened her. Or threatened her in some way. If that was the case, Hayden would kill the bastard when he caught him.

Staring down at her as she sat on the edge of the overstuffed iron bed, he noticed she was oddly nervous. Her fingers had tightened into the folds of a blue quilt covering the thick mattress. "Are you feeling all right?"

"Just a little tired."

Unable to fathom that cool light still lingering in her eyes, he headed for the door. "Why don't you get into bed while I fetch us a hot meal."

She stood up, clutching her arms. "I'm not that tired."

He slid a meaningful look down her body. "You will be."

Red brightened her cheeks. "I don't think we should, um, you know, where anyone could just walk in."

Listening to the rowdy patrons shouting and laughing from the saloon below, and the occasional thunder of footsteps and doors slamming down the hall, Hayden understood her fears. "I'll brace a chair under the knob, *chica.*"

She seemed to think about it, then a wicked little gleam flashed in her eyes, and she smiled. "Okay." She gave him a sultry, come-hither look as she turned her shapely backside to him and started undressing.

Hayden nearly broke his neck racing down the stairs to order their meal. At last she'd warmed up. Damn, he didn't think she'd get that miffed with him just because he went into town without her.

After he'd set the tray down and placed a chair beneath the doorknob, he tried not to rush her as he inhaled his chili, then gulped his glass of milk—and hers.

Brianne hid a smile as she lazily chased a bean around her bowl with a spoon and nibbled delicately on a slice of corn bread. And she couldn't help but wonder how anxious Hayden would be to share her bed again . . . after tonight.

Finally, knowing she couldn't put off the inevitable any longer—not that she wanted to—she set her bowl aside and dusted her hands. Hugging the blanket she had draped around her, she scooted back so she could face him on the bed. "Hayden—"

He reached for her and pulled her against the warmth of his chest. "You've hardly said a word all day, don't start now."

The moistness of his mouth caressed her cheek, sending crazy tingles down her spine. Even though she was furious with him, her body remembered all the delectable things his was capable of.

Knowing she had to gain control of herself or once again succumb to his lust—and her own, she eased out of his hold and used her most innocent voice. "Where were we married?"

"Why are you so obsessed with the wedding?"

She toyed with the hairs on his chest. "I just want to remember."

He let out a long breath. "In front of a preacher."

It was all she could do to keep from wrenching the hair beneath her fingers. The lying cur. She cleared the anger from her voice. "Did anyone stand up with us?"

"Just the clergyman's wife," he rapped out as if he had to force the words. Which she knew he did. The skunk.

She gave a dreamy—if exaggerated—sigh. "I wish I could recall the details." She straightened up. "Hayden! We could do it again. Right now." She scrambled backward. "We could pretend we're in the preacher's parlor and repeat our vows."

He groaned. _"Chica,_ I'm not in the mood for games."

"It's not a game to me," she said in complete seriousness, wishing she was big enough to blacken his eye. "I want this very much." _More than you know._

"We need to get some sleep. We've got to leave early."

"It won't take long—if you stop arguing."

He released a disgusted breath. "Okay, _chica._ I guess it's the only way to shut you up."

Brianne simmered slowly, but she didn't reply.

He turned to the side so the flickering light from a lantern on the dresser touched them both, then he took her hands.

"Not like that." She tucked the blanket securely around her breasts, then bounced up onto her knees in the center of the bed and pulled at his fingers, urging him up with her.

When they were both on their knees, facing each other, she nodded approvingly. "That's better. Now go on."

He rolled his eyes, then clasped her hands. "We stood like this," he said, glancing down at the mattress, "er, more or less—in front of the preacher, then said our vows." He reached for her.

She leaned away from him. "Would you repeat them to me?"

"What?"

She bit her lower lip to keep from smiling at his shocked expression. "I know this is silly of me, but I really want to hear the words, to visualize what it was like."

His jaw tightened. "No."

"Please."

"I can't remember them."

"Try."

"I don't think—"

"Please."

A slow sigh eased from his lips. "I don't recall the words, Brianne." He tightened his fingers around hers, making her achingly aware of his warmth. "But maybe I can improvise."

He paused, as if gathering his thoughts, then cleared his throat. When he spoke, the sudden sincerity in his voice took her by surprise. "In front of heaven, man, and all that's truth, I promise to worship you until my dying day." He brushed his thumbs over her wrists and hands, while his earnest voice held her mesmerized. "If it's within my power, I'll give you a decent home, try my damnedest to make you happy." His hands trembled. "And protect you with my life. So help me God."

Shivers skittered over her flesh. Hayden's vows, though a little rough, couldn't have sounded more genuine if they'd been said before an entire congregation. What was he trying to do to her?

Fortunately, he seemed to shake off the seriousness of the moment. He drew her to him. "And I'm gonna love you till I drop." He pressed provocatively against her. "Starting now."

Knowing she would fall under his spell at any moment—

who was she kidding? she already was—she quickly strengthened her resolve to unman the cunning traitor.

She threw her arms around his neck. "Oh, Hayden. That was so wonderful." She pushed forward. At the same time, she brought her knee up hard—straight into his groin.

"Aghhh!"

She sprang back.

He buckled forward, clutching himself.

"Hayden? Oh, dear. I'm so sorry. I didn't mean to— Are you all right?" She patted him consolingly on the shoulder. "Can I do anything?"

"No," he hissed between clenched teeth. "Just don't touch me." He lunged off the bed, barely making it to the chamber pot before he retched.

Guilt cut into her. She hadn't meant to hurt him that much. "Would a cold cloth make it better? I could—"

"No!"

"I was just trying to help."

"If I had any more of your kind of help, *chica*, I wouldn't live to see sunrise."

She winced under the truth of his words. "Well, what *would* you like me to do?"

"Get as far away from me as possible . . . and go to sleep." Moaning low, he crawled onto the bed, then curled on his side with his rear to her.

"Hayden, I'm really sorry."

He took a long time to respond, and when he did, his voice sounded strained, yet unbearably sad. "So am I, *chica.* So am I."

— 25 —

The next morning, Brianne's conscience nagged her. She felt sick over what she'd done to Hayden, especially when she saw how difficult it was for him to walk. How his face tightened when he saddled their horses, or when he had to stretch to tie on their gear.

Luckily, she didn't have time to dwell on her vile deed. He was in a hurry to leave. Obviously so he could get rid of her. Only he didn't know that she planned to escape him at the first opportunity and start *again* for Uncle Lecil's.

She didn't want to see her father. Not ever. Regardless of Hayden's reason—or need—for taking her to Santa Fe.

As they rode along the Rio Grande, weaving their way around pine and cottonwood lining the banks, her thoughts returned repeatedly to Hayden. She warred with feelings of guilt and satisfaction. One part of her knew he deserved what she'd done, while the other cursed her for hurting him. She loved him. She hated him.

Finally, near noon, he called their laborious jaunt to a stop by a towering waterfall, one of many she'd seen in the mountains along the river. She didn't even bother to admire the lovely foliage-lined setting before she collapsed on the grassy, shaded bank.

As she sat there catching her breath, she watched Hayden scan the area around them, then kneel carefully before the pool at the base of the falls and scoop up a handful of water. While he drank, she realized that something was different about him—besides being in pain. And the fact that he hadn't spoken more than ten words since morning.

His whole manner had changed since last night.

"Hayden? What's wrong?"

"Nothing," he snapped without turning.

Brianne cringed under the force of that single word. He'd been like this all day. Every syllable clipped. His tone harsh, abrupt. "If there's nothing the matter, then why are you so snippy?"

"Leave it alone, *chica*. I'm not in the mood for any more explanations . . . or mock wedding ceremonies."

"So that's it. You're upset because I asked you to repeat our vows last night, aren't you?"

He rose slowly and faced her, his features tight, but she couldn't tell whether it was from pain or anger. "No. I wouldn't have minded repeating them." He stabbed her with an icy look. "*If* I'd ever said them to begin with."

She gasped. "What are you saying?"

"No more games, Brianne. You know exactly what I mean. You remembered everything yesterday." He bunched his hands. "Did you think I couldn't see through your little *accident* last night? You wanted to hurt me, to make a fool of me because you thought I used you." He laughed brittlely. "Well, you did hurt me. But I got news for you, sweetheart. No one can make a bigger fool out of me than I've already done myself, by getting involved with you."

Wounded by his cruel words, she knew if she didn't retaliate quickly, she'd burst into tears. "You're right, Hayden. I did remember everything." She stood, then walked up to him. "But the pain you suffered last night is nothing compared to what you've done to me." With all her might, she slapped him.

He didn't even attempt to avoid the blow, and somehow that made her angrier. Not even the red imprint of her hand on his cheek gave her satisfaction. She struck out again.

Hayden caught her hand. "Enough."

"It'll never be enough! Nothing I could do to you will make up for what you did." Tears ran freely. She kicked him. Her other fist slammed against his chest. "You vile bastard! I'll never forgive you for this. Never!"

"Don't . . ."

She ignored the half-whispered plea. "God, I was so naive. When I think of how I tried to save our marriage— how you let me make an ass of myself." She swung again, striking his shoulder. "I should have damaged a lot more than just your manhood."

He grabbed both of her hands, holding them still. He stared at her long and hard, then sighed tiredly. "You did, *chica.* Much more than you know."

Determined not to be affected by the pain in his soft-spoken words, she yanked her hands free and wiped at her tears. "Why, damn you? *Why?* What did I ever do to you? Why would you do this cruel thing to me?" She felt her voice crack and turned away. Tears of hurt and frustration rolled down her cheeks.

He caught her by the shoulders and shook her. "I didn't try to hurt you. God, that's the last thing I wanted. But I had to use you to get to your father. I know it's hard to understand when you feel like your soul's been ripped out, but damn it, Brianne, *he* is the man who killed my brother. Maybe not by his own hand, but he's still responsible. And I would have done anything to get him." His fingers bit into her arms. *"Will* do anything."

She jerked away. "All right! I can accept that. I know what a despicable, lawless bastard he is. But why say we were married? Let me believe it? *Make love to me?"*

Hayden shook his head. "I wish I could answer you straight, but I honestly don't know. Oh, not about the making love part, *that* was beyond my control. But as for the other, I thought at first because it would be easier if you

213

came willingly, thinking you were my wife. But now, I can't help wondering if it wasn't because I *needed* to make you mine . . . just for a while."

"Until Santa Fe," she concluded.

"Until I was forced to let you go," Hayden corrected.

Brianne felt her anger slip. "So what happens now?"

"Good question," came a voice from the shadows.

Hayden jerked her behind him and went for his gun.

"Don't do it, boy. I'd hate to have to kill y'all before you've answered the question." The barrel of a rifle appeared from a spot between two trees.

Hayden moved his hand away from his holster. "What do you want? Why have you been following us?"

Brianne edged closer to Hayden.

"I kept my distance because I respect what you're doin'." The man stepped into the light. "But that was before y'all tore out my niece's heart."

Brianne squealed. "Uncle Lecil!" She barreled into his arms.

Hayden stared in surprise at the tall, gangly man with wavy blond hair. He looked like a lumbering cowpoke who didn't have a care in the world—if you didn't count the deadly gleam in those irongray eyes, or the rifle pointed at Hayden's chest.

"How'd you find me?" Brianne asked excitedly, stepping out of the man's long arms. "And where's Mama?"

"She's restin' up back at my ranch." He touched her cheek affectionately. "She sent me to fetch you from that hellhole you call a home. She didn't know you'd already run off."

Relief poured over Brianne. Her mother was alive. Safe. And she'd sent for Brianne. A sob broke, and she buckled to the ground. "Oh, thank God."

"Why have you been following us?" Hayden repeated, kneeling beside Brianne to place a comforting hand on her back. He glared up at the towering man. "And why the hell didn't you make yourself known before now?"

The older man pinned him with a disgusted look. "Y'all don't listen, boy. I said I respect what you're doin'. When I stopped in Henrietta for a drink, I saw you draggin' a gal through the saloon and remembered you." He quirked a smile. "Had a little trouble recognizin' my girl, here, though. She's grown a might in the last couple years. Anyway, after I saw y'all, I checked with my old pal, Coke, of the Texas Rangers, and he told me you were after Logan. I didn't know why y'all needed Bree, but I figured I'd just keep an eye on you—long as my little gal didn't get hurt."

"Coke?" Hayden frowned. "You remembered me?" His eyes widened, and he sprang to his feet. "Lecil Stoker! You were with the Rangers when I joined."

"Yep. I quit to raise cattle not long after that."

"Shit. No wonder I couldn't catch—" He waved a hand. "Never mind. What I want to know is why you came after Brianne instead of just sending for her?"

Lecil braced the rifle butt on the ground and leaned on the barrel. "If y'all got a cup of coffee to spare, I'll tell you why."

Sniffing, Brianne wiped her eyes and rose. "I'll make some."

When they all had a steaming cup in hand and were seated around the campfire, Lecil leaned back against his saddle and explained his presence.

"The night my little sis disappeared, she was on her way to my place." He glanced at Brianne. "She and your pa had a big row that mornin', and she finally decided to leave him. She waited for him to go off to a meetin' that was supposed to last until midnight, then her and the maid, Maria, started packin'. You'd already gone to bed, so she was waitin' until they were finished before she woke you."

Brianne felt warmth for her mother steal into her chest.

"But your pa came home early. Caught your mama in the stables, tossin' the last 'a her bags into the wagon bed. However, he didn't see Maria. Thank the Almighty."

The older man's hands drew into fists. "The bastard beat my sis. Damn near killed her. In fact, he thought he had. That's why he lied later and told everyone she'd disappeared on her way to my place and was believed dead. Too, him thinkin' he'd killed her was what saved her life. That night, he dumped her in the wagon and took her out to them maze 'a canyons not too far from his hacienda, then left her and her belongin's in a thicket of hedges. If Maria hadn't followed on Suzanne's horse, my sis would never have been found in time."

The blood left Brianne's face.

"Is she all right?" Hayden asked quickly.

Lecil nodded. "She's comin' along. Got an injured spine, though. That's what took her so long to get to my place. She had to cross the northern plains slower than a snail could crawl lying flat in a buckboard."

Brianne stifled a sob.

"How did Maria get her out of the canyons?" Hayden asked in wonder.

"Made a litter, then hitched it up to her horse and dragged my sis all the way to some little pueblo to get help. When Suzanne came around, she begged Maria not to say anything to the folks helpin' her. She didn't want anyone knowin' who she was until she could get Bree safely away from Art. Guess she figured the bastard'd turn on the young'un. Anyway, after that, Suzanne had Maria sell the horse and hire a couple of drifters to take them to my place in Fort Worth."

He sent Brianne an apologetic smile. "I would have come sooner, but I was away on a cattle drive when your ma made it to my house. I only got home about three days before I saw y'all in Henrietta. I was on my way to get you, Bree—and pound the crap out of your pa."

"I'll help you," Hayden said viciously.

"Speakin' of ass whoopin's . . ." Stoker lifted a thick brow. "Y'all do realize you've got one comin' from me, don't you?"

Hayden stiffened. "No. I didn't know that."

Lecil eyed him coldly. "Y'all didn't really think you could bed my niece and walk away clean as a whistle, did you?"

Hayden felt his guts curl. Then, knowing he had it coming, he quirked his lip to the side. "No. I guess I didn't at that."

Brianne blushed to her toes and jumped up. "I refuse to listen to this." Grabbing a blanket, she stomped off.

Lecil hadn't taken his eyes off Hayden. "Well, when do you want it, boy? Now or later?"

"Later. I'd prefer to meet Logan with a clear head."

A grin cracked the older man's face, creasing the leatherlike skin in his cheeks. "So be it." He took a swig of coffee and stretched out his long legs. "Now. What's your plan to capture Logan? And why'd you need my niece?"

Hayden briefly explained the circumstances from the beginning. Then, having considered a course of action for many days, one that would keep Brianne safe and still accomplish his objective, he added, "I was going to take Brianne to the canyons and meet up with the Hawkins Gang, then wait for Logan—or wait to be taken to him. But I've changed my mind. I have an idea that might work better, or at least just as well."

—— 26 ——

*T*he next morning, they left early and rode hard, stopping only when necessary. Both men, Brianne decided, were obviously anxious to reach Santa Fe—and it didn't do a bit of good for her to argue with them about not going, though she'd tried several times.

Finally—and much too soon for Brianne—they came to Cabezon, a thumblike mountain that was the core of an ancient volcano and the southern landmark just out of the city.

Brianne felt a measure of relief when Hayden called a halt and started making camp. She wasn't in any hurry to confront her father. Not even with Hayden and Uncle Lecil there to protect her. She hadn't seen her father's face since the night she ran away, and she didn't want to. She'd covered hundreds of miles trying to avoid that very thing. She gave her head an ironic shake. Yet, here she was, right back on his doorstep.

Removing the blanket from the back of her horse, she tightened her fingers in the soft folds. Everything she'd done had been for nothing.

"What time y'all goin' in?" her uncle asked, sprawling out on his bedroll on the other side of the fire.

Brianne opened her mouth to shout never, but Hayden spoke first.

"Soon as it's light." He turned on his side and propped his head up with one hand, meeting her eyes across the flames. "I wanna get this over with as quick as possible."

Because he wanted to get rid of her? Or because he wanted her through the ordeal as quickly as possible? She prayed it was the latter. After she'd heard Hayden's conversation with Uncle Lecil last night—even though she'd tried not to—she knew Hayden had spoken the truth. He hadn't set out to hurt her. He was doing his job the best way he knew how. But that didn't give him the right to take advantage of her illness. Of her naive gullibility.

Turning her back on him, she closed her eyes.

Brianne woke to something warm moving against her cheek. Her eyes sprang open. She sucked in a breath when she realized it was still dark—and Hayden's arms held her close as he carried her toward the base of Cabezon.

"What do you think you're doing?" she snapped, trying to wiggle out of his hold.

His grip tightened. "We're gonna talk. Without interruption from your uncle."

"I don't want to talk to you."

"I'm not giving you a choice." He turned into the trees, his stride steady, determined.

Brianne wanted to punch him. He had to be the most infuriating, pigheaded human being God had ever put on this earth. Clamping down on a string of expletives she would like to level on Hayden's head, she turned her cheek away from his chest.

It seemed like he carried her for hours before he at last set her on her feet in a small glen.

"Uncle Lecil isn't going to like this," she snapped, hands on hips, and very thankful that she hadn't undressed before she'd climbed into her bedroll.

"He won't know. He's sleeping."

"What's so important that you had to steal me away in the middle of the night?"

Hayden stared into the dark. "I figured we wouldn't have a chance to say much before we went into town tomorrow." He faced her. "I'm pretty sure I already know, but I want you to tell me why you ran away." His tone softened. What you did to get the scars."

"Why?"

"I could say I'm just curious. But the truth is, I *need* to know why Logan hurt you."

Her chest grew unbearably tight. "You hurt me, Hayden. Much more than he did."

He closed his eyes for a brief moment, pain etching his features. "I'm sorry for that, *chica.* I never meant for that to happen, and I wish I could take the hurt away. But I can't. I can only feel it as deeply as you do." His gaze held hers in the dim moonlight. "Now answer my question."

The determination in his voice didn't surprise her. Hayden was a man used to getting his way. Also, she knew he wouldn't let her return until she told him.

Spinning around, she crossed her arms over her chest and rubbed a chill from her flesh. Still, she hesitated. Finally, reluctantly, she answered. "My father was angry."

She felt more than heard Hayden walk up behind her.

His hands closed over her shoulders. "What happened?"

Strangely comforted by his closeness, she leaned into him. "Like I told you before, my father has had one ambition for his whole life—to be the first governor of New Mexico if—*when*—it becomes a state. He's so protective of his reputation, he'd do anything to prevent a hint of scandal. For some reason, though, he's always had it in his head that I'd be his ruination if I wasn't kept in complete control."

Her voice turned bitter. "For as long as I can remember, I was labeled a whoring slut, though I'd never even been courted by a gentleman. There wasn't one who'd venture within fifty feet of me the way Father glared at them all the time. If I came in late from riding Chester, Father would accuse me of a secret tryst and take a strap to me."

She couldn't suppress a shiver or the sudden tremor in her voice. "After Mama disappeared, his cruelty increased by bounds. Not a day went by that I didn't receive a slap for a wrong look or word."

She pressed closer to Hayden, needing his secure warmth, and he closed his arms around her. "The night I ran away, Father had told me to clean the stables before he left for a meeting in town. Since he'd let all of our hired help go—probably so he could punish me more freely—everything else had been left up to me, too. The cleaning, washing, everything, even cooking, which I knew nothing about. By the time I got to the stables that day, it was dark."

A knot lodged in her throat, and she swallowed. "I-I was bent over, raking out the last stall, when the lantern went out and someone grabbed me from behind. He threw me on the ground." She began to shake. "Oh, God, Hayden, I can't talk about this."

He turned her in his arms and held her close, soothing her spine with the tips of his fingers. "Yes, you can," he said in a rough voice. "You need to let it out, *chica.*" He tightened his hold. "And I need to hear what's caused you such grief."

Brianne pulled in a hard breath. "T-the man t-tried to tear m-my clothes off. He kept kissing me, biting me, *touching* me." Tears slid down her cheek. "He never said a word, but I'll never forget the way his hands groped, clawed, or the horrible smell of his breath. Like bitter mint."

"Bitter mint?" Hayden's voice turned to steel. "As in horehound candy?"

She nodded, her cheek brushing his chest.

"Did he—" Hayden swallowed. "Did he try to force himself on you?"

"He was trying to, but my father arrived at that moment. The man raced out the rear door of the stables just as Father lit the lantern. He only caught a glimpse of the man's boots. Then he saw me lying in the hay with half my clothes torn off." Tremors shook her. "I-I tried to explain how the man had attacked me, but Father wouldn't listen. He accused me of arranging a rendezvous with my lover."

Tears ran freely. "I begged him to listen. But he wouldn't.

He tied me to one of the stall posts. Oh, God, those ropes were so tight. I couldn't move, couldn't get away." She closed her eyes. "Then he got the razor strap. But it wasn't like the other times. This time he didn't stop. He kept cursing me, hitting me again and ag—" A sob choked her.

Hayden hugged her to him, his body trembling. "No more."

Brianne had come too far. She couldn't stop. "I guess I must have fainted after that. I don't remember anything else until I woke up in my room around midnight—and found the door locked.

"When I'd gathered my senses, I managed to peel my shredded clothes off and change. I had never known such pain, but I knew I couldn't stay in that house another minute. Nothing mattered but getting away from that monster and finding my mother. But without money, trying to get to Uncle Lecil's in Fort Worth was nearly impossible. I was forced to steal, beg, lie, cheat, anything to survive . . . or snare another ride.

"And the men . . ." She shuddered. "Everywhere I went, they stared at me. Made sly remarks, tried to touch me. Finally, I stole a boy's shirt and britches off a clothesline to disguise myself. When I reached Wichita Falls, I was so happy. I only had a hundred or so miles to go to reach Uncle Lecil's. But I couldn't get a ride, and I was so hungry . . . I tried to steal a chicken, and you know what happened then. Because of my maniacal father, I was forced to sleep in gullies, under porches, in stinking barns." Her composure shattered. "Oh, God, I hate him!" She buried her face in Hayden's chest and cried. "I hate him."

She was barely aware of him lowering her to the ground, or of him pulling her onto his lap, rocking her. Months of anguish poured from her heart, drowning out his gentle words and comforting touch.

At last, exhausted, she closed her eyes and let Hayden's strong body absorb her pain.

When she awoke the next morning, she was in her own bedroll. For a heartbeat, she wondered if it had all been a dream—a nightmare. But one glimpse at Hayden's hard features told her it hadn't been.

Feeling more exposed than she ever had in her life, she rose and mechanically set about packing up her gear. And she avoided Hayden. After last night, what he'd learned about her, she couldn't meet his eyes, couldn't bear to see the pity.

When the horses were saddled and the bedrolls tied into place, Hayden kicked dirt over their smoldering campfire as Uncle Lecil mounted up.

Brianne started toward her horse.

"Wait." Hayden placed a hand on her arm.

Uneasily, she looked up at him.

He was watching her uncle. "I need to speak with her alone before we go in, Stoker. I'd appreciate it if you'd ride on ahead. We'll catch up in a minute."

Brianne wasn't sure she wanted to be alone with Hayden. Not after last night. But when her uncle sent her a questioning glance, she nodded.

As he rode off, she took a deep breath and drummed up all her control. She would not let Hayden know how vulnerable she felt. She faced him. "Well?"

His eyes met hers and held them, and she nearly melted under the impact of those blue, blue eyes.

"I love you, Brianne."

The breath left her. Never in a million years had she expected him to say that. *"What?"*

His solemn expression didn't change. "You're hard-headed, *chica*. Not hard of hearing."

"But—"

"That's all I wanted to say." He spun around and mounted his horse, leaving her standing there with her mouth open.

Confused, pleased, and feeling as though she'd just survived a twister, she climbed into the saddle. Why had he told her that? And why now?

Hayden still wanted to kick himself as they rode into Santa Fe. He knew Brianne would soon figure out why he'd told her how he felt. But shit, after what he'd learned about her last night, *about Logan and that candy-nipping Pedro Torres,* there was a good possibility Hayden wouldn't make it through the day. Brianne would, he'd see to it. But possibly not himself. His hands tightened on the reins. And when he went down, he'd take both of those bastards with him.

Still, he knew it had been selfish of him to tell her he loved her. But there might not be another chance, and he'd wanted her to know. Just in case.

Loud voices off to the right drew his attention, and he saw the tree-shaded plaza that centered Santa Fe. In the background, a lengthy building called the Palace of the Governors lorded over the plaza. Native tradesmen crowded around newly opened shop doors on the north and west, while oxen bawled against the restraints of full wagon loads as their Mexican and Indian owners bartered boisterously, each apparently bent on being the first to sell his wares.

Seeing the sheriff's office on the left, Hayden steered his party in that direction, then reined up before the adobe building just as a bell rang out from San Miguel Church.

The sheriff hadn't arrived at his office yet, so Hayden motioned Brianne to a bench next to the wall, while he and Stoker stood by the rail to finalize their plans.

"You know without Pedro and the others to back him up he's gonna make a run for it," Hayden pointed out to Lecil.

"No, he won't," the older man disagreed. "That prissy ass is too wrapped up in his political career for that. He's goin' to try to take us. It's the only way to save his hide and his precious reputation. Wouldn't surprise me one bit if some members of the Hawkins Gang weren't already at the hacienda."

Hayden had heard many stories about Stoker's cunning since he'd been with the Rangers, and he relented to the older man's wisdom. Besides, Stoker knew Logan. "Then we'd better stay with our butts to the wall and well outta the bastard's reach."

Lecil glanced at Brianne. "But that's not our only worry. Bree's the biggest threat to the bastard. He'll try to kill her."

Fear for Brianne knotted Hayden's midsection. "Not while there's a breath in my body." He watched her sitting there on the bench, so damned desirable in her jeans and yellow shirt and with her head bent as she swiped at her pant legs. Obviously, Hayden wasn't the only one worried. "She's nervous as hell."

"What makes you say that? She looks as calm as a floatin' duck on a warm pond."

"See the way she's slapping at the dust on her clothes?"

"Yeah."

"She put those on clean this morning, just before we left. Since we came up only a short distance into town over rocky ground I don't see how there can be any dust on them."

"Very good, Caldwell. I'm impressed."

Boots sounded on the walkway behind them.

"If you're still hankerin' to play Malo Navaja, Caldwell, you're too late," a strong voice rumbled. "They hung the bastard last week."

Hayden turned around to see the sheriff, a gigantic man with shoulder-length brown hair beneath a flop-billed hat. Above the pocket of his dark blue shirt hung a shiny tin star. "Not this time," Hayden returned, smiling. "It's good to see you again, Tate."

"Sheriff Tate!" Brianne jumped to her feet.

The big man whirled sharply, shocked. "Bree? That you, girl?" A smile exploded across his leathery face. "Well, I'll be horn-swaggled. It *is* you!" He grabbed her in a bear hug that Hayden feared might crack her ribs.

When he released her, Brianne took a few healthy breaths.

"We thought you was dead," Tate rasped. "Your pa's sure goin' ta be right proud to see you." He scratched his head, his expression suddenly a mixture of concern and confusion. He stared at her, then a revelation seemed to dawn on him. "If you're alive—and I ain't complainin' none 'bout that—then who's that other gal we buried?"

Hayden cleared his throat. "I think I can help you with that, Tate."

The sheriff lifted a scraggly brow, then opened his office and motioned them inside. "Let's hear it, Caldwell."

Within a few minutes, Hayden and Stoker had explained everything to the huge lawman. "The way I figure," Hayden surmised, "the woman you found in Brianne's bed was probably a girl the gang—or at least *one* of them—picked up somewhere. Obviously, Logan needed her to cover Brianne's disappearance until he found her and got rid of her."

Tate shook his head. "Who'da ever thought it of Logan? Such a pleasant man. So respectable." He sat for a moment, deep in thought, then rose to his full imposing height. "Well, guess there ain't nothing left to do but go get him."

Brianne rose with the men.

"Sit down, *chica*. You're gonna wait here."

Hayden saw the flash of defiance enter her eyes. Damn. "Listen. I didn't mean to come off sounding bossy. But bringing Logan in is gonna be dangerous, not to mention unpleasant as hell." He nodded toward the other men. "None of us want you in the middle of it."

"I *am* in the middle of it."

Hayden didn't know anyone more stubborn. "Don't argue, woman. You're staying."

"We'll just see about that," Brianne snapped, heading for the door.

Hayden swore, then snatched her up by the arm. "You mule-headed— Shit!" He dodged her knee.

"Let me go!"

Ignoring her command, he hauled her over to the sheriff's desk and picked up a ring of keys.

"What do you think you're doing?"

Not bothering to answer, Hayden marched her to a cell and thrust her inside, swiftly closing and locking the door.

For a frozen moment Brianne stared at the bars in shock, then exploded in a torrent of fury. "You low-life bastard! Let me out of here! Damn you, Hayden. Let me out!"

He tossed the keys on the desk and smiled, then lifted his Stetson off the hat stand.

"Don't you dare leave me here like this," Brianne threatened.

Slapping on his hat, Hayden turned for the front—and came face-to-face with Lecil Stoker.

The older man glanced over Hayden's shoulder at Brianne, then gave a slight shake to his head and opened the door. "Gotta hand it to you, boy. You've got a stroke of genius in you." He chuckled. "But I wouldn't want to be in your shoes when she gets out."

Brianne stood fuming in the middle of the sheriff's cell, listening to the men's footsteps rumble on the boardwalk then fall silent as they stepped onto the street. Just who did Hayden Caldwell think he was? How dare he lock her up like this. She hadn't really wanted to go with them. Curse it all. She was just going to walk them to the door—until *he* started ordering her around.

Hayden couldn't be that big a fool. Good heavens. Seeing her father was the last thing she wanted. If she never saw him again, that would be fine with her. Disgusted, she flounced down onto the stiff cot and crossed her arms. She would stay here because *she* wanted to—*not* because Hayden Caldwell forced her to.

For several long minutes, she sat there, tapping her fingers, dusting off her pant legs, listening to the sounds bustling from outside, to the clock ticking on the wall next to the rear door.

She did everything she could to keep herself occupied, but her thoughts returned again and again to Hayden. Even though his deceit and high-handedness were uppermost in her mind, she kept seeing him as he was on the trail. Now she could recall the signs of discomfort he'd displayed every time she questioned him. He hadn't liked what he'd obviously felt he had to do.

She remembered his words to Uncle Lecil. *I didn't want to hurt her, Stoker. But, I didn't have any choice.*

She stretched out on the cot and clasped her hands behind her head. He certainly *did* have a choice. He could have told her the truth in the beginning instead of frightening her to death. *But if you hadn't been scared senseless,* her logic reasoned, *you might have given away his ruse to the gang members.*

Rising, she paced to the window and glared out. Okay, so he's not perfect. He took the easy way out—for him. He really did try *not* to take advantage of her. Her cheeks burned at the memory of her seduction attempts, and her anger started to climb, but Hayden's recent words doused the flame.

I love you, Brianne.

Her fists knotted. Damn him. Why had he gone and said that?

Because there's a chance he might not make it through this ordeal.

Cold settled around her chest. Just the thought of never again seeing that arrogant swagger, gazing into those smoldering blue eyes, seeing that heart-stopping smile, feeling the strength in those powerful arms, or the intimate heat of that solid male body stole her breath.

Her knees grew weak, and she bowed her head in prayer. "God. Please don't let him die. For all his miserable faults, all his arrogance and bullheadedness, I do love him. Just keep him safe."

Helplessness washed over her like a flash flood, and she gripped the bars on the window. "Damn you, Hayden Caldwell!" she shouted to the street. "Don't you die on me. Do you hear me? Don't you even *dare.*"

—— *27*——

*H*ayden felt a rush of excitement as they crested a knoll and saw Logan's hacienda centered in a small valley less than a mile away. From where they were, Hayden thought, it resembled the type of house a Spanish Grande might live in, neat, clean, with gentle arches framing the front portico. Shade trees, lining the inside wall of a tall adobe fence, surrounded the building.

Removing his hat, Hayden wiped the sweat from his brow. "Looks like pictures I once saw of a desert oasis."

Tate mopped his face with his neckerchief. "Yep. It's sure pretty, all right. But, like the assemblyman, looks can be deceivin'. Only got 'bout fifty acres of land that goes with it, and water gets real short on that piece durin' the summer."

"How far are we from town?" Lecil asked.

The sheriff glanced over his shoulder as if measuring the distance. "'Bout five miles or so." Then he nodded toward some mountains up ahead, on the other side of Logan's hacienda. "We're 'bout twenty miles from White Rock Canyon, where the Rio Grande cuts through the Jemez Mountains. That's where Logan's men are supposed to be waitin' for you. Which still remains to be seen."

Hayden scanned the distant hills, then Logan's place. Odd, he thought. There didn't appear to be any horses or cattle grazing in the pasture, even though it was fenced with barbed wire. "Why doesn't he have a place in town if he's not going to run stock? Seems like it'd be handier living close in."

"Yep. That's what I thought, too. Never did understand why Art wanted such privacy. But from all you and Stoker have told me about how he treated little Bree and Suzanne —and his association with them no 'count outlaws—I think I'm beginnin' to see. Sure wished my deputy hadn't taken ill. We could use an extra hand 'bout now." Tate frowned suddenly. "Speakin' of them other outlaws . . . how many are there?"

"Three left, not counting *el jefe*. They were about two, maybe three, days ahead of us. If they're still in the canyons, as soon as Logan's behind bars, I'll go after them." Recalling how Frank and the others had behaved around Brianne, Hayden thanked God she was safely out of the way.

"We'll go after them," Lecil stressed.

"Well, we ain't gonna get nothin' done sittin' here jawin'," Tate said, spitting out a wad of tobacco. "Let's go."

Hayden eyed the quiet hacienda again, and suddenly felt a ripple of apprehension. It was too damn quiet.

"I'll go around back," Lecil said as he hauled in on the reins and dismounted in front of Logan's walled yard. "Place's got a rear gate that leads to the stables."

Sheriff Tate nodded and withdrew his rifle. "Let's get at it."

Hayden checked his Peacemaker, then palmed it. Blood surged through his veins with each step toward the door.

When they walked beneath the curved arch onto a covered porch, Tate motioned Hayden to the side, out of sight, and knocked.

Hayden cocked his gun.

"Si?" a heavily accented voice inquired from within the open doorway.

"Where's Logan?" the sheriff demanded.

Hayden stepped into view, surprised to see a small

Mexican servant. Hadn't Brianne said her father dismissed all the servants?

"Senor Logan, he is in *la sala*—the parlor."

Tate shoved his massive weight past the smaller man and strode quickly inside.

Keeping his eyes trained on the many closed doorways that lined the tiled entry hall, Hayden followed.

"Why, Sheriff Tate. What a pleasant surprise," Art Logan's smooth cultured voice rang out as Tate lumbered through an archway.

Hayden closed in behind him, quickly searching the room noticing several glass doors, most of which were open, before settling his attention on assemblyman Logan. The smokey scent of a fine cigar lingered in the air.

The older man lowered the book he'd apparently been reading and set it on a small table. He rose, his neatly trimmed gray head tilted at an angle. The cut of the brown pinstriped suit he wore fit his bulky frame to perfection, and as he stepped around the table, Hayden couldn't help but notice the mirror shine on his cinnamon-colored boots. A real Dapper Dan. But the brittle harshness in his hazel eyes, and the cruel curve to his mouth, gave Hayden a glimpse of the real man.

Tate raised his rifle. "Step back, Logan, and get those hands up."

"What's the meaning of this?" the assemblyman sputtered as he edged toward one of the open doors, his hands lifted high, stretching the front of the suit over his round gut.

"Make another move toward that door, and your suit's gonna have a new buttonhole—just about chest high," Hayden warned, his fury barely contained when he thought of how this man had brutally beaten Brianne. How this man's orders had ended his brother's life—and destroyed Kathy's.

Logan instantly stilled.

This was too easy, Hayden thought warily. The bastard was too calm. Keeping his gun trained on the man's burly chest, Hayden met those cold eyes. Satisfaction glinted maliciously.

Hayden's skin began to crawl, and he risked another glance at the open doors.

"I'm arrestin' you for murder," Tate rumbled. "Little Bree jist showed up in my office."

Logan gasped. "My daughter's alive? Oh, thank heavens!"

"Cut the crap, Logan," Hayden grated, barely containing the urge to blow the bastard to hell. "We know about the woman you butchered and left in Brianne's bed."

Logan's cleanly shaven face paled. "What are you talking about?"

"I'm done talkin'," Tate announced reaching for a pair of handcuffs.

Every instinct Hayden possessed sprang to life. He swung his gun to the open doors.

Cold steel pressed into the center of his spine.

"Ah, *senor,* a sudden move could prove fatal, no?" Pedro Torres stated coolly from behind him. "Hand the *pistola* to *el jefe. Muy* easy, no?"

Tate whirled around.

"Don't do it, Sheriff," Logan said smoothly, a small revolver suddenly appearing in his hand. "I really would hate to clean your blood off my floor."

Tate lowered his weapon, his face tight with rage.

Pedro jabbed the barrel of his gun into Hayden's spine. "The *pistola, senor.*"

Realizing he had no other choice at the moment, Hayden handed his Peacemaker to Logan, but at least he still had the razor tucked in his belt and the derringer in his boot.

"And *el navaja,*" Pedro demanded, as he stepped around to face Hayden, his brown hand extended.

Hayden's spirits sank. Did he know about the derringer, too? Resisting the urge to slice off Pedro's fingers, he placed the folded instrument in the outlaw's palm.

"Take the cuffs," Logan ordered Hayden, "and put them on our big friend here." He motioned toward the sheriff with the Colt.

Wanting to wrap them around the fat bastard's neck, Hayden complied. But as he worked he wondered what the hell was taking Lecil so long.

A gunshot exploded from the rear of the house.

Hayden stiffened.

Logan's face spread into a winning smile. "Ah, I see Frank and Lou found the other one."

As if to prove his words, Frank Hawkins strolled in through an open doorway, a smoking gun held in his hand. "Christ, El Hefty. That one out back was a mean buzzard."

A sick feeling gripped Hayden. *Lecil.*

Logan didn't smile. "Quit caterwauling and tie this bastard up." He gestured to Hayden. "Then get my wagon out of the stables and load up the body—and our friends here."

"What are ya plannin' ta do?" Frank asked as he bound Hayden's hands tightly behind him.

"Goll dang, Franky. Ain't you got no sense," Lou piped up as he stepped in the room. "The boss cain't have no bodies found around here. He's gotta git rid of 'em."

"Smart man, Lou," Logan said approvingly, his softspoken tone at odds with his cruel features. "As soon as Pedro, here, gets Brianne, we'll take a little trip into the Pajarito Canyons."

A coil of fear tightened in Hayden's gut. *Brianne.* He struggled with the ropes on his wrists. Oh, God. No. Please don't. Not Brianne.

Frank shoved him forward. "Get movin'."

Pedro smiled broadly. *"El jefe,* he and others go. Pedro, he be right behind him with *senorita."*

Logan gave him a cold stare. "You'd better be."

Praying for Brianne's safety as he never had anything in his life, Hayden walked with Tate out to the wagon. But when he saw Lecil's body lying on the porch, blood soaking the front of his shirt, rage nearly choked him. He hadn't known the man very long, but he meant a lot to Brianne. A chill as cold as death shrouded him. Brianne. She didn't stand a chance. Feeling a surge of panic, he again fought to free his hands.

Frank and Lou loaded Stoker's body and rolled him over to the side of the bed.

Logan's gun jabbed into Hayden's kidney. "Get in."

Silently, grief and hatred closing his throat, Hayden climbed into the buckboard.

"Are we gonna wait for Pedro?" Frank asked, eyeing Tate.

"No." Logan mounted his horse. "Pedro's trustworthy." He glared at Hayden. "Besides, he wouldn't miss the chance to dispose of *another* Ranger."

Pain hit Hayden in the chest like a fist. *Pedro had pulled the trigger on Billy Wayne.* And all this time, Hayden had been within arm's reach of the whoreson's throat. Fury burned him. The muscles in Hayden's arms quivered with the need to kill.

"Yeah, Pedro'll be along. Less he decides ta git him a little taste of that gal first," Lou supplied with a guffaw.

Logan shrugged. "It doesn't matter. She'll be dead before sundown, anyway."

Hayden's rage exploded. He twisted wildly, clawing at the ropes. He'd tear Pedro's heart out with his bare hands!

But the effort was futile. The bindings were well knotted. Hayden inhaled several times, trying to regain control, knowing if Brianne stood a chance of surviving, he had to get his mind off Pedro, and what the Mex might do to her. Hayden took another breath and cleared the anger from his throat. "I thought you boys were gonna wait in the canyons."

"We were," Frank supplied. "But El Hefty rode out ta meet us. Tol' us ta keep watch fer ya instead." He cackled. "El Hefty's right smart. When he seen 'em hang the real Navaja, the boss figured ya fer a lawman. Been twiddlin' our thumbs waitin' fer three days now, while Pedro was hol' up in the hotel across from the sheriff's watchin' so he could warn us. He jist beat ya here. Too bad ya left the gal behind, though."

"Shut up," Logan interrupted sharply. "Lay the bastards down by their friend and cover them with hay. Let's get this distasteful business over with. I've got an early meeting at Fort Marcy first thing tomorrow."

Lying on his side next to Lecil, Hayden was forced to focus on the older man's body as the outlaws struggled with the sheriff.

Tate slammed into the wagon bed behind him, but Hayden barely noticed. He stared disbelievingly at Lecil's back and watched with amazement as the man took a nearly imperceptible breath.

Brianne stood in the cell, her hands gripping the window bars as she stared out. She'd come full circle. Here she stood, locked in another jail . . . waiting for the outcome of her very existence. She thought of Hayden and the others and knew if anything happened to them it would be her fault. If she hadn't stolen the chicken, she wouldn't have ended up in a cell with Hayden. He wouldn't have found out that Brianne Logan was still alive, and none of them would be here risking their lives.

"Buenas dias, querida."

Brianne gasped and whirled around.

Pedro Torres walked to the desk and picked up the keys. He smiled, revealing a piece of candy wedged between his teeth. "Pedro, he has come to rescue you."

She stared speechlessly at him. Rescue her? Ha! "I don't need rescuing, thank you."

He unlocked the cell and threw it wide, making certain he filled the opening with his body. "Come, *nina*. We must go, *pronto.*"

"Get away from me," she cried, edging along the side of the wall. "What do you want? W-where's Hayden?"

Pedro frowned. "Hayden?" Dawning struck him. "Ah, the lawman who plays killer. He is on de way to meet his Maker."

"No!" she screamed and flew at Pedro.

He grabbed her roughly, wrenching her hands up behind her. *"Si, muchacha, si."*

The odor of his candy sent her into a panic. It was the same scent she'd smelled *that night!* Oh, dear God, it was *him!* Visions taunted her from every direction. His foul breath, the cruel fingers digging into the tender skin of her breasts. She could again hear his ragged breathing, feel the stiff thrust of his engourged manhood against her leg. The stomach clenching fear. She bucked and kicked out wildly. "No! No!" Suddenly a fist came out of nowhere. Pain exploded in her jaw, then everything spun into black.

28

It was noon when the wagon finally pulled to a stop. Sweat beaded on Hayden's brow, his damp shirt clung to his chest and arms, and the cloying smell of hay made him sick, but with Stoker's somewhat hindered help, he had nearly worked his hands free. Tate had been too far away for Stoker to help, and if Tate had tried to move, Frank or one of the others would have seen the hay shift.

Hayden felt the wood creak beneath his cheek, then a loud thud in the dirt. Frank had jumped down. The wagon dipped again, and hard hands scraped at the hay covering Hayden's body, then lugged him up into a sitting position.

He blinked in the sudden brightness. After a moment, his gaze focused on an L-shaped recess in a canyon wall directly ahead of him. He eyed the area closely, hoping for any chance of escape. There wasn't one.

With towering rock walls on two sides and an acre of aspen trees, hedges, and tangled berry vines on the other, the only way out was the trickling streambed they'd apparently been traveling up for the last quarter hour. And that was blocked by Logan and his men.

"Hey, El Hefty? Whatcha want us ta do with the dead one?" Lou asked.

"Toss him into that thicket." Logan pointed to the bushes.

Hayden, still seated beside Tate in the wagon, watched as Frank and Lou complied, praying they didn't notice the warmth of a body that should have been cold long ago.

Obviously they didn't since they dumped Lecil roughly into the hedges and returned to drag Hayden out of the wagon bed, then Tate.

"You're not goin' to get away with this, Logan," Sheriff Tate spoke up as he regained his balance.

"Yes, I will," he responded smugly. "Your body's going to be left where it can be found quickly." He shook his head in mock sympathy. "Sad thing, our sheriff getting murdered by a gang of cutthroats. When they find your remains, I'll be safely ensconced in my hacienda, absolutely shocked at the brutality of it all. Of course, I'll rage and vow to procure stiffer laws to deal with such vile criminals."

Knowing Lecil was hurt but stubborn as hell, and, being a Ranger, was probably at this moment readying for an attack, Hayden stalled for time. "And how will you deal with Brianne?" he asked, then suddenly feared the answer.

Those cold eyes met his. "As far as Santa Fe's concerned, she's already dead and buried. It's only necessary to ensure that *this* body is never found." He raked Hayden with a leer. "Or yours." He pointed to the rear wall and spoke to the Hawkinses. "Stand them over there. It's time for an execution."

Hayden didn't even struggle as Frank shoved him into the shale, but he was praying Stoker made his move soon. Not that he gave a damn about his own safety, but he had to get to Brianne. "What about the people in town who saw her?" Hayden asked, stalling for time.

A smile twisted Logan's face. "None of those low-life peons would recognize her. I kept her away from them. I wasn't about to have her coming up pregnant with one of their bastard whelps. Only our good sheriff here, and a select few of my influential political associates have been permitted an introduction. Why do you think it was so easy to substitute another woman's body for hers?"

"Why would you want to?"

"Because," Logan stretched out the word as if talking to an imbecile. "I had sent out invitations to a social gala, intending to find an influential husband for the chit. When she ran, I was left with no choice. I had gained a great deal of sympathy from my peers when my wife *disappeared* and was assumed killed by outlaws. But a second disappearance from a member of my family would have caused suspicion. I had to produce a body—and find the bitch before someone saw *and recognized* her." He smirked at Hayden. "All those robberies you partook in with the Hawkins Gang were merely conveniences. Pedro was tracking Brianne, the whole time. But if it hadn't been for *you*, we might never have found her."

Hayden paled.

"Who was the other gal? The one you buried?" Tate interrupted.

Logan flicked a hand. "Some runaway soldier's brat."

"Where—"

"Enough talk!" He turned to Frank and Lou, his expression tight. "Kill them." Moving off to one side, he crossed his burly arms.

"I thought ya was goin' ta let Pedro have the honors," Lou remarked.

"I'll let him spit on the corpse. That ought to satisfy him."

Frank chuckled. Then both men drew their guns.

"Hey, Pa," Frank said. "You can have the sheriff." He narrowed his eyes on Hayden. "I still owe this one fer pullin' that razor on me."

"Sure thing, son. But what say we make a contest of it first?"

Frank didn't take his eyes off Hayden. "How?"

"We could cut 'em down a little at a time. Ya know, first an arm, then a leg, maybe the balls next. See which one can last the longest."

Frank cackled. "Ten bucks says the Ranger's still standin' when the sheriff falls."

"You're on." Lou raised his gun and took careful aim.

Frank did likewise, his barrel pointed at Hayden's right arm.

Hayden braced himself for the pain, instinctively tightening his muscles. He watched Frank's finger ease over the trigger, then ever so gently begin to squeeze.

Hoofbeats splashed in the creek.

Frank and Lou both whirled around.

Pedro Torres rode into view, carrying Brianne wrapped in a blanket. "Ah, *amigos,* you do not wait for Pedro."

Logan stepped forward. "Put the slut over there with the others. You can join in on Lou and Franky's game." He smiled. "Ought to be quite a sight, watching you cut the little bitch down . . . piece by piece."

Terror nearly choked Hayden. He couldn't just stand there and watch them kill Brianne. Just the thought of those bastards riddling her small body with bullets nearly gagged him. Hayden opened his mouth to say something—*anything.*

"Ah, *el jefe,*" Pedro interrupted. "The *senorita,* she give Pedro *mucho* problems." He carefully unwrapped the blanket to expose Brianne. "Pedro, he is forced to silence *la muchacha* for little while."

The blood drained from Hayden's face. His heart began to pound savagely. In frozen shock, he stared at Brianne. Her head was arched back over Pedro's arms. Blood dripped from the corner of her mouth, and a swollen bruise darkened her jaw.

Hayden started to shake uncontrollably. That rotten sonofabitch! Something inside him snapped. *"I'll kill you!"* he roared insanely. Arms still tied behind him, he blindly charged forward, bent on destroying anything in his path. His head drove into Frank's spine.

A gunshot exploded.

Fiery pain slammed into Hayden's arm, and he dropped to the ground.

"Stand him up," Logan ordered, the Colt smoking as he stared down at Hayden. "And bring the bitch here."

Pedro dismounted awkwardly and carried Brianne to the

leader, dumping her at his feet, while Frank hauled Hayden up and shoved him toward the wall next to Tate. Hayden and the older man shared a defeated look.

"I'll take care of the girl when you're finished with them," Logan said harshly.

Hayden pulled his gaze from the sheriff and worked frantically at the loose bindings around his wrists. He had to get his hands free. Brianne's life depended on it.

The Mex pulled his gun. "Pedro, he want to kill de Ranger."

"No," Frank argued. "He's mine."

Hayden slipped his hands free.

At the same instant, gunfire erupted from the brush.

Hayden charged Torres.

More blasts echoed through the canyon, but Hayden barely heard them. He wanted to kill Pedro with his bare hands. He drilled a fist into the other's face, knocking him to the ground, then dived on top of him. Again and again, he battered Pedro's nose and mouth.

Another round of shots rang out.

Pedro sprang to his feet and drew the razor. He flipped it open. "Ah, *senor*," he purred, spitting blood. "You are not so brave now, eh?"

Hayden rolled to his feet, keeping a healthy distance between himself and the weapon. "Make one wrong move with that, Mex, and it'll be your last."

Pedro curled his mouth into a smirk—then lunged. His hand swept out in a wide arc, the razor aimed at Hayden's throat.

Hayden caught Pedro's wrist, and in one swift, smooth motion, swiped both their hands across the front of Pedro's own neck. "That's for Billy Wayne," Hayden hissed. He cut him again, deeper. "And that's for Brianne."

For a stunned moment, Pedro didn't move, as if he hadn't comprehended what had happened. Then his eyes widened, and he began to gag. He jerked free of Hayden's hold and clutched his bleeding throat. He made a choking, gurgling sound, his mouth open in a desperate appeal for air, then slowly, his body arching grotesquely, he folded to the ground.

Hayden turned from the grizzly sight to see Frank and Lou lying dead near his feet, Tate and Stoker standing over them.

But Logan was gone—with Brianne.

"Hayden? Damn it, Caldwell, are you all right?"

Vaguely Hayden recognized Lecil's voice, but the picture of Brianne in Logan's hands and what he would do to her kept stealing his ability to think.

Ignoring the pain in his arm, Hayden stiffly walked over to one of the horses and started to mount.

Stoker placed a hand on Hayden's shoulder.

Hayden withdrew sharply. "Don't touch me." He felt as if he were made of glass, and the slightest jar would cause him to shatter. He met Lecil's concerned gaze, then glanced at the bleeding wound high on the older man's chest. "You need a doc," he said offhandedly. "And I need your gun."

Lecil complied without hesitation. "I'm going with you."

"It's *my* job," the sheriff argued.

Sickness curled in Hayden's stomach. "No," he countered both men with finality. "It's me he wants—that's why he took Brianne. He knows I'll come—and I won't disappoint him. I owe the bastard." Woodenly, he mounted and reined the animal toward the stream. "Better get Stoker to a sawbones, Sheriff." He didn't turn as he spoke again. "Which way did Logan go?"

"Into the Pajarito," Tate supplied a little testily.

Fearing Logan would kill Brianne before Hayden could find them, and too numb to respond any further, he kicked the horse into a trot. He would follow the stream, inspect every inch of the banks until he saw where Logan turned off.

And he would pray.

Brianne shook uncontrollably and curled into a tighter ball on the ground. Fiery pain burned where her father had kicked her. "Why?" she panted. "Why did you do it? I'm your daughter, for God's sake! What did I ever do to make you hate me so much?"

"Hate you?" her father raged. "That's putting it mildly. I *despised* the very sight of you. I would have killed you long ago if I thought I could have gotten away with it. Every time you called me *father,* I wanted to spit."

Brianne frowned in confusion. Holding onto her ribs, she pushed herself up into a sitting position.

Her father snorted. "You've seen your face, and you've seen mine. But do you see any resemblance between us?" He clenched his hands. "Hell no, you don't. Because you're not mine. Your whoring mother was pregnant by an arrogant Texan named Aaron Gregory, when I married her."

Brianne's world reeled. *Not his daughter?* "What are you saying?"

"You heard me, bitch."

Regaining her balance, she tried to understand. "What happened to my real father? Where is he?"

"I saw to it the bastard hung," Logan answered smugly, then he smiled. "Even though I knew he was innocent."

Her brain slowed to a walk, none of his words were making sense. "You loved my mother that much?"

"Hell no. I *had* to marry your mother. Her father was a congressman. He could make my career. *Did* make it. But back then, she wouldn't give me the time of day as long as Gregory was around. Only after he was dead, and I told her that Aaron had asked me to take care of her, did she reluctantly agree to marry me." He sneered. "She thought it was her beloved Aaron's last wish. But I paid a price, believe me. I didn't know the slut was already pregnant. Oh, not that she didn't tell me eventually. She did. A week before the wedding. By then it was too late to call off the ceremony without causing a scandal. One scandal I couldn't afford."

He drew his gun.

Brianne gasped and scampered backward. "W-what are you doing?"

Art Logan smiled wickedly. "Calling your lover." He slowly fired three shots into the air. "Caldwell won't give up following me till he's dead. So I'm going to oblige him." He lowered the barrel to her.

Horrified for Hayden and herself, Brianne closed her eyes, waiting for the bullet that would end her life.

Logan chuckled. "Afraid, are you?"

Her lashes flew up.

"Don't worry, I'm not going to kill you." He smiled, not a nice smile. "I need money to start over in Mexico, thanks to you. So you're going to pay the way."

"How?" she asked shakily.

"I've got a friend in El Paso who'd give *mucho dinero* for a new *puta* for his cantina. With all that silvery hair and white skin, he'd get double the rate for a piece like you."

Terror knocked through her chest.

"But for now," Logan added, "I don't have time to mess with you. Your lover should be arriving soon." With a hideous smile, he drew back his fist. . . .

Almost an hour had passed since Hayden had heard the shots, felt the waves of panic for Brianne's life. But he'd forced himself into numbness. He had to find Logan. And Brianne. He couldn't allow himself, not even for an instant, to believe Logan had harmed her.

A thin stream of smoke coming from behind a distant bend in the gorge brought Hayden up abruptly. But he wasn't fooled. Logan had set a trap.

Easing out of the saddle, he tied his horse's reins to an aspen tree, then cautiously approached the curving wall on foot. Around the bend, another ravine emerged. Cut into a deep V the weed- and rock-littered valley led upward to yet another mountain with several caves lining the base.

Hayden knew Logan had to be in one of them. Making his way up the incline, Hayden followed the line of smoke until he saw the ground level out before the row of deep caves, and a small fire near one opening. Off to the side a protruding boulder canopied a circular rock-lined pit. Below that, Brianne's motionless body lay wrapped in the blanket.

The air squeezed out of Hayden's lungs. *Her face was covered.* He quickly pulled his gaze away. He had to deal with Logan first. But a rapid search of the area told him the assemblyman was nowhere to be seen.

"Are you so yellow you have to hide from me, Logan? Or do you plan to shoot me in the back?" Hayden asked mockingly.

"I'm merely cautious."

The sound of the man's voice ricocheted off the canyon walls, but Hayden couldn't tell where it came from. "Then why don't you face me like a man?"

"I'll consider it—as soon as you drop the pistol." He paused. Waited.

Hayden didn't move.

"Now, Caldwell," Logan ordered. "Or I'll kill you where you stand."

As if Hayden cared. His only reason for living lay wrapped in a blanket not ten feet away—and she was probably already dead. *No, she isn't,* his heart cried. Swallowing the pain that threatened to split him in two, and knowing the only way he would draw the bastard out was by disarming himself, he slipped the gun from his holster and tossed it in the dirt.

Logan's chuckle filled the ravine. "That was a stupid move. What's to stop me from killing you now?"

"You could have done that before I threw down the gun," Hayden pointed out.

Logan stepped into view from the dark recess of a cave. "True. But it's more enjoyable to watch the face up close. To see fear in the eyes, sweat on the brow . . . the body twitch in death."

Steadily, Hayden met the man's gaze. "So what are you waiting for? Get on with it."

Logan seemed momentarily disconcerted. "So you're not afraid to die, huh?"

"I'm already dead, Logan. I died with Brianne."

Logan's expression went blank. "She's dead, all right. I killed her. And I enjoyed the hell out of watching every bullet I fired sink into her body," he taunted, waving the gun he held. "But I'm disappointed in you, Ranger. I thought

244

you had more gumption. Especially after all you went through in an attempt to catch me."

Hayden felt his heart stop when Logan confirmed his worst fears. Brianne was dead. His eyes burned, then darkened with hatred. His hold on reality slipped. He studied the weapon, praying Logan would be stupid enough to come a little closer. That's all Hayden wanted. . . .

"Get over there by Brianne," the assemblyman ordered.

Hayden didn't move.

Logan raised the gun threateningly. "Move."

Hayden remained still.

Anger flared in the older man's eyes. He pulled the trigger. Dirt exploded between Hayden's feet.

Hayden didn't flinch. He just stared at him calmly. "If you want me, Logan. You're gonna have to come get me."

"I'll kill you where you stand!" he bellowed furiously.

"Go ahead."

For a moment, Hayden thought he'd pushed him too far. The man's hand shook. The cords in his neck bulged.

Suddenly Logan stilled. "Ah, now I see. You want a quick, easy death, is that it?" He walked toward Hayden. "Hardly any pain?" He fingered the barrel of his pistol. "But an easy death won't make me happy. You see, you've not only destroyed my gang, my means of earning campaign money, but you've destroyed my entire life—my career. I want to see you suffer."

Without warning Hayden lashed out, catching Logan across the wrist with the side of his hand, knocking the six-shooter from his grasp.

Logan dove for the gun.

Hayden jerked him back by the shirt and slammed him into the mountain wall.

With a move so fast Hayden barely saw it, Logan palmed a small gun and fired.

Pain burned across Hayden's already injured arm. Blood gushed from the open wound. He lunged for the gun on the ground and sprang to his feet.

Logan fired wildly.

Hayden aimed true. A bullet slammed into Logan's gut. He fired again. Another caught the assemblyman in the chest. Hayden's brain shut down. He fired again and again.

It was several minutes later before a distant clicking sound penetrated his mind. Hayden looked blankly down at the Peacemaker in his hand and realized he'd been pulling the trigger on an empty gun for some time.

Logan's bullet riddled body lay in the opening of the cave.

Stiffly holstering the six-shooter, Hayden took a moment to gather his scattered senses. Logan was dead. Billy Wayne was dead. Hayden began to shake. Brianne was dead. "Nooo!" The weight of the world crumbled in on top of him. His legs wouldn't hold him, and he dropped to his knees.

Low, animallike sounds came from his throat, sounds he couldn't stop, couldn't control. His chest caved in, and he couldn't breathe. "Brianne," he rasped out brokenly. "Oh, God. *Brianne!*"

Brianne sluggishly came awake to the sound of someone calling her name. She blinked, trying to clear her fuzzy vision. When images came into focus, she stared in confusion at the rock canopy over her head, then at the mountainous canyons surrounding her.

A guttural moan drew her attention, and she glanced to the side.

Hayden sat on his heels with his clenched fists pressed into his upper thighs, blood coating the sleeve of his shirt. Her gaze lifted to his face, and her breath caught. His head was thrown back, his throat working roughly as tears slipped down the tortured lines of his face.

Her own tears threatened to fall. She had never seen anyone so devastated, so broken. It wasn't right. No one should hurt like that. She pushed herself up to her knees, wanting desperately to go to him, to ease the pain. "Hayden . . . please . . ."

His head snapped around. "Brianne?" His eyes widened

246

in shock, searched her hurriedly, then blazed with unbridled joy.

The next thing she knew, she was in his arms, his face buried in her hair, his arms crushing her against him, his body shaking wildly. "Oh, sweet Christ, *chica.* I thought I'd lost you."

——— 29———

*B*rianne carried a glass of Madeira to her uncle seated on a chaise in the parlor of the hacienda.

"Thank you, Bree," her uncle said, raising his hand in a painfully slow motion.

Now that the ordeal with her father was over, and she knew everyone was all right, she smiled more readily. "You're welcome." As she handed him the drink, she turned that smile on Hayden who sat in a nearby chair with a half-full glass of the spirits. Suddenly, she was very glad she'd washed up and changed.

"You must have hide tougher than a bull's," he remarked teasingly to Uncle Lecil.

"Hell, Caldwell. During my years as a Ranger, I was shot up more than a post used for target practice. One measly little bullet isn't going to do me in."

"Well, I, for one, am damned glad of it," Sheriff Tate said, wiping the last of the dust off his rifle.

"I'll second that," Hayden added. "If it hadn't been for Lecil firing when he did, I'd have most likely caught someone's bullet between my eyes. Hell, he only had one gun and about two seconds to hit both the Hawkinses."

Uncle Lecil chuckled. "Glad to be of help. But I'd prefer not to cut it so close next time."

"Cut it close?" Brianne echoed.

Her uncle nodded. "I couldn't fire until things broke loose with Caldwell and Tate. Otherwise, I probably wouldn't have gotten more than one or two before one of Logan's men got me. But it was nerve-wrackin' as hell waitin' for Hayden. From where I knelt, I could see him workin' his bindin's free."

"Where'd you get the gun?" Hayden asked.

Lecil grinned. "Y'all should know the answer to that, boy. Every Ranger carries a spare. Even ex-Rangers."

"Not that you always have time to get at them," Hayden mumbled.

Brianne smiled adoringly at her uncle, then at Hayden. She was so glad they were both safe. And Sheriff Tate, too, of course. But in truth, she didn't love him quite as much as she did the other two men in her life.

"Want some help with those corpses out back?" Hayden asked the sheriff.

"Naw." The lawman sheathed his rifle. "You and Stoker, here, have already done enough. Besides, I don't think little Bree'll mind if I borrow the buckboard for a spell." He turned to her. "Will you?"

Brianne shuddered at the thought of the four bodies in the wagon, and how easily it might have been one of the men now seated in the parlor. "No. Of course not."

Sheriff Tate rose. "You sure that's all of them?" he queried Hayden.

"Yes. There were two others, but one was killed in a robbery, and the other, an Indian . . ." Hayden shrugged. "I don't know who killed him."

Uncle Lecil cracked a smile. "If y'all are talkin' about that big Comanche, I'm afraid I had to put a knife in his back when you were still in the gorge. I found him leanin' over the ledge with his rifle pointed at Bree."

Hayden swung his head sharply toward her uncle. "Wha—"

"Good riddance, I say," Sheriff Tate interrupted, slinging

his Sharp over his shoulder. "And I'm headin' out. Got a passel a paperwork to do after I leave the undertaker's. I'll be needin' to figure the rewards you two got comin' on the Hawkinses, too."

"Send my share to Kathy Caldwell, down in San Antonio," Hayden instructed.

"Who's that?" the lawman asked before Brianne could.

"My brother's widow." Hayden's gaze claimed Brianne's. "Kathy has two small children. She's gonna need all the help she can get."

Brianne felt a chill run through her. It wasn't bad enough that Hayden's brother died because of Art Logan, but the younger Caldwell had left behind two babies and a wife. Empathy for Kathy and the children swelled. And in that instant, Brianne forgave Hayden everything. She understood what drove him. Why he'd had to use her. But she also knew, because she knew Hayden, that he'd despised every moment of the deception.

"I'll see she gets the money. And I'm off now." Tate nodded good-bye. "See you good folks later."

After his departure, Brianne rose and crossed to her uncle. "I think you could use a bed about now, too." She patted his hand. "The doc said that wound in your chest needs to start healing. Come on, I'll show you where to lie down." She arched a brow at Hayden. "You can bed down on the sofa."

Leading her uncle into the bedroom that had previously belonged to Art Logan and her mother, she urged him inside and shut the door, then headed for her own room. She still didn't know how to take the news about Aaron Gregory, her real father, but right now, she needed a long, hot soak and a decent night's sleep.

Knowing she could reach the kitchen without going through the parlor, she set the water to heat, then returned to her room and laid out a clean nightgown and towel.

Once her bath was prepared, she sank down in the soapy water and scrubbed vigorously, then leaned her head on the rim. God, she was tired.

The door latch clicked.

Her eyes sprang open.

Hayden stood in the doorway, wearing only his jeans and a white bandage on his left arm. Slowly, he stepped into the room.

"What are you doing in here?"

"I want to talk to you."

"Can't it wait until tomorrow? I'm exhausted."

"I won't be here tomorrow."

Brianne lurched upright in the tub, then realizing her breasts had risen out of the water, she snatched a towel from the floor and covered herself. "What?"

Hayden's gaze lingered on her wet shoulders. "I'm gonna meet up with Char in Socorro and head back to Texas. That's what I came to tell you."

"I thought you were taking me with you."

"Where the hell'd you get that idea?"

She rose and wrapped the towel around her, then stepped out of the tub, oddly aware of the fact that she wasn't quite so modest around Hayden anymore. "When you said you loved me, I thought—"

"That I meant to marry you?"

"Well, that does usually follow." She walked to the bed. "Not this time."

He was leaving her? She brushed a lock of hair out of her eyes that had escaped the coil on top of her head. "Let me get this straight. You love me, but you're not going to marry me?"

"Right."

She started to shake. How could he do this to her? Damn him. Lifting her chin, determined not to let him see how his words affected her, she pulled off his ring. "Then I guess I won't be needing this." She handed it to him, willing her fingers not to tremble.

He just stared down at his palm, a muscle throbbing in his temple.

"Why?" she whispered.

He closed his hand around the ring, then brushed a finger down her cheek. "After what I went through today when I thought you were dead? You know the answer to that." He bent and brushed his lips over hers. "I love you too much to ever let anything like that happen to you again. I couldn't live through it. And if anything happened to me, I couldn't bear the thought of you suffering like Kathy." He touched her with his eyes. "There just isn't any hope for us, sweetheart." With a last prolonged look, he turned and left.

Brianne sat frozen on the edge of the bed. Hayden wouldn't marry her because he loved her too much to see her hurt or killed. Or see her suffer over his death.

But he didn't love her enough to quit.

Hating him almost as much as she loved him, she tore off the towel and jerked on her nightgown. It's just as well she found out the limitations on his love now, before it was too late. Feeling close to tears, and angrier than she'd ever been, she flounced down on the bed. She punched her pillow several times, then yanked the blanket over her.

For what seemed like hours, she lay there, alternately cursing, crying, hating, and loving him. Finally, disgusted, she sat up. If Hayden was going to leave her tomorrow, then by God, she wouldn't spend *this* night without him. She'd have one last memory to carry her through a lifetime.

Rising, she stalked out the door.

Making her way through the dark house, she headed for the parlor. When she reached it, she found Hayden sitting on the sofa, staring into the flames of a low-burning fire. The tortured look on his face tore at her heart.

Silently, she moved next to him. "Hayden?"

He glanced up, startled. "What?"

"I know you're leaving tomorrow, and I understand why." She touched his bandaged arm. "I won't try to change that. But, please, before you go, give me one more night." She knelt in front of him and placed her hand on his chest.

His heart pounded roughly beneath her palm. "You're destroying me, *chica,*" he said tightly. "It's hard enough to leave as it is."

She traced his lips with her fingers. "I won't try to hold you."

"I love you enough to let you go," he said defeatedly. "You have to understand that."

Her heart constricted. Hayden was desperately trying to do what was right in his own mind, and she knew she'd never be able to change him. Nor did she want to. Any change had to come from deep within Hayden. She felt his breath on her hand, the moistness, the heat, the promise of pleasure. "I do understand," she answered truthfully, dying inside.

He brushed his tongue over her skin. "Be very sure this is what you want, *chica.*" His arm slid around her waist and he pulled her up onto his lap, letting her feel his fiery hardness.

Minor eruptions exploded between her thighs, and she wrapped her arms around his neck, parting her lips to take his. "I am." She needed him as she'd never needed anything in her life—if only for this night. Nothing had ever touched her heart, her soul, the way this man did, and she desperately needed him to know.

Shakily, she rose. "Stand up."

His eyes darkened, and he slowly complied.

Holding his gaze, she reached for the buttons on his jeans.

He lifted his fingers to her breasts, but she shook her head. "Not yet. I want to go slow, and I can't do that when you touch me."

His nostrils flared slightly, but he lowered his hands.

When the last button slid free, she stared at the heavy rise and fall of his chest, the ripple of muscles across his tight stomach, and the smooth line of hair that slipped below the open front of his jeans. Suddenly, she had the uncontrollable urge to taste that spot.

She sank to her knees, then bent forward to place her lips against his hot stomach. His flesh rippled, and the soft hairs moved beneath her mouth.

Encouraged by her obvious power over him, she eased onto her heels and stared up into his eyes. "I love you, Hayden. More than my life."

He sent her a smoldering look that singed her toes. Yet he also seemed to understand the demons that drove her. He gently brushed the backs of his fingers over her cheek. "I love you, too, *chica.* Too much to lose you."

Basking in a warm glow, she lifted unsteady hands to the material hugging his hips, then slowly edged it down.

His heavy sex sprang free.

She held her breath, awed by the magnificent power before her. She ached to touch him, but felt shyness overcome her.

He dragged in a shuddering breath. "If you stop now, I'm a dead man."

Moved by the blatant need in his voice, she pressed her palms to his stomach, entrapped by his smoldering eyes while her fingers explored the texture of his skin, the ridges and hollows near his hips, the tense muscles in his thighs. She felt him tremble, and lowered her attention to that part of him that had given her so much pleasure.

She steepled her fingers over his shaft, then let them trickle down its long length.

His body jumped, and a deep moan rose from his chest.

Her own senses flamed. The need to feel his strength, to give him pleasure, staggered her. She closed her hands around him and squeezed gently.

Hayden's stomach hardened. "Damn."

Slowly, lovingly, her hands trembling around his member, she slid her tongue over his taut abdomen.

He drew in a sharp breath. "Brianne . . ."

Warmed by his response, and hungry for more, she closed her lips over the tip of his sex.

"Oh, Christ," Hayden groaned thickly. He gripped her by the shoulders, his hands shaking, and dragged her to her feet. Savagely, his mouth took hers.

The desperation in his kiss, in his fevered haste to remove her gown, took her breath away. And before she could gather her senses, she was lying naked on the rug in front of the fireplace, Hayden pressing down on top of her, his mouth wildly plundering.

His loss of control shattered hers, and nothing could have prevented her from parting her legs to receive him.

He thrust deep, and she felt the impact all the way to her soul. She loved him. Would rather die than live without him.

Her thoughts faded as pure feeling claimed her senses.
He drove into her.

Heat burned through her core.

He withdrew and plunged.

Fiery sparks burst.

He quickened, impaled, and sank into her erupting depth.

She burst into a million blazing fragments, swirled through hungry flames of pleasure, then slowly, oh so slowly, shuddered into smoldering cinders.

It seemed to take forever for her breathing to return to normal.

Hayden raised his head to search her eyes, his smiling with love and wonder. *"Chica,"* he said on a winded breath, "I don't think I could make it through another explosion like that one."

Feeling more at ease than she ever had before, she flicked a finger down his cheek. "If you don't get off me soon, we may just have to test your theory." Already she could feel the embers starting to glow. She moved against him suggestively.

A wicked little gleam lit his eyes, and he kissed her long and thoroughly. When he pulled back, he grinned sinfully. "I'm too tired to move, so if I don't survive, just remember that I died a contented man."

Brianne yawned and stretched, feeling happy and well loved. She smiled sleepily when she thought of the night just passed, and the several times she and Hayden had shown their love. The man was insatiable.

Opening her eyes, she stared up at the canopy over her bed. *Bed?* She shot upright. What was she doing in her room?

Wildly she searched for Hayden. He was nowhere in sight. She threw back the covers and rushed into the parlor. His clothes were gone, his boots, his gun.

No. Oh, please, no. She spun around to check the stables, but something lying on the rug before the fireplace caught her eye. She stared helplessly at the object until pain brought her to her knees. For a long moment, she couldn't bring herself to touch it. When she finally did, her hand shook, and tears tumbled down her cheeks.

Sobbing beyond control, she clutched the perfect yellow rose to her breast, knowing in the deepest part of her that Hayden had just told her good-bye.

30

*B*rianne stood on the back porch of her uncle's ranch in Fort Worth, staring out over the wide expanse of summer green pastures. Longhorn cattle grazed lazily in the distance. Occasionally, horsemen would emerge from one of the many thickets of trees, returning a stray to the herd.

It had been three months since she'd seen Hayden. Three months of heartbreaking agony that had at last settled into numb emptiness. A thousand times, she'd relived the days they had shared, the warmth, the anger, the love, the laughter, and sadness.

The yellow rose was now safely pressed between the pages of the Bible she carried to church every Sunday. A memento of a love that was never to be. She smiled. Even if it was stolen from her mother's rose garden behind the hacienda. Her smile disappeared, and she brought a hand to her stomach. But the rose wasn't the only gift Hayden had given her. He'd also given her a part of himself. His child.

Another smile, a sad one, touched her lips when she recalled how at one time she'd have done anything to hold Hayden. And now, when she actually had a reason, she couldn't do it. He had to love her enough to stay—which he obviously didn't.

Swallowing another rush of hurt, she recalled how not long after she and Uncle Lecil had returned to Fort Worth, they'd learned that the Texas Rangers had disbanded. Hayden was out of a job. But Brianne hadn't held onto hopes of him coming to her. He would get a new position, possibly as a sheriff, a marshal, or even a bounty hunter. Anything that brought criminals to justice. That was a part of Hayden. A need within him that far exceeded his need for her.

She hadn't told Uncle Lecil or Mama or Maria about the baby yet, and not because she was afraid to, even though she knew Uncle Lecil's reaction would be volatile. But because she wanted, just for a little while longer, to hold the proof of Hayden's love close to her heart, cherish it.

"You're still thinkin' about him, aren't you?" her mother asked softly from the kitchen doorway.

Startled, Brianne turned around to see her mother staring up at her with kind violet eyes.

The older woman maneuvered her wheelchair onto the porch, and Brianne felt a sudden rush of warmth, not only for her mother's presence, but at the doctor's news yesterday. Suzanne's spine would heal properly, and someday soon—with proper care—she'd walk again. Of course, Maria had clucked like a mother hen, vowing Suzanne would be treated better than America's President Grant.

Distantly, Brianne noticed how much younger her mother appeared since Art Logan's death, or perhaps it was because Suzanne finally unburdened the truth of Brianne's birth. A few years ago, Brianne might not have understood the kind of love her mother and Aaron had shared, but now she did. All too well. "I don't think I've ever *stopped* thinking about Hayden," Brianne answered her mother's question honestly.

"Are you goin' to tell him about the child?"

Brianne inhaled sharply. "How did you know?"

Suzanne smiled, her features soft and clear like her voice.

"Darlin', I, too, once carried a baby. I haven't forgotten the signs. It really wasn't hard to figure."

"Do Maria and Uncle Lecil know?"

Her mother shook her head. "Not your uncle. And I'm not lookin' forward to him findin' out. I love my brother dearly, but he tends to get a little crazy when it comes to things like honor and responsibility. When he does learn the truth, it wouldn't surprise me if he went after your Hayden and dragged him back to the ranch—tied and kickin'." She grinned. "But I think Maria knows."

Brianne managed a small smile, but alarm had already set in. "I can't let Uncle Lecil know. And because of *honor*, I can't tell Hayden."

"Don't you think he has a right to know?"

She shook her head. "I can't, Mama. It would only hurt us all. Most of all him."

"How are you goin' to explain your sudden weight gain to your uncle? Not to mention a child suddenly appearin' out of nowhere?" Suzanne teased gently, as she always did to cheer Brianne when she was upset.

"I'll go away somewhere."

Suzanne's eyes grew wide with panic, and she clutched Brianne's hand. "No. Darlin', please don't do that to me. I couldn't bear to be separated from you again."

"Then I'll—"

The sound of horses thundering to a stop out front drew her attention.

"It must be Uncle Lecil." Brianne pulled from her mother's grasp and gripped the handles of the wheelchair, then guided it inside.

As they entered the parlor, Maria set her knitting aside and rose.

Uncle Lecil came in the front door, peeling his hat off as he walked toward the sofa. "Put on a pot of coffee, would you, Bree?"

Surprised by his appearance in the house at this time of day, and that he'd asked her instead of Maria, she stared dumbly. "Is anything wrong?"

"Nope. Just want some coffee."

"Okay." Still baffled, she glanced at her mother and the maid, then shrugged and headed for the kitchen.

After retrieving a tin coffeepot hanging on the wall, she carried it to the drain board and began pumping water into it. She'd never known her uncle to set foot in the house except at mealtime or to sleep. What was going on? Sighing and knowing she'd find out when Uncle Lecil was ready to tell her, she reached into the bag of coffee and tossed in a handful of grounds, then set it on the cookstove to boil.

"I like mine hot enough to take your breath away."

Brianne froze.

A pair of familiar warm arms encircled her waist from behind. Soft lips nibbled her ear. "And I like my women the same way."

"Women?" Brianne spun around.

Hayden smiled down at her lovingly. "Just a figure of speech, *chica*. There's only one woman in my life."

Brianne's heart took flight, but she quickly clipped its wings. Suspicious, she attempted to step away. "What are you doing here?"

Hayden didn't release his hold. "Would you be disappointed if I said just riding through?"

Pain knifed through her, but she held her stance firm. She wouldn't let him see how she hurt. "No, of course not."

His beautiful mouth drew into a slow smile. "Liar." He pulled her to him, his features suddenly serious. "I'm here because I've been damned miserable without you."

A thrill shot through her. "A-aren't you working?"

"Yes."

Disappointment nearly smothered her. "Since the Rangers disbanded, you're probably a sheriff or marshal, or something, now."

"Or something."

"I-it must have been hard for you when they let you go, after spending so much time with them, I mean."

His fingers massaged her spine. "They didn't let me go. I quit—but I owed it to McNelly to see the problem settled on the Nueces Strip first."

Surprise held her immobile. "You quit? Why?"

"After that night we spent together, you have to ask? Did you really think I could just up and walk away from you?"

"Isn't that what you did?"

He squeezed her side. "I tried to," he answered honestly. "But I couldn't. My life *and* my job were empty without you. Besides, I could hardly marry you and not have a place to bring you. A home."

She tried to still the wild pumping in her chest. "And now?"

He pressed her close and brushed his lips over hers. "Now, I'm a horse breeder—or soon will be. I just bought a little place about three miles from here. Between handing out the money for that and the hundred dollars I owed Char, there's barely enough left to buy the stock, but we'll manage."

"A hundred dollars to Char?" Brianne's head was spinning.

Hayden smiled. "Yeah. A little bet I really won, but paid anyway."

"Why would you do that?"

His gaze roamed over her face. "Guess I figured it was worth it. Anyway"—he shrugged—"I've been working like a horse beneath a whip for the last week trying to make the place liveable." He slid his hands up her back. "And trying to get rid of the guilt I felt for leaving you. I don't know which pained me worse, being without you, or hating myself leaving . . . for hurting you."

"Oh, Hayden." She clung to him, so happy, she feared it was all a dream. "After all you've done for me, you've more than made up for it."

"I'd like to say I did everything for you, *chica*. But the truth is, I think I did it for me. To end the aching, the long, lonely nights . . . the emptiness." He kissed her cheek. "Before I came to my senses, I even went to see Kathy, hoping to remind myself what it would be like for you if . . . well, you know. Anyway, was I in for a surprise. Kathy had dug her heels into her and Billy Wayne's dairy farm, and she was making a go of it. Hell, I thought she was some hired hand when I first saw her. That gal's got a lot of spunk. She still misses Billy like hell, but she's damned tough. I know she's gonna be okay." He nuzzled her ear. "Know what she told me?"

"What?"

"She said she'd rather have had the short time her and Billy spent together, than none at all. Even the pain was worth enjoying his love for a little while."

Tears dampened her eyes. "That's beautiful. And I know exactly how she feels." She cleared her throat, a little embarrassed. "Um, why did you choose horse breeding?"

He brushed a drop from her lash. "A Ranger's got to know horses if he wants to survive. Figured it's what I knew best—next to catching outlaws."

She stared at him, her chest suddenly feeling heavy. He would give up his life's work for her . . . or would he? "I don't know, Hayden. Oh, not about you being sincere. I know you are. Right now. But what about later? What would happen if someone stole one of your horses? Could you really be content to just sit back and let someone else handle it?"

"I didn't say it would be easy, *chica*. And I know I'll be tempted. But the answer to your question is yes. As long as no one touches you or one of our children, I'll be content to let the law take care of anything else." His hold tightened. "As long as there's not another Pedro Torres out there."

"He didn't hurt me, Hayden. You above all people should know that."

"But when I think of—"

"Shh." She touched a finger to his lips. "It didn't happen." She trailed her nail over his provocative lower lip. "Are you sure about us, Hayden? Is this really what you want?"

"I'm more than sure." He kissed her nose. "When I thought Logan had killed you, I had no reason to go on. Nothing meant more than you did. And when I realized you were still alive, I knew I could never bear that kind of pain again. Death would be preferable. This need I have for you scared the hell out of me. That's why I left at first, hoping distance and time would dull the feelings. But it only made it worse."

Her heart began to hammer savagely, and she fought to maintain control. "Are you any good at horse breeding?"

"I've got a good eye for fillies." He grinned roguishly.

"How are you at fatherhood?"

Hayden went deathly still, then stepped away. His gaze searched hers. "Why?"

The rough sound to his voice touched her. "Because in about six months you're going to be put to the test."

Hayden closed his eyes, then grabbed her to him. He shook as he held her. "Oh, God, *chica*. No man has a right to be this happy."

"Everythin' settled between y'all, now?" Uncle Lecil asked from the kitchen door.

Hayden spun around, then smiled and snuggled her to his side. "Yep."

"You goin' to marry her?"

"Yep. Gonna be a pa, too."

Uncle Lecil nodded, not at all surprised. "Good. Guess we should get to settlin' matters between the two of us, then."

"What matters?" Brianne asked in confusion.

"Y'all were there when I told the boy he's got an ass kickin' comin'. Nothin's changed, and it's high time I gave it to him."

Her gaze darted to Hayden.

His eyes flashed with a hint of respect, mixed with amusement. "Now?"

Uncle Lecil crossed his arms. "Good a time as any."

Hayden nodded seriously, but when he bent his head and kissed her, she felt a chuckle feather her lips. "Get out the healing salve, *chica*. I'll be back in a minute."

Dear Reader:

Your opinion is very important to me. If you have comments or questions about *Rawhide and Roses,* or any of my other books, please write to me at the address below.

Sincerely,

Sue Rich

Sue Rich
P.O. Box 625
Ash Fork, AZ 86320

P.S. Your self-addressed stamped envelope would be greatly appreciated.

Journey back to lush, turbulent
eighteenth-century Scotland in
another wonderfully sensual tale
from the bestselling author
of BORDER LORD

Arnette Lamb

Border
Bride

"Arnette Lamb ignites readers' imaginations
with her unforgettable love stories."
—*Romantic Times*

POCKET
STAR
BOOKS

Available from Pocket Star Books

840